Morbid Relations

Jonathan Whitelaw

To James

Hope you enjoy this as much as my copy –

JW

Ringwood Publishing
Glasgow

First published in Scotland in 2015
by
Ringwood Publishing
7 Kirklee Quadrant, Glasgow G12 0TS
www.ringwoodpublishing.com
e-mail mail@ringwoodpublishing.com

ISBN 978-1-901514-19-3

British Library Cataloguing-in Publication Data

A catalogue record for this book is available from the British
Library

Typeset in Times New Roman 11

Printed and bound in the UK
by Lonsdale Direct Solutions

Acknowledgements

Despite enjoying long-winded speeches, I'm not going to contribute one here. Too many people contributed to the writing of this novel that I'd like to express my unending thanks to individually. If I were to note them all, the Acknowledgments Page would be longer than Chapter One. But I am grateful for their contributions, support and good humour.

I would like to thank my family, across Scotland, Northern Ireland and England, who have always encouraged me to read and write, as they do, and to them I am eternally indebted. From my earliest recollections of laughing at The Beano comic, to trying to tackle War & Peace and everything in between, I wouldn't have been able to start this wonderful journey without their motivation, encouragement and dedication.

A special thanks also to Laure Deprez, Sandy Jamieson and Isobel Freeman of Ringwood Publishing. Their support in the publication process has been fantastic and again, without them, I wouldn't have had the stage with which to tell this story of mine.

And, as always, I thank Anne-Marie, for being my muse, my sounding board and the best thing that ever happened to both my writing and me as a human being.

Dedication

This book is dedicated to my beloved Anne-Marie. Without her constant support and faith, none of this would have ever been possible.

About the Author

Jonathan Whitelaw is a journalist. After working on the frontline media of Scottish politics, he first reached global audiences with articles appearing in broadsheets, tabloids and magazines like The Sun, STV, Daily Mail and The Author. Subjects he has covered have varied from the arts, culture and sport to fashion, music and radioactive waste, with everything in between. He has also contributed to a number of independent almanacs and collaborative works of fiction. Morbid Relations is his first novel."

'We participate in a tragedy; at a comedy we only look.'

Aldous Huxley

Chapter 1

'So, the new King has been born, a boy, obviously. It's funny, don't you think, this country is ready to bow down to a creature that can't focus its eyes yet.' The audience remained perfectly silent. I thought fresh material floated these days. And you couldn't get much fresher than that. The kid's umbilical cord was barely cut.

'But, yeah, it's a real mind bender, you know, when you think about it. I mean, just think what the poor mother is going to be put through. Crying, teething, the early starts. It's a wonder she's stayed married to him for so long already.'

Little ripples of laughter from the back, but it could have been polite conversation. What the bloody hell was wrong with these people? I was giving them gold and getting squat back. Ingrates.

'But, I have every sympathy for her, I really do. I mean, it can't be an easy gig being married to a multi-millionaire, heir to the throne, after all. You've got to look at that leering face every time he wants another regent.'

'You're shit!' somebody shouted and got the biggest laugh of the routine. It was time to wrap this thing up, end of the line.

'Well,' I said with a sigh. 'I've had better nights. I've been Rab Argyll and can I just say, I've never met a bigger bunch of ungrateful shitheads in all of my life. Goodbye and I hope you all rot in hell.' That got a reaction all right.

The boos and bottles began to fall from the depths of the shadows. I took a dive off to the left and, between fits of panting and panic, I found it difficult to keep the smile from my face. Ducking through the narrow little corridors and passageways that ran throughout the building, I didn't stop for ceremony; promoters, angry owners, colleagues wishing me well or trying to throttle me, I ignored them all until I came to the fire exit.

1

A blast of cold air slapped against my face, hitting me like an invisible wall. The door clanked shut behind me as I moved down the alleyway, boots crunching on the frosty snow.

I came to a stop near the end and dug around for my cigarettes. When I finally found them, along with a fountain of change that had spilled out of my pocket, my phone began to vibrate, much to my surprise. Nobody called me during a show; nobody called me much at all anymore.

Pulling it out, I didn't recognise the number but something told me it was bad news. Maybe it was a survival instinct, or a hunch, I was certain that this call would mean disaster if I answered.

I did, naturally, and it was, of course.

I stood perfectly still and learned, from a trembling voice, that my mother was dead.

Chapter 2

Taking a trip down memory lane wasn't my style. Looking back to the past was something I tried to avoid like the plague. What was the point? What's done is done, you can't go back.

Everybody knows the type, the grumpy old man sitting in the corner of the pub, telling his stories of glories gone by. I knew I would never be one of those. I probably wouldn't live that long, for one thing.

All of my thinking was beginning to get boring. For distraction, I decided to stand up and stretch my legs, my back and anything else that had been folded up like an accordion in the cramped seat of the train.

'Excuse me, love,' a middle-aged woman said from behind me, dragging with her a large, bulky suitcase. Pressing against the seat, she scooted past, carrying with her the smell that all women of that age seemed to have. Moderately priced perfume and scented soap.

'Thanks, son,' she said in a thick Glaswegian accent.

'No worries,' my own not quite so native. She smiled and moved on a little down the cramped middle aisle of the train before stopping.

She straightened her shoulders and turned around. My stomach churned, an inevitability washing over me.

'You're him, aren't you?' the woman said with a smirk, looking over her expensive spectacles. She flashed a smile that said she was probably once an attractive woman. Only once.

'Excuse me?' I asked, trying to buy a little time to think. It was useless of course; I could never come up with an excuse good enough.

'You're him, that comic, him from the telly.' She snapped her fingers, puckering her lips and trying to pull a name from

3

the depths of her wine and home cooking ravaged mind. 'Rob, Rob Argyll. It's you, isn't it!' she was shouting now, a few of the other passengers coming to life around her.

I could have curled into a ball and fallen into a coma right there. Instead my autopilot clicked into action, using the same lines my brain had become used to saying whenever I was recognised.

'Rab actually. Hi, how you doin'?' I reached out and took the woman's hand in both of mine.

'I knew it was you, I bloody knew it, it's good to see you, we're big fans of you son, big fans,' the woman's face had brightened up, her eyes wide as saucers behind the thick lenses of her specs. 'Me and Terry watch you all the time on the telly, can't get enough.'

'Well the re-run is only on now and then … '

'Our son has your videos, gets them every Christmas.'

'I've only got the one and it didn't sell … '

'And we've been trying to get tickets to your shows but there's never any.'

'I don't do tours unfortunately, I'm more of a smaller gig … '

'Well this is just a big thrill. Wait 'till I tell my girlfriends about this. Wait 'till Terry sees, Terry!'

'No, please, I'm just … '

'Terry!' the woman shouted down the carriage. She waved her hands until a head turned around from a seat near the door.

Some of the other passengers were staring now, others weren't as interested. Funny how some of them acted like this type of thing happened all of the time.

I was beginning to feel out of sorts and more than a little ill, worse than before. The morning had been a whirlwind of bad thoughts and endless frustration with tickets, booking and travel. Now, there was the Great British public to deal with and their endless curiosity into the personal lives of the rich and famous.

Even for the poor and infamous such as myself, there was no getting away from them. They were like a plague of locusts, straight from the Old Testament.

'Excuse me, darlin'' I said, patting the woman's shoulder gently and distracting her from getting her husband, 'I'm not feeling so well, just going to sit down.'

'You don't look well, love, very pale, you want some paracetamol?' she clapped her hand against my cheek. It was the closest to a motherly touch I had felt in nearly a decade. It knocked me for six.

The biting sting of tears began to eat at the space behind my nose and their wetness gathered in the corner of my eyes. A lurch of sickness made my skin creep, vomit pushing up my gullet.

Before I knew it, a steady stream of grimy, brown sick was blasting from my mouth. A terrible groan escaped me as I lurched over onto my knees. Had it not been for the pounding headache now hammering inside my skull, I might have felt better. That was until I realised where the jet-stream of sick had landed.

The middle-aged woman stood in front of me, her face ashen white, mouth dangling open like a corpse. Her arms were spread wide like a crucifix as she looked straight at me, utterly shocked. The apron of vomit that coated her cardigan and travel trousers dripped and shimmered in the moving light of the train carriage.

'I'm sorry,' I breathed, feeling the acid of my own stomach coat my teeth and tongue. 'That's never happened to me before.'

With that the woman burst into tears and charged down the aisle shouting for her husband, her case left long behind in the wake. A few of the other passengers took a customary glance at the chaos and then in my direction before returning to their commute. As if I ever needed reminding, and I never did, I really hated travelling on the train.

Chapter 3

The train rolled into Glasgow's Central Station a little after ten in the morning. The engine hissed and blew smoke out across the platform like some forties romance film, *Close Encounter* or something like it. Typical bank holiday Monday viewing.

The dank wetness and bitter cold of a Scottish winter made the whole place seem almost mystical. As reluctant as I was to admit it, it was good to be home.

I stepped from the carriage and threw my travel bag over my shoulder. There was a smell of sick about me but I was sure there was nothing on my clothes. Twenty minutes in the bathroom, shivering and staring in the mirror had made sure of that. I could still smell it and even taste the faintest hint of the outburst from earlier in the journey.

I headed along the platform towards the waiting area. The old station grew up about me, metal and stone culminating in the great latticework of a transparent roof.

Massive stone archway windows peered out onto Argyle Street to the east and west. Beneath the bridge the pedestrians and buses passed blissfully unaware of how much weight was charging over their heads. Ignorance was bliss after all.

While the technology had changed in the hundred and twenty years since it opened, the same design of the station had remained. Trains came from the south, passengers filtered out of the north, east and west exits, the city just beyond them and easy access to everything they could ever want.

Thinking about it made my teeth itch. This city, its people, it had been a long time. To be thrown straight back in was a culture shock I hadn't quite prepared for.

I wanted to jump back on the train. I didn't have to pay, just hide until somebody found me. Then maybe plead for forgiveness, be thrown off in the middle of nowhere and hope that life never caught me up. Any enjoyment or excitement I had of coming home had quickly worn off.

'Robert!' my name rang out above the constant echo of the station.

I looked up and saw an arm waving above the heads of the other commuters. I didn't want to but my legs pushed on like pistons, determined to drag me forward, kicking and screaming if need be, towards the flailing arm.

'Hi, Gerry,' I said glumly.

'How are you, Robert, here let me help you,' said Gerry with his usual friendly demeanour, reaching for my bag.

'I'm fine, all things considered.'

'I know, I know, come on, I've got the car outside.' We walked a little forward, my head bowed low.

Gerry Dawkins was my brother-in-law of some twenty years, give or take. A short, balding man with a big smile and sharp wit, he had always been kind to me when I was growing up. An electrician by trade, people very rarely had a bad thing to say about Gerry and I could see why. He was giving, kind and always looked on the bright side of things. God knows how he ended up part of my family.

'How was your journey?' he asked, panting a little as we left the station.

'Not bad,' I lied. 'The journey was long, the seat was too small and I felt ill the whole way. Apart from that … '

'Yeah, can be a long time, can't it. Mindy and I were down in the Smoke back in October, went to see *Phantom of the Opera*, took the train … ' Gerry continued his story but I wasn't listening.

One mention of my sister's name had that effect. A pang of guilt made me think better than to be ignorant and I rejoined the conversation.

' … So we ended up coming back a day early, you know what Mindy's stomach is like. How's Tess?'

The guilt quickly turned into apprehension and I felt my scrotum retract almost completely into my stomach. My anus tightened too almost on cue. I felt like a drawstring being pulled too tightly with a short, sharp tug.

'We … We broke up,' I choked, throat suddenly dry.

'Really?' Gerry stopped, his eyebrows arched upwards.

In anybody else I would have dismissed it as a fake showing of interest, a polite, pretend shock that, in the end, was done more through social expectancy than genuine concern. But I knew Gerry was better than that, a lot more genuine.

'Yeah, things weren't really working out. She was working all day, I'd be out at night. You know the way these things go.' I tried my best to shirk it off, subconsciously shoving my hands into the pocket of my long, black coat.

'That's a shame, she was a lovely girl. Are you alright?' Gerry said, starting off again.

'Fine, you know me, Gerry.'

I remained tight-lipped as we walked through the busy morning street. It seemed everybody was out at this time, when they should be working. Students, old folk and a whole host of the able-bodied, all busying themselves as they headed to unknown destinations.

The whole scene reminded me of one of my first gigs. Seventeen years old and nervous as hell, I'd taken to the stage and almost passed out with the heat of the spotlight. The audience moved like a dark, shadowy sea, faceless in front of me but still there, they were always there. More importantly, they weren't going anywhere. It was eat or be eaten and I'd filled my plate to the full.

'Ever notice how pensioners are out during the daytime,' I had started. Complete silence. 'I mean, like always out, really early in the morning. What's with that?' Still silence. 'What I want to know is, how do they get up, dressed and out so early without any help. It's not like that when they're round yours for Christmas dinner, then it's all, help me to the toilet, son, give me a hand up the stairs there, will you?' a few murmurs of laughter but nothing serious.

'Well, I reckon they do it deliberately, just to piss us all off in the morning. You know how it is,' I started to pace back and forth along the stage front. 'You're running for the bus, tie about your neck like a fucking silk noose, stitch running from your nipple to your anus and right up in there,' I mimicked the action, a couple more laughs. 'Only to see the bus and think 'I'm going to make it!' then you realise there's a fucking oldie at the front, dribbling and paying the two quid in pennies,' the room opened up a little more, hearty laughter filling the smoky air. 'Get a fucking move on, I'm on discipline as it is! And they know, don't think they don't know.' I wagged my finger at where I thought the end of the audience may be and leaned on the mic stand, wiping my brow.

'You'd reckon McDonald's would be a bit more forgiving with my lateness too!'

The laughter passed over me like a warm blanket and suddenly I felt braver, more courageous. It was a pity, therefore, that I couldn't remember the rest of the set. The beer and spirits had taken care of that.

'Here we are,' Gerry's voice snapped me out of the daydream. We had reached his car, an old, washed out silver BMW Five Series. As I prepared to climb in, I took a look around the city of my birth. I hadn't noticed until now how beautiful it was becoming, tall glass buildings of New Glasgow looming overhead.

The place was forever changing but it still maintained its

character: tough, working class and forever with a giant chip on its shoulder. There were very few places like it in the world. Probably for the best.

I climbed into the passenger seat and was met with the familiar contents of a family saloon. Dog-eared A to Z, an old ice scraper, window sham covered in dust and lint and the obligatory empty bottle of water, Marks & Spencer of course. I had the strangest feeling I should be noting things down for the act but I couldn't muster the energy.

Gerry thumped into the seat beside me and we set off, ready to combat the mid-morning traffic. My head was pounding, a real nauseating ache that flared up with every heartbeat. The roll of the car, lolling more like a ship on a choppy ocean than the ultimate driving machine, wasn't helping. I gripped the door handle and tried to keep myself from making the same mistake twice in one morning.

'So, how's the act?' Gerry chirped.

'Good, really good. Making progress,' I muttered, swallowing to take away the nausea.

'We saw you on the telly the other night there.'

'Yeah? What was it? Crimewatch?' I couldn't help myself.

'No,' Gerry said in all seriousness, looking a little confused as he glanced between the traffic and me. 'No, it was one of those panel shows, a repeat I'm sure.'

'It will have been,' I said through thin lips. 'I've only ever been on two of them, my first and my last.'

That got a laugh out of Gerry although I suspected it was more to hide his nerves.

'You were very good, had me in fits. You doing any … any more TV work?' he turned on the radio, Radio 2 naturally, and reduced the volume until it was barely audible.

'Nothing lined up,' the words held a finality to them that

clung to the stuffy, blazing warm air of the car.

'Ah,' Gerry replied, tapping out a beat on the steering wheel. It took all of my effort to hear what it was, *Thorn in My Side*, by The Eurythmics. I loved that song, always had done.

'Well, as long as you're working, that's the main thing. That's what I tell our Rob, keep at it and you'll get something in the end. You remember Rob, don't you?'

'Yes, of course,' the image of a dumpy little baby, all snot and saliva came back to me.

'He's twenty next month,' the bouncing bundle of joy immediately evaporated, like a comic book cloud exploding.

'He plays in a band, they're quite good. Worth a listen, I'm sure he'll play for you after the … after the … ' Gerry seemed to be struggling for words. I was kind and threw him a bone.

'The funeral.'

'Aye, the funeral. He'll get his guitar and we'll have a sing-song. Christ knows we'll need it.' A silence followed and I felt Gerry's discomfort.

Maybe he thought he had overstepped the mark, been offensive in his comments. But he couldn't have been more wrong. Back and forth to a hospital every night for months wasn't fun and I had no leg to stand on in that department. I was living in London, hundreds of miles away and had completely sidestepped of any responsibility. In mother's final months, he had been more of a son to her than I had.

But he wasn't bitter with it, at least not to me. Some guys would have thrown that back in your face. I know I would have. Just like I had always thought, Gerry was one of the good guys.

The car raced through the empty lanes of the M8 heading towards the leafy, comfortable suburbs of Glasgow's South Side. In the twenty-five years I had spent living in the city, there had been very little change. The houses all looked the same; the abandoned factories were gaunt skeletons of their former muscular, almost heroic selves.

Most of all the people still wore the sullen, washed out, sick-of-life look on their drab faces.

The motorway had sliced through a lot of the waste but it wasn't a complete regeneration. The concrete snake of road weaved its way through the derelict land and relics from the past. All that remained were pockets of the old city, the last guards from a bygone era. Progress, I thought, always came at a price.

Gerry took the off ramp and prepared to do battle with the outdated gridiron of the city's inner suburbs. Familiarity was a strange thing and I found myself sitting up while street names of old whizzed by.

I liked to think the memories they evoked were all happy but who was I kidding, they were mostly shit. There was a reason I was a comedian and they had more than contributed to my material over the years.

The car pushed on through the traffic as we neared our destination. My sickness began to build up again but I could ignore it for the time being. There was a much bigger hoodoo facing me in a little over ten minutes. Like stepping into a time machine, I was going to come face-to-face with my childhood and adolescence.

I knew my running away wouldn't last forever. I had always just kind of hoped.

Chapter 4

Growing up in Glasgow you had one of two choices. It could be a lot of fun, or total bloody hell.

For me, and the rest of my family, it had been the latter.

Perhaps I was being unfair when I remembered those days, on the few occasions that I did. Maybe they weren't as bad as all that really, maybe it was me just being cynical, being a fully grown adult and all that. The regret of those thoughts flared up now and then like a bad case of lumbago.

When Gerry's car pulled up to the family house, I knew straight away that my rose tinted spectacles were in desperate need of binning. And I couldn't get a new pair on prescription.

Things hadn't changed at all. The house still stood proudly, a defiant solidarity with creeping vines and broken plaster clinging to its outside. A detached Victorian townhouse in the popular suburb of Newlands, as the estate agents called it, the gravel path that led to the front door was littered with sprouting weeds and leaves that didn't know when to stop growing.

Reluctantly, I climbed out of the car and tried to gulp down as much air as possible. The quiet chirping of the suburbs should have been welcoming but I wasn't in the mood. The prospect of what lay inside the old house was much more important. And frightening.

I hadn't thought about what I was going to say to the rest of the family. I hadn't really thought much about anything in the past thirty-six hours. As soon as I had the call, the infamous call, I had walked numbly back to my flat and threw some things in a bag.

The first train to Glasgow still had seats and I had booked my ticket at Euston, running completely on automatic and hoping I hadn't offended anybody or caused an incident on the way. I barely knew what clothes I was wearing, or indeed what

I had packed, the need to be at home throbbing in my chest like a second heart.

It was a strange sensation and one I had never felt before. Was this grief? I didn't know.

Now that I was here, standing at the front porch of the house I had grown up in, the only home I had ever known, I wasn't sure what to say, what to do, how to be. When I had left the place I had made very little effort to return, for good reason. But now, I was back.

My mother's death was all-consuming, clinging to every atom of my mind, heart and my soul, or what was left of it. I didn't want to face it, I couldn't face it, but now I was here. I had no choice; I was forcing myself into the maw like a lemming off a cliff. I knew I couldn't fly, I didn't think I wanted to.

Gerry fetched my bag from the boot and headed up the path, soft loafers crunching on the stones.

'When were you last home? It's probably a while ago now, eh?' he called over his shoulder.

'Dunno, couple of years, maybe more,' I bowed my head, trying to avoid looking at my bedroom window. I knew which one it was but I didn't want to see it. Not until I absolutely had to.

'Well it hasn't changed much. Garden needs done; I'll bring the lawnmower around tomorrow and do it, maybe, depending on the weather. I've just been too busy, what with your mother, and the business, and everything else.'

'Yeah, I know, Gerry. Look, I'm sorry.' My brother-in-law stopped at the door fishing for his keys. He looked up, a sheen of sweat on his wrinkled brow, breath smoking from his tiny mouth in the cold morning air.

'Sorry? What are you talking about?'

I shifted uneasily on my feet, furtive little movements that clicked on the burnt orange tiles of the front step. Why was this so damn difficult? The same nervousness that came on before a date, or if I was exceptionally lucky, sex, made my skin and palms greasy. This was ridiculous; I was hardly asking him out.

I felt queasy and tired but I knew I had to speak to somebody, anybody, before I faced the house.

'I've been on shit form since you picked me up. And I appreciate the lift and dealing with Mum, honestly Gerry, you're a good man. Better than me.'

Gerry shook his head and found his keys, expertly pulling the right one out from amongst the others. He smiled and nudged my elbow.

'Don't be silly, pal. You've had a time of it lately. What else would I have done?' His voice was warm and soothing, moving through the bitterly cold air like a wave of warm butter. This man was a saint in human clothing. At that moment I felt closer to tears than I ever had done.

Only the sound of the door clicking open stopped me from sobbing all over his Pringle jumper.

'Robbie!' moaned Mindy as she draped herself over my shoulders. It took all of my strength not to topple backwards into the flowerbed.

My sister made some fawning noises and stood back up. Her face was made up in the same way it had been since she was fourteen, eyes dark and ringed with mascara, the hint of blusher around the high cheeks, a family trait, and bright red lipstick that looked painful.

'How are you, my darling brother, it's so good to see you.' She wiped at her nose with a rolled up piece of tissue. There weren't any signs she had been crying. An actress with her props, I thought, as we shuffled into the hallway.

16

'I'm alright, Mindy, fine actually. Felt a bit dodgy on the train, but I'm alright now.'

She stood there watching me, nodding and pretending to look interested. When she realised I was finished talking, she snapped back into her grieving daughter act, shaking her head and sniffing uncontrollably.

'Terrible, isn't it? Just terrible,' she said over and over.

'Terrible,' Gerry agreed.

'So terrible.'

'Yeah, terrible.' I had the feeling this would go on until I toed the company line. To my surprise, it came to an end as soon as I said so.

'How was your journey?' Mindy asked.

'Was alright, like I said, didn't feel very well, had a bit of a dicky stomach, fine now though.'

'Oh, Robbie.' Mindy threw herself at me again and clung onto my shoulders.

Hugging wasn't one of Robert Argyll's strong points. I tried to avoid it as much as possible. It wasn't that I was against the whole thing, far from it. More that it was hugely overused. My sister was the typical over-hugger and she was filling her boots.

Mindy was the oldest of the three children and five whole years my senior. Growing up we had never been close, despite the small age gap. While I preferred quiet solitude and a small group of close friends, Mindy had always been the popular one. Amateur dramatics, dancing and a good sporting all-rounder, she had her pick of the men, and women, from school.

When our younger sister Wendy arrived, we seemed to grow even farther apart. Perhaps it was a sex thing, the old girls v boy match-up. I had always been made to feel like the outsider of us all, constantly out of the loop. Not that it had

17

bothered me much; it served as ammunition to my animosity, a stroppy teenager's best friend.

My relationship with my older sister was prickly at best and not something I tended to tell strangers about. After all, who needs to know about a sharp faced, acid-tongued lawyer at the best of times, least of all when she's blood.

'You must be hungry. Come on, let's eat.' Mindy took my hand and headed towards the kitchen. I tried to retract but her grip was far too strong. Somewhere in the back of my mind my pity for Gerry grew.

The sound of voices flittered through the hallway, creeping out from behind the living room door. By my estimation there were at least five more people I would have to contend with before I got some peace. Typical then that I was facing the toughest time of my life and I still had to be 'on'.

Mindy released her iron grip and I sat down at the long kitchen table that dominated the small room. Much like the outside of the house, the kitchen had barely changed since I had last set foot in it. The smell of burnt toast still lingered, as did the musky stench of a clogged drain, a perennial problem that had started not long before my fourteenth birthday.

Whether it was to do with the dead mouse I had shoved down the waste disposal pipe the day before the party or not was still undecided. The jury remained out on that one.

The thought made me smile and I realised it was the first in a very long time.

'Now we've got roast beef, ham, chicken, or turkey, I can knock you up a sandwich or two,' said Mindy in full steam.

'It's fine.'

'Or I can do you a full breakfast, we've got bacon, eggs, sausages, mushrooms.'

'Just tea and a slice of toast, Mindy, thanks.'

18

'Do you want some boiled eggs with that? Soldiers?'

'I'm alright, Mindy.' I looked up from the wood grain of the table and levelled my sister a look of determined grit. She was being overbearing as usual, the matriarchal figure now instilled as the family head elect.

Only a small part of me believed she was doing this through grief. A big portion of my mind screamed she was in her element. Was it right to think that? Was I being unnecessarily harsh on her? She had just lost her mother, as had I, maybe I should cut her some slack. One look back at her fussing made me banish that thought, annoyance replacing the empathy.

Right on cue, Mindy seemed to pick up on my thoughts. I had always suspected she was a bit telepathic. Or I was psychotic, it was hard to tell. She turned towards the window and began to bob her shoulders, quietly sobbing. I sat back in the chair and felt the wooden joints strain.

'Oh, come on, Mindy,' I tried to plead, but I knew it was a losing battle.

'What's wrong, darling?' Gerry came into the room and immediately scurried over to console his weeping wife. He held her shoulders but kept his distance, a wise move.

She spun and pointed a long, well-manicured finger at me. Standing there, in our old kitchen, I couldn't help but think she looked like some old comic witch from a Halloween decoration. The ones Mother had bought from the local supermarket, hastily thrown up after work before the trick-or-treaters arrived.

We were always that house, the one that never gave anything good to visitors. I had always fully expected a backlash but it never came, I guess the kids around our area weren't into throwing eggs and toilet roll. More's the pity.

'You're so unappreciative!' she shouted. 'I'm trying to make you feel better. It's always been the same!'

'Ssshhh, darling,' Gerry tried to neutralise the scenario with an expert, weary ease.

I was about to fight back but I didn't. How could I ever put across my point of view to Mindy? In all of our lives I was yet to do so. Now was certainly no different. Call it a casualty of family harmony or just plain stubbornness, there were some people that couldn't be reasoned with. Mindy Dawkins née Argyll was their queen.

Silence filled the void between the three of us, awkward, sweaty silence. Muffled laughing filtered from the door down the hall, the rest of the assembled mourners putting their upset to one side for the time being. I wished I could share the joke. I'd probably heard it before though.

I slid back my chair with a screech and headed for the door.

'Where are *you* going?' Mindy sneered. I deliberately ignored her and left them both behind, stopping at the living room.

I laid a hand on the handle of the old door, dirty finger marks all around the old bronze knob where a thousand palms had tarnished the metal. Mother had never been house proud, little details like that were always forgotten about with her. My Tess, on the other hand, was the complete opposite. If she could see it, she'd have the Brasso out at the speed of light. I smiled at that notion, the second smile in as many minutes. Something was definitely wrong then, I could never be that happy.

At the thought of Tess, a pang of loneliness crept in. There we go, the happiness short lived as ever.

Thinking about her only soured my mood. I straightened up and let out a thick, heavy sigh and listened to the voices beyond the door. This wasn't the right time to face everyone. I wasn't sure there would ever be a right time.

My bones felt tired, muscles cramped and weak, and my mind was like scrambled eggs. I wasn't back in Glasgow an hour yet and already I had thrown up all over a stranger, spilled more emotion onto a man I wasn't even close to and pissed off my sister to no end. Not bad going, all things considered.

Another wave of laughter went around the room behind the old wooden door. How I'd heard it so many times before and yet I was barely able to crack my own chuckle when needed. Irony was a cruel mistress and she hated my stinking guts.

I turned on my heels and started up the broad stairs that led to the first floor of the old house. Memories of juvenile adventures flooded my mind as I stepped over the third step, knowing that it creaked loudly enough that the living room could hear. I bounded up the rest two at a time.

'Where are you off to, now?' Mindy called, walking like a ghost from the kitchen, Gerry faithfully by her side.

'Going to my room,' I grunted, the bolshie pubescent act complete.

'That's right, just hide away as usual,' Mindy sneered but it was already too late, I had reached the landing above and tuned the rest of the world out.

The doors stood looking at me like headstones, an image still a little too close to the bone. The carpet had thinned enough that it barely covered the floorboards anymore, the dark red and green of the McGregor tartan now all but gone.

My room was straight ahead, ten paces from the bathroom behind me, seven from the end of the stairs and thirty-two from the front room. The statistics were still etched into my memory from the bored, rainy Saturday afternoon I had spent mapping out the whole world from my front door.

This time I made my room in a little under six steps, I must have been eager. Not that I felt very enthusiastic; I knew what I'd find on the other side.

The door opened with a creak, a new addition, and revealed the place I had called my home, my sanctum and my 'Batcave' for the majority of my life. I was a little surprised, it looked almost exactly the way it had when I left it years ago. The *Star Wars* and AC/DC posters were down from the walls but the wallpaper was the same, now with sky blue patches where the posters had once been.

My bed was still there, not the original, but close enough. A tall, two-door cupboard stood in the corner and a writing desk sat beneath the window. Many a happy evening was spent at that desk, drawing and writing, making things up in my head. Escapism, pure and simple.

The desk was no more a wooden table top than it was a portal to anything I wanted. Epic space battles, adventures on the high seas, nothing was out of bounds or outwith my reach.

There were many more unhappy ones, too. Revision, studying, punishment exercises, and all the other bullshit paperwork school made me do. On my own time no less, what a nerve.

The view beyond the window was a familiar, completely benign one that screamed reassurance and imprisonment all at once. Across the street were the Campbells, the twin peaks of their upstairs bedrooms just visible behind the spindly branches of the leafless oak tree in their front garden. It mirrored our house in every way, but I was certain there were massive differences inside.

One red faced memory struck me as I looked out at the street. I remembered sitting at that desk looking at a dirty magazine I managed to get my grubby little hands on. Not so much a *Penthouse* or *Mayfair*, more like the lingerie section of one of Mother's catalogues. Either way it got the job done.

Young, spotty, and bursting with sperm, I was ever curious about my own body. When the delights of the fantasy had weaved their magic, I leaned back to enjoy my post-coitus-for-one relaxation.

Unfortunately, the comfort was replaced by immediate

shock. I had caught sight of the Campbells' youngest daughter Fiona walking their beagle past the front gate. The panic of being spotted and utter self-loathing was altogether too much. But rather than act, or move, or do anything, I simply sat still with a face that looked somewhere between a ghost and a rabbit before it gets smashed to pieces by a lorry.

I touched the same seat where the masturbatory mayhem had occurred and ran a hand along its back. Fifteen years had passed but that same shame and embarrassment were still there, fresh and raw. One of many, many reasons why I hated these trips down memory, or rather agony, lane.

Footsteps thumped up the stairs beyond the door. A heavy knocking on the wood was enough to break my concentration.

'Knock, knock.' The door swung open a little revealing the scabby, untidy hair of Wendy, my kid sister. Fresh-faced and bright-eyed, she was always the best looking of the three kids. Mindy was always a little sour, even as a baby. I was altogether plainer looking, apart from my high cheekbones. Oh, how the critics liked to point those out on me.

'You alright, big bruvver?' Wendy said in a caricature cockney accent.

I walked over and slumped into her waiting arms. Any energy I had now sapped out through my feet. I sunk my face into the space between her neck and shoulder, her hair smelling of sweat and herbs as it rubbed against my cheek like a brittle sponge. She wrapped her arms around me.

I smelled her skin and gripped her tight, feeling her ribs running along the contours of her back. It felt good to be close to somebody, to feel something again, it had been so long since it last happened that I was almost nervous.

'It's good to see you, sis,' I breathed.

'I know Rob, I know,' Wendy whispered back. I pulled her a little tighter and cried for the first time since our Mother had gone.

23

Chapter 5

Sleep was a wonderful creation; it made almost everything seem that little bit better and easier to handle. By the time I stirred, it was nearly nine o'clock. The sulphurous glow from the street outside bled through a gap in the drab, brown curtains, breaking the darkness.

I yawned and stretched and slid my legs over the edge of my bed. My stomach rumbled, bubbling away angrily. I needed food, plain and simple but there was nothing further from my mind. A stale bacon roll, more grease than dough, in Euston Station had offered a mediocre breakfast; everything else had ravaged my appetite for the rest of the day.

It rumbled again, louder this time, like it was telling me, ordering me to eat. Did nothing want to give me a break? Now, my own bowel was turning on me.

'Alright, blimey,' I said quietly, heading out into the landing and towards the downstairs world. Oh, the joys.

The kitchen was the house's hub, the congregation point for everybody in the family. Back door, front door, call to arms, they made their way to the same room. From the most difficult problems to the joy of celebration, the action always unfolded around that familiar table.

'Good evening,' I said rather ominously, even for me.

Five faces turned to stare at me, the conversation stopping in an instant. I hadn't enjoyed this much attention in a long time. Was it bad that I quite enjoyed it?

Wendy was there, tucking into a bowl of steaming soup, the spoon halfway to her mouth. Gerry stood at the sink, elbows deep in boiling hot water, the edges of a pair of bright yellow Marigolds peeking out from amongst the suds.

Mindy was, of course, sitting at the head of the table, where Mother always sat. If the Queen of Sheba wanted her throne, I thought, then she could have it.

The other two faces I didn't recognise. One was a man, tall and dark, who looked like a corporate banker, or words to that effect. Long hair was tastefully slicked back behind his ears, curls gathering above the collar of an obviously expensive shirt.

He stood up and rounded the table, confidently offering his hand.

'Dave Thatcher, pleased to meet you.' I gave him my own in return and felt the solid, rugby club grip crush my fingers.

'Pleased to meet you,' I managed, looking bewildered. 'Who … '

'David is my boyfriend, Rob,' Wendy said, slurping at her soup.

'Boyfriend?' I asked, looking back and forth between the two of them.

'Yes,' they both replied in unison.

Wendy had a boyfriend? And not just a boyfriend, a man, a wolf, one that looked like he was going places, even when he sat perfectly still. When the bloody hell had this happened?

'When the bloody hell did this happen?' I blurted.

My sister slammed her spoon down into her bowl, sending splashes of thick, orange tomato soup all over the tabletop. She ignored it and stared at me as Gerry hovered about her, wet cloth in hand.

'Don't be so fucking rude, Robert,' she said, her dark eyes focussed hard on me, head tilted to one side.

'Wendy,' Mindy said with a groan.

I felt bad, of course, knowing that ignorance was one of the very many things I hated. To display it with such vulgarity wasn't just hypocritical, it was bloody stupid.

'You're right, I'm sorry,' I bowed my head a little.

'Don't apologise to me, apologise to Dave,' she nodded towards the broad shouldered, corporate shill who towered over me.

This was great, already in his debt. Hardly the best of starts.

'I'm sorry, Dave, it's very nice to meet you,' I said humbly, bowing a little farther than was necessary. 'So glad you've decided to bang my sister, welcome to the family.'

'Robert!' Mindy and Wendy shouted at the same time as I slid into a chair. Dave remained standing, his cheeks a little ruddier than before.

'Unbelievable,' Mindy said quietly to herself, making sure I heard her.

I cracked my knuckles and resorted to the other new face at the table. If I had burned all my bridges already with the suit, I figured I might as well go for two.

'And you are?' I asked, nodding to a timid looking girl who had remained perfectly silent.

'I'm Angela, one of Wendy's flatmates,' she answered, like a witness in a murder trial. Maybe it was Mindy, solicitors have that effect on people. I knew I felt like that when I was around her.

She was pasty white with faint freckles that dotted her nose and cheeks. Long, shiny, ginger hair hung from her head like great crimson curtains. Altogether plain and simple, her breastbone poked out from beneath the untidy rim of her baggy t-shirt and cardigan.

A student then, or at the very least a graduate researcher. I winced internally at how easily I had judged her.

'And what do you do, Angela?' I said, bored of trying to hide my boredom.

'I'm a PhD student at Glasgow Uni with Wendy.' Got it in one. 'I heard about your Mum, you must be pretty … um … '

'Upset,' Mindy interrupted, eyes like a hawk peering out from beneath her makeup.

'Yes, upset,' Angela continued.

I slid my hands forward onto the table and drummed my fingers loudly. Every pair of eyes in the room focussed on me, fearful of what I might say next. The feeling was so strong, I could almost taste it.

'Yes, I'm pretty upset, Angela. But thank you for asking, you're a star,' I winked at her and smirked, but she remained stoic, eyes darting everywhere but at mine, desperate not to look at me.

'Don't be such a prick, Rob, you're in a foul mood, get over it,' Wendy said, speaking out the corner of her mouth, the other side filled with soup.

'Sue me,' I said firmly. She shook her head and dipped a large chunk of crusty bread into the remnants of her bowl. My stomach rumbled.

'What's the arrangements, then?' I said, sucking in air through my nose.

'Arrangements?' Mindy answered, assuming, as she always did, that I was talking to her.

'Yes, arrangements. You know, for the funeral? When are we burying the old girl?'

'Robert,' Mindy tutted, Gerry dropped a plate into the sink.

'What?' I pleaded. 'That's what we're doing, isn't it?' What was I doing? I had no control over the words coming out of my mouth. Something was urging me on, forcing me to keep talking.

'Actually, I believe she's being cremated,' said Dave.

The blood in my veins boiled in an instant. I could feel it scorching the muscles and fibres beneath my skin, like molten lava. Who the holy hell did this jumped up, half-witted, rugby bum boy think he was talking to? Telling me how my mother, my own mother, no less, was being seen off.

Was that it then? Was I the last person to know everything? Just because I wasn't there, because I hadn't seen my old Mum in three years, barely spoken to her in almost as long and left the rest of the family to take care of her throughout the illness.

I was relegated to the second division? The Championship? Well that wasn't the case; I was Premier League, baby, Champions League, top flight. I deserved to know.

By the time the adolescent fantasy had worked its way through my brain, the conversation had moved onto something else. Only the distant rumbling of my stomach made me realise I was back in the land of the living. Cold, hard and hungry reality.

'We'll need somebody to pick up the flowers,' Mindy was babbling.

'The humanist lady says she's had a look over the notes, if you want anything added then just let her know before Wednesday,' Gerry continued.

'Auntie Pauline and Uncle Paul aren't coming up from Liverpool, he's got a bad back,' even Wendy seemed to be on the mailing list.

'I'm bloody starving,' I said, getting up and heading to the fridge.

'There's some chili in there, Rob and some sandwiches from lunch,' Mindy directed. 'Not that you bothered to eat any of them.' I went to glance around the edge of the door but decided against it, I was too tired and too hungry.

'The cars are arriving on Wednesday morning, nine sharp. They'll be coming here of course.' Mindy's meticulous planning needed only to be praised for her to be happy.

Hauling the pot of chili from the ice-cold fridge, I nudged the door closed and thumped my way back to my seat. A damp sandwich hung from my mouth like the big floppy tongue of a Great Dane. I dropped the pot onto the table with a bang as the others watched me. Centre of the attention, as always.

'What?' I asked, but nobody answered. I ignored them and pulled the ring of a can of coke, the brown froth bubbling out of the hole.

'Where's the after "do"?' I said, slurping loudly.

'What?' asked Mindy, 'The refreshments?'

'Refreshments,' I repeated, 'Gathering, whatever you want to call it.'

The others looked at each other. Something wasn't right here. I felt their cold stares and stopped my inspection of the pot.

'We thought … ' Mindy started but she trailed off.

'Thought what?' I asked, looking about the room.

'We thought you'd like to do a bit of … talking. A speech, something like that.' She stared at me then turned away and headed for the sink to be beside Gerry.

Dave cleared his throat but didn't follow up with any words. Angela fumbled with her hands beneath the table. Wendy was surprisingly quiet, even though her soup was now little more than a thin layer coating the bottom of her bowl.

'Hey,' I said. My mind was reeling. Any cobwebs from my nap were now long gone as I realised there was something afoot. 'What's going on here?' I raised my voice.

'Now, calm down, Rob. Don't be dramatic,' Mindy tried to placate the situation in her usual, motherly tones. It was too late for that.

29

'What do you mean don't be dramatic? You're wanting me to do a fucking routine at my own mother's funeral! Fucking hell,' I stood up and marched towards the back door.

'We're not asking you to do a show, Rob,' Gerry, of all people, called over to me as I went.

'No, of course not,' said Mindy. The others had remained suspiciously quiet. 'We're just wanting you to speak to the family and seeing as you're used to public speaking, what with your job and all, I thought you'd be best for it.'

Being patronised was one thing, I could handle that. Having it done to me by my family was something completely different. I knew I had slipped away from them, but I didn't think I had drifted so far that they treated me like a performing seal now.

I had to get out of there before I put my fist through the wall, or someone's face. I darted for the back door and pulled it open, marching into the darkness. The movement sensor triggered the backlight and it snapped on, shining bright enough to blind me a little as I dug around my pocket for a cigarette.

'Tell you what, why don't I do a whole fucking set, the full two hours, how does that sound?' I shouted back into the warmth. 'Save everybody forking out the ten quid or whatever it is for a ticket.' I clicked the lighter over and over trying to get a light.

'I'll even do some signings afterwards, get the cousins to bare their chests and I'll put my signature on their breasts. How does that sound?' The lighter still wasn't working.

Somewhere in the darkness, over the wall at the bottom of the garden, my shouting made a dog bark. Good, I was glad it was disturbed; I wasn't going to suffer on my own.

I couldn't explain the anger that was surging through me. My temper wasn't the softest, I knew I had a short fuse. But this was something new, even to me. Everything was shaking, quivering, like I didn't have any control over my own body.

'In fact, I'll do it in the nude! How does that sound? Billy bollocks in front of great aunt Petunia, see if the old cow notices! What's wrong with this fucking thing!' I clenched my fist around the lighter and threw it into the darkness, the cheap plastic rattling somewhere in the night.

A tired and infuriated gust of breath escaped my lungs, bringing with it a long groan that sounded something like a reanimated corpse. The reality wasn't far from it. I placed my hands on my hips and stared upwards towards the brooding, bruised clouds. Things were spiralling out of control at an alarmingly quick rate and there was nothing I could do.

That was what scared me the most, the complete lack of control. Strange then, I thought, how these moments came to you. Control was what I craved; I always had done, over and above anything else in life.

As a child I loved to play with my train set, LEGO, anything that would give me the complete and utter dominance over the lives and actions of the toys.

The same hunger for rule shifted from playing with toys to playing with girls. That acne-riddled Robert had always been seen as coming on far too strong with the young ladies I went out with. One date and, as far as I was concerned, we were as good as married.

In retrospect, I could sympathise with those conquests, but it was a very different story at the time. Broken hearts and closed minds were how I spent my formative teenage years. Then again, who didn't spend them like that?

Adulthood hadn't been any kinder, if anything, it was even worse. More years, more money, more problems, just ask my exes. I was hardly selling out venues up and down the country, yet my professional career was ironically the only place I had any control.

Now, I stood in the freezing cold of my old back yard, arguing with myself over something that barely mattered. Then again, I was the only one left who bothered to fight with me. Everybody else had learned long ago that it was a lost cause, pointless.

'Unbelievable,' I said into the night. 'I hope you're all happy!' I shouted back towards the house.

There was no use fighting it, I knew I'd have to do the routine. Certain expectations came with having appeared on TV, even if it was just once. Maybe this was what it was like to be a celebrity, I hardly knew or had any desire to find out.

I trudged back into the kitchen and shut the door quietly. The murmur of conversation was kept low as I moved towards the chili.

'Have you calmed down?' Wendy asked, cocking her pierced eyebrow.

'As calm as I'm probably going to get, yes,' I said solemnly. 'I'll do a short, very short set at the dinner, but I'm telling you all now, it's only because I'm sick of arguing.'

A wave of nods rolled around the room, each of them in turn silently agreeing, or at least pretending to. Even Dave the shill looked humbled by the generous offer from a one-time comedy show panellist.

'How long will it be?' asked Mindy, the first one with courage to break the silence. Typical.

'Pardon?' I asked, feeling my brow wrinkle.

'The set, how long will it be?'

'I don't know, is there a limit?'

'Well, do you have a rough estimation, is it going to take half an hour, an hour, ten minutes, what?' my sister probed deeper and deeper.

'I don't understand,' I pleaded, genuinely bewildered. 'I haven't really thought about it much, you only sprang it on me, just there. I need time to put something together.'

Mindy rose from the table and lifted Wendy's empty bowl. She glided across to the sink and dumped it into the murky water, Gerry already donning his rubber gloves once again, ready for action.

'Well, it's just … ' she faltered for a moment, puckering her lips as she searched for the words. I got the nausea plague one more time in the pit of my stomach.

'… We're on a very tight schedule, what with other speakers and well-wishers wanting to pay their respects. Is five minutes enough?' she crossed her arms and leaned against the worktop.

The others glanced back at me, eyes moving the same way they did at Wimbledon, following the ball as it flies over the net. As it happened, I reckoned there was more tension now in the old kitchen than there had ever been on Centre Court. The pulsing, throbbing vein in my temple was a fine indicator.

I clenched my fists, a growing habit, and gritted my teeth enough that my jaw hurt.

'And if you could keep it clean, there are going to be kids there, the cousins are bringing their children of course,' Mindy continued her list of demands. 'And nothing too controversial, no politics or religion or anything like that, you know how the old ones hate you slagging off the church.'

There were few occasions in life where time seemed to stand perfectly still. Everything slows down to a bare minium and the world at large feels like it's frozen in a block of ice. Birds hang in mid-air, cars appear to be motionless on busy roads, even people stop dead, mouths ajar and gawping in the middle of a sentence.

For me, those moments never came around often enough. But sometimes lady luck smiled favourably and cut me a little

33

universal slack.

I don't remember how the chili pot got into my hands, nor do I recall the actual throwing motion that sent it flying across the room. By the time the hard metal clattered against the worktop beneath the kitchen window, I was already shouting at full volume.

The clang of the pot smashing against the hard surface rang out like a boxing bell, end of round one. The world and everything in it raced back into real time. I already missed the stillness of the moment. It never lasted long enough.

I stopped shouting and stood panting, sweating and feeling altogether too dramatic.

All eyes were once again on me, although their expressions were noticeably different. Angela had retreated so far into her own cardigan, she looked more like a turtle than a human being. Wendy held a casual, non-plussed look of sad expectation, her beau Dave had leapt to his feet, chest shoved out from beneath his immaculately pressed shirt, Hugo Boss of course, ready to spring into action like the cavalier heroes of old.

Gerry had ducked for cover, Marigold hands covering his bald head in a vain attempt at protection. The sleeves of his sweater were soaked to the elbow in frothy dishwater.

And then there was Mindy. In fairness to myself, I hadn't been aiming for her in particular, nor had I been attempting to cover the kitchen in day old chili. Beheading a family member with a cooking pot was hardly the best way to prepare for one's mother's funeral, even I knew that.

While the rest of the party looked disinterested, frightened, and just plain confused, Mindy remained her calm, composed, and ruthlessly efficient self. Her eyes stared back at me from across the room, two shinning orbs of swirling, dark hazel that screamed authority and demanded respect, whether it was deserving or not.

The remnants of the chili began to slide down the back wall,

34

splattered against the glass like the prop from a low budget zombie movie. When I felt suitably relieved of my anger and frustration, I slid my feet together and stood to attention.

'Are you quite finished?' Mindy asked, her voice like a cold blade slicing through every pore and orifice in my body. It carried the same steely determination I imagined made Gerry's life a plain misery on a day-to-day basis, like living with a retired sergeant major or, heaven forefend, a pensioned off cop.

'I think so, yes,' I squeaked, voice brittle and hard from the shouting.

'Then I think it's time you went to bed, Robert. Don't you?' The eyes darted back and forth again, championship point Miss Argyll.

'Yeah, that sounds good.' Game, set, and match, Miss Argyll, a straight ace with no chance of return.

I turned and headed out the door towards the hallway, legs feeling weaker than ever. The climb up the stairs was a slog and by the time I got to my room, it was almost impossible to breathe.

Pushing through the old door, I staggered towards the desk and let it prop me up, shoulders slumping. My arms shook under the weight and strain of my own body, the anger ebbing out of me with every laboured breath. I felt it rising from the depths of my soul, or what remained of my soul, climbing up from the pit of my stomach.

I looked up but couldn't see the window or the street for the tears, water blurring my sight enough that everything seemed like a black and orange kaleidoscope with a shattered lens.

First came the sobbing, then the weeping, before I was finally reduced to little more than a quivering, snotty wreck. I collapsed onto the floor and hugged my knees, wishing they weren't mine, hoping they were somebody's, anybody else's.

But they weren't, and they never would be. I was alone.

Tears streamed down my cheeks and burned my lips with their saltiness. I couldn't cry enough, couldn't get the pain from within me out of my core, my very fabric. Everything hurt, every wince was like a dagger jabbing into my ribs. My mouth hung open, muscles locked into a frown but no noise came out, I was silent.

Everything that had gone on, thirty-two years of hurt and pain and missed opportunities, flowed out of me then, as I lay on the floor of my old room.

But it didn't feel good, it felt awful, simply awful, the worst feeling I had ever had. A shallow emptiness in the pit of my core now sat where my stomach should have been and brought with it a terrible sense of loneliness and isolation. At last, I realised what I had been denying myself for so long. I was detached from the world, strung out on my own little lifeline that clung desperately to the edge of the rest of existence

Seconds ticked past like hours, my mind hammering home just how much despair there was inside of me. From the very darkest reaches of my memory, the broken promises and untruths told to save face, to the crippling anger and depression that clung to my adult self like a second skin. They all flowed out through my tears, emptying me completely.

Yes, the darkness was soothing and much better than the light, but it was also the loneliest place in the world. Everything made me feel sick, the thought of any interaction with the rest of the human race was enough to send shivers up my spine. Life itself felt like a party where I knew none of the guests. That was my lot, and only now in the confines of my childhood home could I bear to bring myself to face it.

The carpet soaked up and absorbed everything I let out, like it always had done since I could first remember. It smelled of every grazed knee, every punishment exercise, every afternoon spent grounded while I watched the neighbours enjoy the delights of summer.

For the times I had been confined to my room for talking back or when I was left broken hearted, the carpet, the bed, the desk, the whole room had always been there for me. Beyond the door, the rest of the house, always there, the only constant in my life that I had ever truly relied upon. I could rely on it always, nothing else ever came remotely close. And as I mourned the death of my mother, it was there for me again.

Silent and dead, but still very much there, my little piece of the world that wasn't ever going to leave me. I could never thank it enough for everything it had done for me, the idea it would never know only made it that bit more special.

I lay still for a long while, watching the window as my sight gradually returned. My cheeks dried and tightened, salt still lapping at the edges of my tongue. I listened to my heart thump, time and time again, behind my rib cage and let a million and one thoughts pass through my mind like a Calcutta cow market.

Eventually, after two minutes or two hours, I wasn't very sure, I pulled myself up and rested my head on a pillow. I closed my eyes and rubbed my nose clean before drifting off into what promised to be a torrid night's sleep.

Chapter 6

Sleep was never a huge priority in the Argyll household. Most of the family saw it as an inconvenience between dinner and breakfast. There were places to be, people to see, or so they insisted on thinking.

Breakfast was the usual chaotic rigmarole it had always been. Between flying bowls of cereal and the chorus of sizzling bacon to the inevitable rush of two or more family members trying to get out through the front door, keys and clothes and sanity still intact.

When I was a teenager, I used to lap it up with great delight. Sitting in my KISS t-shirt and boxers, smelly toes poking out from holes in my two-day-old socks. I would watch the rest of them dash about like headless chickens knowing that the rest of the day was mine to lounge around at my own leisure.

Mother would be endlessly fussing over Wendy's school uniform, an argument every morning over the length of her skirt, the amount of make-up, the fact she was wearing a safety pin through her nose. My sister would put up a good fight, but she would always lose out to matriarchal superiority.

Father would brood over his morning coffee and copy of The Herald, Scotsman, Times and Mail. He read all the fine print, arming himself with conversation for the rest of the day. As the clock hit eight, he would rise like a Kraken from the depths of the ocean, sweep through the kitchen giving each child a kiss in turn before making his exit, gone until God knows what hour.

Mindy remained at home for longer than was probably necessary. Her methodical mind working out that it was cheaper to stay in Glasgow while she studied than to disappear to some unknown city a hundred miles away. Even as a selfish teenager with no idea about anything, I had known it was because she was scared.

Scared she might get out from underneath our vigilant parents' wing and start enjoying herself. Twenty years old and still a virgin. Even at that age, and still a virgin myself, I knew something wasn't right there.

She would finish up whatever pretentious lecture she was giving from the kitchen stool before heading off to the lands of higher education. Only mother would bid her goodbye, siblings completely uninterested in anything and everything she had to say.

Mother and Wendy would always be the last to leave, the school-run, once the pride and joy and show stopping event of the morning. The older the kids got, the farther it was relegated down the league table and the more it became a damned inconvenience.

A kiss on the head with a warning about too much TV and they would both be gone, leaving behind them the wake of a fully functioning family. I sat amongst the debris like the outsider I was.

Years had passed since the last time all that had happened, but I couldn't tell the difference. Only the names and the faces had changed now. Where our parents had fussed, it was now Mindy and Gerry. Wendy remained indifferent while the rest doted on her, the boyfriend Dave still lingering around, altogether unsettling.

I sat silently and munched on the soggy cornflakes I had served myself. All remnants from the chili incident were gone, the window and wall wiped clean of any evidence. Nobody said anything to me; I was like a ghost to the rest of the family. Hardly any change there then.

'Robert, I need you to pick up the wreath from the florists this afternoon,' Mindy finally asked.

'Okay,' I said, surprised at my own relief that somebody had finally bothered to talk to me. Although the craving for attention still remained, the freshness of the previous night's

39

breakdown was still burning a hole in my mind. Now it seemed I was being ushered back into the unit without question. And, to top it all, was being handed something to do with the funeral.

They had to know surely. Didn't they? Had my weeping been loud enough to filter downstairs? I'd spent a lifetime hiding away what I thought of them. It would be almost a shame to have let it all slip out now. Or would it?

'Who's paying for them?' I asked.

'All taken care of, the whole funeral has been paid for. Just pick them up and bring them back here.'

'Fine.'

'Wendy, can you go with him please?'

'I can go myself,' I snapped.

'And who's going to drive you?'

'I'll walk.'

'You don't know where it is.'

'Well, where is it then?'

'Shawlands, Crawford's, on the high street.'

Memories of Mother's Day presents and birthdays came flooding back at the mention of the florist's name. It seemed only appropriate then that they should provide the final floral tribute. I nodded to myself and swallowed my breakfast.

'I'll walk, bit of fresh air will do me the world of good. When do they open?'

Mindy glanced up from the toaster and darted me a look of contempt mixed with feigned disbelief. She nodded towards the clock.

'It's gone ten, Rob, pull yourself together.' Wendy began to giggle, snorting every few breaths in her own, mildly adorable way. Dave looked embarrassed but stayed silent.

40

'You're losing it, Argyll,' she said.

'Sorry,' I said pathetically.

Moments like that were embarrassing, they weakened any sort of stature my moodiness might have built up. They also served as a sign of just how indifferent and detached I was becoming. Not only with the rest of them but with society as a whole. Rock and roll was for younger men, not ones who hadn't been a teenager for over a decade.

Despite my moment of sad lament, a sense of urgency and purpose seemed to take over me. Perhaps it was the chemical release of the cereal or maybe I was coming to terms with things. I wasn't sure, I wasn't sure I would ever know the answer to that great question. Did anybody ever find out?

I resolved that it was the responsibility. That broken moment the night before had shone a glaring light on my inability to cope with responsibility. Not my only shortcoming, not by a long shot, it was surely progress then that I was wising up to reality.

Being trusted with something, focussing my attention on the task at hand. Feeling useful for the first time in, well, forever. It felt good. The last time I had felt that way around these people I had been in nappies.

A quick shower, shave and fresh clothes continued the good feeling, the Beach Boys' *Good Vibrations* playing over the radio as I made my way downstairs helped, too. When I left the front door and headed towards the main road, I was feeling positively elated, even, dare it be thought, happy.

The bustling street of Shawlands was a pleasant change. Not overly busy like in some of the bigger cities, London, Manchester, those sort of places, but just right. Different faces, young and old, passed me by and came as a more than amicable change to the rest of my family.

Old folk, as usual, were clogging the bus stops and bakeries, banks, and butchers. Their constant presence being felt more than ever. Somewhere in the back of my mind, I noted that I should add that to the act.

Crawford's sat on the corner of Pollokshaws Road and Langside Avenue, across from the leafy edge of Queen's Park, one of the city's great Victorian commons. Everything about the place was old, even the service.

Old John Crawford had died years ago, but it was still in the family, his daughter Susan now running things. When I stepped in from the cold, a tinkling bell rang overhead and the proprietor, herself now nearing her sixties, came hobbling out from the workshop in the rear.

'Morning, my love, how can I help you?' she asked, wiping her hands on a soil stained apron.

'I'm here to collect a wreath,' I answered politely, 'under the name Argyll.'

The woman's face turned from jolly to sad in an instant, all the life and colour drained from her rosy, plump cheeks. She tipped her spectacles down onto the end of her nose and peered over at them.

'You're not Robert, are you?' she asked expectantly.

This fame business was becoming something of a repeat offense. Any more of it and I might actually have to start behaving like a jumped up, self-obsessed twat. Who was I kidding?

'That's me,' I said. Susan stepped over and clapped a firm pair of hands on my shoulders.

'I'm sorry to hear about your mammy. She was a lovely woman, really lovely. Kind, so kind.'

Something twanged in the back of my mind as I listened to Susan Crawford talk about my departed mother. Unexpected and wholly strange, a dizzy light-headedness took over and I began to feel faint.

In that instant my happy mood was extinguished, gone, vanished in a puff of smoke. I shouldn't have been so surprised, good things hardly ever lasted long in my life. Why should it have been different this time?

I could feel tears welling up in my eyes again and I tried to choke them back as best I could. What the bloody hell was happening to me?

'Excuse me, I'm sorry,' I breathed, voice cracking at the end of the sentence.

I swayed a little on my feet and searched the shop floor for something to hold onto. There was nothing, only tall pots of exotically coloured flowers and plants that I couldn't afford, hanging and sprouting from every possible angle. Designer vases stared down from high shelves and the wafting perfume of a dozen different species stuck in the back of my throat.

My legs were about to give way when something strong and solid stopped me. I cleared my eyes, blinking hard and saw that Susan was holding both of my hands in hers. She was like a rock, a boulder, unshifting against the pressing tide of emotion. It came and went in intervals within the ocean of my despair. If I had ever needed somebody like her, it was now.

We sat in the small break area at the back of the workshop and just talked. No subject was off limits and it all seemed to flow so naturally that I wasn't even sure I was actually there. I had never spoken so easily to a stranger before. I pinched my arm to remind me that I was awake and not passed out on some hospital bed, tranquilised into a coma and suffering a psychotic episode.

Susan made a wonderful herbal tea and kept a fresh pot nearby at all times, never letting my mug empty. We demolished a packet of dark chocolate digestives and were halfway through some Jaffa Cakes when the phone began to ring. My generous benefactor got up and moved to the workbench strewn with cuttings and shoots of a thousand different plants meant for even more occasions.

'Yes, he's here,' I heard her say, ears pricking up immediately. 'No, he's alright, just needed a cup of tea. He'll be home shortly, alright? Bye now, bye.' Susan clicked the phone back down on its receiver and placed her hands on her hips.

'Am I wanted?' I said slowly.

'Seems you made a promise to pick up your mammy's wreath and head straight home,' Susan replied. 'But you've been sat nattering away to me all this time. Your sister Mindy's worried something happened to you.'

I gave a small snort of a laugh and rubbed my forehead with an open palm. The smell of natural herbs from the tea came from my fingers, the underside of my nails dark with melted chocolate. Funny how I could take solace from something as simple as a cup of tea and biscuit, yet be utterly deplored by my behaviour towards the people I truly loved. Was supposed to love.

I was the comedian; I should have been able to see the funny side.

'You're going to be fine, you know,' Susan said loudly, as if answering my own self-loathing and doubt.

I looked up and feigned a smile, shook my head and pulled on my coat with a lethargic groan.

'You will, you know.' The florist who I barely knew came over to me and took my hands once again. I felt a lump in my throat but resisted the urge to be overcome once again. Twice in one day was more than enough; I couldn't submit this poor woman to that again. I couldn't put myself through it, either.

'You've got to be strong, Robert. Not for your mother and not for your sisters but for yourself, son. Do it for yourself, get back a little of that respect you don't seem to have anymore.'

She stared at me earnestly, her dark green eyes growing glassy at their edges. 'Promise me you'll try.'

'I'll try,' I managed to squeak. Clearing my throat I made a second attempt at it. 'I promise I'll try.' I nodded like a child who had been caught being up to no good. I was well practised in that; it was almost a proud tradition of mine.

'Okay, well, here,' she released her grip and fetched a box from beneath the workbench. 'It's all in there, sorted and ready. Pass on my condolences to the rest of the family and just, just keep on fighting. Alright?'

I took the box and nodded again, sniffing a little. Susan clapped me on the shoulder and walked me to the door. I said my thanks one more time and started up the street, heading for home.

Chapter 7

Home was a strange concept. When you really sat down and thought about it, there was very little to distinguish between a home and any other place where an individual spends an extended amount of time.

That rather scientific, sterile definition aside, I found myself thinking about the idea more and more. The only difference between a house and a home was the emotional attachment. I knew that. I wasn't stupid.

As glaringly obvious as that might have been, it didn't make things any easier to take when I really thought hard about them. A death in the family was always bound to throw these types of thoughts up. The basic ability to cope dictated it had to happen; otherwise I would have a breakdown.

That's what the textbooks said. It was altogether different in the real world, as old and tired a cliché as that sounded. Sometimes these old phrases were right on the money, there was a reason they were so popular.

Fighting these emotions was becoming a moment-by-moment struggle, but I was convinced I was coping. Failure wasn't an option; father had drummed that into me. On the rugby pitch, in the classroom, everywhere. Some children would have risen to the challenge, others resorted to good old-fashioned rebellion.

I was, of course, the latter. And how I rebelled, I had never really stopped. Always on the other side, quick to argue, never relenting when it came to putting my point across. Half the time, or maybe more than half, I was only doing it out of spite. If I had cared as much as I had made out, I'd probably have become a doctor, or a lawyer, or a highflying businessman. A success.

Staring across the old living room now at Dave, the corporate shill, I wondered just how different our upbringings had been. Was he the complete opposite from me, the positive to my negative? Where I had said 'no', did he say 'yes', curtailed and whipped into line and shaped by a pushy Dad who would have had no problem sharing a whisky with my own father?

I could see that conversation now, what a pair of old bores. Sipping from their expensive glasses, warbling away about the city, the government and everything else old men talk about. There would be no football chat, only rugby and maybe the occasional reference to cricket, if they were feeling particularly British.

Then the light-heartedness would give way to the serious stuff; the family. The real meat and potatoes of any middle class conversation.

'David's just come back from a three month trip around Europe,' Dave's Dad would scoff. 'Finding himself or some such. I would have minded but for his finals results, a first in economics from St Andrews, you know,'

My father would be forced to nod politely while the sickening feeling of inevitability grew in the pit of his gut. He knew that the next question would be directed at him and his own son and, the embarrassment that followed.

'And how's your son, Robert?' Dave's Dad would gush.

'He's just Robert,' my father would answer, almost apologetically.

'And what's he doing with himself?'

'He's a comedian.'

'A comedian?' the term would be more like an accusation than a question.

'Yes, he's a stand-up comedian, one of those chaps from the television.'

The awkwardness would be almost unbearable, pressure

growing for my father to look properly shamed while still maintaining an air of dignity. He would invariably try and aim the conversation towards the golden shores of Mindy and her legal frolics, but it would never be enough. The damage was already done, he had lost.

No wonder the old bugger had keeled over from a heart attack one day. It must have been a lot of pressure, being embarrassed by your only son.

'Yes, keeled over from a heart attack,' my attention was taken away from my daydream momentarily and I snapped back into the present.

Dave's leering face sat across the living room from me, hair slicked back and looking more predator-like than ever. His suit was sharp, lapels cut into distinct angles, everything looking deadly. Then again, anything would look like killer fashion next to my beat up old two-piece, a relic from my first foray into the world of work.

At least our ties were the same; you didn't get much variance on a simple, black tie. This was a funeral, not a fashion parade. I sounded like Mother, or worse, Mindy.

I was feeling strangely at ease as we waited for the funeral cars to arrive. Strange really, on the verge of the most painful moment of my life, that I would be bordering on the sedate, catatonic even. Bloody typical, I couldn't even get this right.

'Just fell over one day and never got back up,' Mindy was telling the story of our father's death for the millionth time. Nobody was paying particular attention, we had all been there for that drama and promptly tried to forget.

The only one who had been missing was Dave and I doubted he cared. Still, he was doing a good job of pretending to look interested. I didn't imagine he had a problem doing that, the weasel.

'Terrible tragedy, he was only sixty,' she sniffed after the sentence and awaited the praise. None came and she moved over to the window to search the street for the hearse.

Weddings and funerals, I thought, always the same, the only time there is a large gathering of a family, friends and well-wishers. The stories are always the same, retold time and time again as if everybody had forgotten them. Like the tall tale of Father's passing.

Mindy had taken it upon herself to be the master storyteller and that one was her favourite. What she always forgot to mention was that he was found in the flat of his mistress. The old bugger had been playing away from home with a woman half his age and she'd polished him off. Literally.

All personal and familial ties were broken in an instant for me. I might never have gotten on with the old man, or Mother for that matter, but there was a difference between not loving a parent and not caring. He had betrayed the trust of the whole family, not just our Mum. And for what? Two pumps and a squirt with some tart from his office.

At least the whole incident had provided some fresh material for the act, still in its early days at that point. Every cloud and all that.

'Cars are here,' Mindy announced from the window. The assembled party began to shuffle and head for the door, Dave leading the charge.

Gerry hovered around Mindy, holding out her coat, always vigilant, always ready to keep his wife as happy as she could be. I wondered if he knew that would probably be an endless task.

Wendy downed the last of her drink, a gin and tonic more parts gin than tonic, despite being ten thirty in the morning, and stared at me. She looked sad, the saddest I had seen her since this whole escapade had begun. Behind those dark eyes we all shared, I knew that she was a hurt individual, one that needed mending.

Who didn't in this family? But just then I could see her real age, her real problems. Wendy put up a good pretence being the happy-go-lucky forever student type. When you stripped all of that bullshit bravado away, she was a lonely little girl who had just lost her Mummy.

I moved to give her a hug, but Dave's arm slipped over her shoulders like a tentacle. He turned her away and ushered her out the door before I could say or do anything. I was mad and getting madder, but I had to keep it together. Susan the florist's words still echoed in my mind like a toll bell, be strong, not for them but for myself.

Breathing helped, it always did. It kept things going, pushing on, blood pumping and everything else. I cleared my mind and headed for the front door, desperate for some fresh air.

Light flakes of snow were falling from the dirty grey sky, dusting the streets and walls with a thin layer that looked like icing sugar. I marched down the gravel pathway and prepared to see Mother for the last time.

The hearse rumbled with a low purr, an elegant machine that glistened in the mid-morning gloom. The funeral director stood next to the bonnet with one of the drivers, hands crossed in front of them and a look of experienced mourning etched on their grey faces.

I tried to take in as much detail as I could before the inevitable happened. As I pushed on down the pavement, it finally forced itself into my field of vision. There, in the back of the car, was the coffin.

To my surprise I didn't feel as bad as I thought I would. Viewing the box that contained the remains of my departed Mum was as scientific and straight to the point as it sounded. All personal attachment was removed and I was struck by just how inanimate the whole thing seemed.

I felt a little robbed, hurt, that there wasn't anything else.

Despite the damp squib of a reaction, like a firework that didn't go off, I couldn't keep my eyes from the wooden box.

'You alright, pal?' Gerry said beside me. I flinched but relaxed immediately when I saw his friendly face peering at me from beneath the rim of his black trilby.

'Yeah, I am actually. Thanks, Gerry, got caught a little off guard by the box, you know?' I thumbed towards the coffin. My brother-in-law nodded, colour draining from his cheeks.

He swallowed hard, then gasped a bit for air. Instinct forced him to adjust the scarf around his neck.

'Yeah, it gets to you, doesn't it?'

'You bet.' I nodded towards Mindy, who was climbing into the back of a car. She stopped and looked above the door, eyes glistening with tears in the shadow cast by her own wide brimmed hat. 'How's she holding up?' I felt obliged to ask.

'She's not good. Things aren't good at home though, Robert, not good at all,' Gerry shook his head and for the first time since I met him, I thought I saw him look truly unhappy. The endless well of positivity was gone; in its place was a husk, something empty. That happy, chirpy, always aiming to please demeanour that made him so popular had vanished. I felt for him.

'Why? What's the matter?' I asked. He shook his head again and tried to palm the situation off.

'It's nothing, just a bit of business, that's all. Really, it's nothing. This isn't the time or the place, I'm sorry I brought it up. I am.'

He looked shattered, gaunt in the pale light of the winter's morning. Whatever was eating away at him, Gerry wasn't able to cope and I had a sudden urgency to step in and be a hero. Every dog had its day after all, maybe this was mine.

'Gerry!' Mindy shouted, still halfway in and out of the

limousine. He gave me another, teary-eyed glance and trudged off, defeated to be with his wife.

I watched him clamber into the car, the door slammed shut behind him. Once again I was alone, left out in the cold on what should have been the moment where my family were around me, together. Who was I trying to convince here, we Argylls were about as warm as a Siberian toilet seat, at night, in the open. Boom, I still had it.

The second car very kindly let me have a seat as transport to the crematorium. Me being the only son wasn't qualification enough, it appeared, to get a free lift to the service. Instead, I had to hang around looking like an abandoned puppy.

We passed through the suburbs, but I wasn't interested in any of that. Childhood haunts, places I had been with friends, spent sleepovers at, what a load of bull. This whole trip had opened my eyes to more than I was prepared for. I'd had enough of that nostalgic rubbish.

A large crowd had gathered at the Linn, a popular south side haunt for those in need of a fiery pathway to the next world. Former Celtic and Scotland manager Jock Stein had been cremated there following his heart attack in 1985. Ever the man of the Scottish, although mostly Glasgow, public, Stein had presided over the national team's efforts to reach the 1986 World Cup in Spain only to collapse after the qualifiers.

I was no Scottish football fan, but I liked to give credit where it was due. Long before the overpriced mediocrity of the modern day, it used to be something worth watching.

Past history aside, the Linn had been chosen as the venue for another important ceremony, or at least, one of two that day. A sign on the notice board at the entranceway indicated we weren't the only ones planning a bonfire with a dearly departed family member that day. The McGinley clan would also have to go through this pain-in-the-arse rigmarole.

When the cars pulled up, the pallbearers stood nervously at

the rear end of the hearse. Myself, Gerry, and Dave the shill were joined by two cousins of mine, Tim and Stewart, twins who stayed across the city in Milngavie.

The two lads were Mother's sister Rita's kids and they were always made to feel that way in our household. We had enjoyed almost carbon copy upbringings, private school, and university. Yet somehow, they were always distanced. The two families never seemed to click.

I put that reason down to why neither of them exchanged any eye contact with me as we pulled the old girl out from the hearse. The sixth pallbearer was from the funeral directors and I conceded it was nice to have somebody around who knew what they were doing.

'Nice and gently, onto your shoulders and take your time,' said somebody from behind me, the funeral director himself presumably. Either that or one of the throng of mourners was interviewing for a new job in the funeral business.

Lifting a coffin is one of the worst things a person could ever do. The social fear of dropping the bloody thing was bad enough, the added weight of the box almost unbearable. All I could feel was the biting sting of the wood as it jammed into the base of my neck. Dave was my partner, I could feel his muscular arm grab onto me from the other side. Even his grip was better than mine, the show-off bastard.

We marched into the crematorium at a snail's pace and I could feel my hands getting slippery with sweat. I focussed on Tim's ginger, very ginger, crown bobbing in front of me, making sure I didn't catch sight of any of the gathered congregation. Somewhere in the distance I heard organ music, but I didn't know the tune. I didn't know anything, my mind was utterly blank.

The coffin was laid down on a plinth at the head of the chapel and we all breathed a silent sigh of relief. While the others moved off towards the pews, I stayed perfectly still.

My legs wouldn't move, they were frozen. My feet were like two blocks of ice, dead and cold, my hand clinging to the edge of the lid.

I gazed at the top of the coffin, but I wasn't looking at it, I wasn't looking at anything. I just stared blankly ahead, examining every knot of the wood grain, every curve and straight divot of the bronze plaque that was screwed down tight to the surface.

For a moment I thought I was having a heart attack, or a stroke or both at once. My body ceased to function, all power shut down, even the autopilot. It was like the worst stage fright I'd ever experienced, magnified into one terrifying, blood freezing moment.

A thought had suddenly dawned on me. This was the last time I would ever see Mother. We had never gotten on, but I'd always believed we would resolve our differences, everything that had been bad between us. Before the end, before the last breath of hers, or mine, things would be put right and we could enjoy each other's company, the way it should have been.

But now, as I stood staring at her coffin, I realised that was never going to happen and I didn't want to let go. This box, this wooden, odd shaped storage device was all that I had left of her.

I could never see her again, not properly. Those days were gone now and I couldn't ever get them back.

My heart was ripping in two, literally aching from the thought. Everything that I could have said, should have said now would never be done. As if that wasn't enough, all the things I did say, those terrible things in the heat of the moment, they couldn't ever be undone now.

While I might have been apologetic towards the way things had turned out, it didn't mean anything anymore. There was nothing I could do to rectify any misdoings, any problems or grievances we had let fester over the years.

These were what devastated me most of all. I may not have been close to my mother, but in some large way, that I wasn't willing to admit to myself, I had always wanted to apologise to her for the way things had turned out. This wasn't about blame, I may shoulder the bulk of that, but Mother wasn't perfect either.

None of it mattered anymore. It was too late. Like everything else in my selfish, obsessive, overly analytical life, I had missed the chance to make things better, to sort them out. And all for what? Some lonely existence that had alienated everybody from ever getting close to me.

Standing over Mother's coffin, seeing her name inscribed on the plaque, I at last realised what a terrible son I had been. It was little consolation now, time was up.

A sharp pain shot up my hand and I came to my senses. I was still tightly grasping the edge of the coffin. Only Mindy's gentle touch on my shoulder finally broke my grip as she helped me to my seat. I couldn't see a thing through the tears.

Chapter 8

Jumping from one form of blindness to another isn't a recommended move for most. It's especially stupid when the second loss of sight is due to alcohol, and lots of it.

The reception moved all of the action, and its players, to a small bar and hotel near the house. The Tinto Thistle had been the usual pilgrimage for all grieving Argylls since my grandfather's passing when I was barely on solids. It had changed over the years of course, but still retained a nostalgic air. Indeed, I had never been in it for any other occasion other than the aftermath of a funeral.

Even my father got the dignified send-off that he never deserved in the Tinto, although I had tried to forget that whole sorry escapade. Not that anybody seemed to be bothering with that now, they all looked thoroughly entertained.

The atmosphere in the limousine had been sour on the way back from the crematorium. Once again, I found solace in one of the family cars, but was made to feel like an outcast with glaring looks from Wendy and Dave boring into the back of my skull. I wasn't sure they were aware they were doing it anymore. It still hurt though.

I had managed to pull myself together before we reached the hotel and ducked into the toilet for a splash of water and a private tear. I looked at myself in the mirror, skin around my eyes blotchy and red, sockets burrowed deep into my skull. I looked like shit and didn't care.

When I had been ushered to my seat in the crematorium I couldn't bear to watch the coffin descend into the furnace. Perhaps it was my imagination playing tricks on me at the time, but I could have sworn I heard the inferno raging beneath the floor.

The service had been short and succinct, the product of a humanist minister. Mother had never been big on religion and we had been raised the same way. I had bowed my head and stared at my scuffed shoes while the woman droned on about people she didn't know, places she had never been, and events that had happened and she hadn't heard of up until a few days before.

It wasn't her fault and I certainly wasn't blaming her. As I looked at my laces, counting each in turn, I had realised I was as much of a stranger as she was.

And that hurt, that hurt like all the daggers of Hell were stabbing me in the chest all at once. To think that there were people in the chapel who knew more about my mother, been with her, lived their lives around her more than I had was sickening. I was ashamed of myself.

I hadn't been blind to it, that was one of the problems. Everything I had done, all the missed birthdays and anniversaries, the humdrum visits at Easter and every other time, they were all my doing. I had made that decision to stay away, hiding like a stupid, self-absorbed coward.

I was never interested in the rest of the family. I had convinced myself they wanted nothing to do with me, either. But I admitted now, in the privacy of the men's room, that had been nothing but an excuse. A way of making me feel that little bit better about what I knew was wrong.

There had been no end to the depths I would sink to. I hated myself, I hated my actions. Above all else, I loathed what I had put everybody through in the process.

By the time I had re-emerged, freshened but no more re-energised, most of the guests had arrived and taken their seats in the smaller of two dining rooms that the hotel offered. I was lumped beside Tim and Stewart and their end of the family while the others milled around with aunts, uncles, second cousins, third cousins, great aunts, friends, well-wishers, hangers-on, serial funeral goers, and a partridge in a pear tree.

The usual awkwardness abounded and I took a small

comfort in knowing that the family trait extended to the farthest regions of the bloodline. Fumbled words, speaking at the same time, the general fluffiness of polite conversation with somebody you hardly knew. All a total nightmare, but it had to be done.

The booze made it a bit more amicable. Two and a half pints down with the prospect of at least another three on the horizon. God bless whoever came up with the idea of 'rounds', it was a social lifesaver.

By the time it got around to my speech, or set, or whatever it was meant to be, I was relieved to be returning to something I knew better. I still didn't feel like it, nor did I want to parade in front of the room, but I'd said I'd do it, didn't I. It was a small wonder Mindy had trusted me with anything, let alone give me a forum, a soapbox with no filter. Well, plenty of filters. Actually, it was all bloody filters.

My older sister had opened proceedings by taking to a small dance floor that occupied the front of the room. She thanked the guests and babbled on about how nice it was to see so many faces turn out for the occasion. With all that patronising nonsense out of the way, she gave me a little nod and I headed for the stage.

One of the waitresses who buzzed around the room handed me a cordless mic. This was all a bit slick, I was expecting to have to shout. Disco lights and a DJ booth and we would have had a full-blown school dance on our hands.

'Good afternoon, ladies and gentlemen,' I said, trying to settle into this uncomfortable role. I was feeling awful, the booze wasn't helping and I was starting to sweat. 'Thank you all for coming here today. I want to say on behalf of my family, and myself, that I appreciate your efforts.' The assembled group of mourners began to pay attention, stopping their efforts of eating the hotel out of supplies.

'Still, it's better than a day at work or school right?' they all scoffed, that got them going alright, the pigs. 'So, yeah, it's not been a great trip back home. But I suppose none of them ever, are they? You come back for funerals and weddings, sit beside people you don't see for decades and hope that you don't forget the names of their kids. Honestly, we're better leaving it at Christmas cards.' The whole dining room was laughing now.

Fat uncles, henpecked cousins, children squabbling with themselves in the corner. All the while I was standing at the front like some old, drunk crooner. I only needed the loose bow tie, the wonky fedora, and a penchant for beating up women. A set of blue eyes wouldn't have gone amiss, either.

'I must say though that the vicar did a great job of the service, don't you think?' I started clapping, 'Come on, yeah, give her a round of applause,' a couple of claps, but the laughter began to die down a little. Faces were turning slack, had I pushed it too far already?

'Can't be easy for her though, not the best way to spend your working life, putting people into ovens. She should have become a baker, would have been a lot more fun and she could at least get her leg over once in a while!'

That had done it. The punch-line fell flatter than the Belgian skyline and people were beginning to shift uncomfortably in their seats. Nobody was looking at me now, instead searching for any excuse under the sun to get out of the dining room before I said anything else.

'What?' I said, sweat lashing down my forehead. I felt like Lee Evans after a workout.

Mindy was sitting near the edge of the dance floor, making subtle gestures to her throat to bring the whole thing to an end. At least I thought that was what she was doing. In my semi-pissed and fully pissed off state I decided to use it as my swan song. Nothing like going out with a bang, was there?

'Right, oh well, it looks like I'm being ushered off here,

rock and roll.' Conversation was bleeding back into the gathered mourners now, they were already beginning to forget I'd even said anything.

'Thanks for coming, and I believe you're getting a real treat now,' I said as Rob, Mindy and Gerry's son, was making nervous steps towards the stage, guitar in hand. 'Stay lucky,' I said, bashing the mic against my arm and sending a long, high pitched whine out across the dining room.

Rob nodded at me. I handed him the mic and made for the exit and, beyond that, the bar.

'Good luck, kiddo,' I said, clapping his arm.

'Yeah, sorry, thanks, sorry. Thanks, Uncle Robert,' he murmured. Rob was a decent enough kid, one of those guys who would always apologise. Anything he did was sorry this, sorry that. Not spineless, just downtrodden, a bloody pity at such a young age. Then again, having somebody like Mindy for a mother, the poor sod didn't stand a chance. Even in the womb, I'm sure she made him feel inadequate in some way.

I could only imagine the horrors she had said to him about the whole pursuit of music. More was the pity, but I was short of that, as I always was. Pity and regret weren't my strong points; he should pull his bollocks out of his mother's handbag and get on with it if he was that bothered.

He tuned up his acoustic guitar, plucking the strings. I left him to it, deciding immediately that I wasn't going to listen to his set. Call me callous, I just didn't care. Putting your mother in a wooden box then setting it on fire did that to a man.

I hurried to the bar and made sure to steer clear of Mindy and the others. If I could drink myself into a stupid oblivion, then I wouldn't care what she or any of the rest of them said. The sad truth was that I cared in the first place.

The bar was busy with mourners and they were all forthcoming with plying me with more alcohol. The only problem was the accompanying sympathy, plenty of 'get better soons' and 'such a terrible shames'. I was the mourning son after all, I suppose it was my duty.

Binge drinking aside, I was glad when a hand clapped my shoulder and broke the monotony of a story I was telling to a friend of my father's who I had probably met twice in my whole life.

'Gerry,' I said with a sluggish smile, turning to meet the hand.

'How you doing, Robert, you alright pal?' he asked.

'I'm good, Gerry man, real good. You got a drink?' I sauntered around to face him, leaned a little on the bar and narrowly avoided falling flat on my arse.

'No, I'm fine, pal. Listen, there's someone here to see you.'

A shot of adrenaline coursed through me like I had been struck by lightning. Everything tightened, from my jaw clamping shut to my buttocks clenching tighter than Superman's buns of steel. My mind caught up a second later and I subconsciously began to frown.

'Who is it?' I asked, barely louder than a whisper.

Gerry looked about the busy room as if checking that the coast was clear. He licked his lips and generally looked like a bad secret agent. What was this all about? He was hardly James Bond, he was telling me about a visitor, it was a funeral, these things were meant to happen.

Then it struck me, like a hammer blow to the chest. Whoever it was, he wasn't sure if it was right for me to see them. That meant it could only be one person.

My heart began to thump hard, filling my ears with a drumbeat loud enough that it drowned out the rest of the room's background noise. A numbness trickled down my arms from my shoulders and I struggled to push myself off the bar.

Standing on wobbly feet, I tried to pull myself together, fixing my shabby hair and unfastened collar, even rolling down my sleeves.

'I'm ready,' I said, sounding like an old Hollywood hero. Well, maybe not that heroic, perhaps something from a cheesy daytime soap. More *Doctors* than *Dunkirk*.

Gerry straightened up too and smiled weakly. He turned and headed towards the main exit of the room, I followed him like a swaying, slightly drunk pet dog. How the mighty had fallen.

'Now, I did say that you were speaking with the family,' he shouted over his shoulder as we pushed past a couple of hotel guests and two young children, Tim's, I believed, who were swinging from the banister of the tall staircase. 'You know, that you were doing your duty, keeping everybody at bay, at ease, doing your bit.' Gerry kept warbling, but I couldn't have cared less.

It wasn't his fault; there were bigger fish to fry. I felt nervous, tense, queasy. Nothing new there, then. But this time it was different. Almost like there was an added risk, something I could lose if I wasn't on my best behaviour. The stakes were high and I hoped I was holding a pair of aces.

'But he insisted on coming in and seeing you.'

I stopped dead. He? He who? Who was he? What was happening here?

'He?' I blurted. Gerry stopped and turned a little. He looked confused, not half as much as I felt.

'Yeah,' he said.

'Gerry,' I replied with a bemused laugh. 'Who the bloody hell am I going to see here?'

'Robbie!' came a big, booming, bombastic voice from the main entrance of the hotel.

The burly, heaving sight of Jack 'Jacky-Boy' Johnson filled the doorframe. He outstretched his arms and wrapped them around me, pulling me closer in as tight a bear hug as I had ever been in. When he finally released me, I slumped back onto my feet and gasped for air.

'Good to see you, Jacky,' I just about managed.

It wasn't a lie, I was happy to see him. Since we were five years old, Jack had been my best friend. At times he had been my only friend and for that I would always love him.

A huge, sprawling man with a barrel chest, wispy, faded blonde hair and big features, Jack and the Johnsons lived a couple of streets up from us in Newlands. His parents were both doctors and he had been huckled into the profession, or at least they had tried to. When that went awry, a young Jack being more stubborn than an angry mule in heat, they had effectively disowned him.

When he was eighteen, he packed up his things, drained his savings account and never looked back. Five-years later he was a millionaire, shrewd investment and foresight in the Internet company boom of the mid-nineties had successfully put him in a tax bracket higher than I could ever aspire to reach.

No formal education, other than the torturous years at school with me, the man was a walking testament to cunning and wit.

Deep down, though, he was a good man. Beneath all the bravado and loud showmanship, Jack was actually quite a sensitive, honest person and a perfect candidate for good egg of the year. Not that you could tell from his behaviour. Several low profile relationships with some higher profile celebrities had successfully been kept under wraps, thanks to a kind whisper in the ear of some newspaper editors. Jack the Lad didn't have a look-in when it came to Jack the Johnson.

And he seemed to be relishing in the eccentric, millionaire playboy mood. Multicoloured Pringle sweater and a pair of claret chinos that seemed to ooze from his gut. Only he could turn up to a funeral dressed like that and nobody would have the courage to question him. That was the power money bought you.

'Good to see you, too, you long streak of piss,' he pawed me on the shoulder and smiled. 'Sorry to hear about your old lady, Robbie, Gerry here was telling me you've taken it pretty well.'

I looked at Gerry who smiled politely. Good old Gerry, always looking out for me.

A sad thought crossed my mind then. These two were probably the only people in the world who gave a rat's arse about me. What did that say about my character?

'It's been a tough old time, yeah. But what can you do,' I kicked my heels on the polished floor of the reception area.

'I know, buddy. Anyway, let me buy you a drink, I owe you that much. You coming, Gerry?'

'No, I'm going to head back and see if Mindy is coping with the old yins, thanks, Jack,' the two shook hands and Gerry retreated into the dining room again to be with my sister. Poor bastard.

'Right then, to the bar!' Jack shouted, charging off. 'Mine's a pint.'

I walked behind my best friend and watched him go. All things aside, and my strange nervousness as to who I thought had turned up, I genuinely was glad to see him. She Who Will Not Be Named could go take a flying leap for all I cared at that moment, I was going for a pint with my bestest buddy in the whole wide world.

'So, how's life treating you then?' Jack asked, the barmaid delivering two pints of lager and two whisky chasers, some expensive single malt I had never heard of but he had insisted upon.

64

'It's alright, I suppose. All things considered.' I replied weakly. It was fast becoming my standard response. In times of trouble you had to go with what you know.

'All things considered?' Jack asked, handing over a crisp fifty-pound note and telling the barmaid to keep the change. I should have known he would pick up on it, the fox.

'Well my relationship's gone to shit, my act is fucking dreadful, and to top it all off my mother is currently a smoking pile of ashes destined to sit on the mantlepiece.'

'Sorry, Rob, hold on a sec,' he held up a meaty finger that looked like an uncooked sausage. He turned to the barmaid and caught her eye. 'Excuse me, darlin', you're not related to Becky Woods, are you?'

The barmaid looked at him, paused for a moment, then smiled.

'She's my older sister,' she said at last, hand clasping the end of her long blonde hair.

'Blimey, you're not little Erica, are you?'

She giggled, cheeks flushing a little red beneath hastily done makeup. She was young, too young and Jack should have known better.

'How did you know?' the flirting had commenced.

'I used to date your sister about, oh God, nearly ten years ago now. When you were only a little nipper. You must be what, nineteen?'

'Eighteen two months ago.'

Jack stepped back and laughed loudly. He wiped his brow of pretend sweat and nudged me in the ribs.

'Time flies when you're having fun, eh, Rob.' he sank his chaser and made a loud rasp.

'Well, you take care of yourself, Erica, and we'll catch up

for a chat later, eh?' he winked and gave his best, leering smile.

'Come on, you,' he said to me, lifting the pints.

We walked over to a small table that sat beside the huge panoramic windows of the bar's far wall. Outside was the car park and beyond it Kilmarnock Road, the lifeblood of the south side suburbs. When we were settled, Jack took a sip from his pint and bashed me on the leg.

'What do you think of that then?' he grinned.

'You're a dirty old man,' I said, half meaning it. 'She's half your age.'

'Don't be such a pussy, man up.' He took a giant gulp from his pint, the glass looking tiny in his hands.

'I'm fine by the way, thanks for asking,' I said, pretending to be irked.

'What?'

'Never mind.'

'Aye, you were saying, how's the act?' He put his glass down and took another quick glance up at the bar before settling into our conversation, ten minutes late.

'It's fine, don't want to talk about it.'

'Sure you do, come on, tell me about it. How's Tess?'

The name still burned. Didn't he know there were certain rules about saying it around me? Of course he didn't, he was my best friend and a normal human being.

'We split up,' I said solemnly.

'Shit,' he leaned forward. 'When and why and was it because you've got a small willy?'

I gave him a look of deadpan disapproval and he sniggered. It took all of my effort not to join him.

'Come on, tell your old pal Jacky. What happened?'

Before I started I needed a drink. I took another sip of my pint, the effects of the others wearing off by the minute, and prepared to pour my heart out. It wasn't that I didn't want to, I just wasn't comfortable.

A battle had been raging inside me since the whole thing had happened and I was permanently stuck in the middle. Stealers Wheel might have had clowns to the left of them, jokers to the right. I was between an endless life as a bachelor and the cold shoulder of a family that didn't want me.

'I cheated on her, plain and simple,' The words tumbled out of my mouth and I felt strangely relieved to free them.

'Shit,' Jack said again. 'You shouldn't have done that, lad.'

'Pot calling the kettle, Jack!' I said, suddenly defensive.

Jack looked hurt but it quickly passed. He drained the remnants of his glass and signalled to the bar for another round. A large burp pushed past his pursed lips and he shook his head.

'Who was she then?'

'Some girl, a tart. Used to follow me around the clubs in Hammersmith. Nobody, absolutely nobody.'

'I see,' he steepled his fingers like a master detective, eyes narrowed on me intensely. I tried not to meet them.

'And did you tell Tess or did she find out through other means?'

'I told her,' the sentence was cold, hard and perfectly logical. The same processes that had gone into my decision to come clean.

'That was stupid, boy-oh, bloody stupid.'

I was angry, I was mad. Who the hell did he think he was talking to? This was the man who had barely kept himself on the straight and narrow, let alone a relationship with another

67

human being. His first jibe had been brave, this lesson in morals was taking the piss.

'You finished?' I asked him. 'What would you have had me do?'

'Did you think about Tess?' he asked. 'Did you think about how hearing you were sleeping with another woman would make her feel about herself?' I let his words sink in. He might have been on to something.

'Did you think that when you were spilling your guts to tell her how you had been sneaking off at night, coming home late in the morning smelling of God knows what, that she would have been waiting for you? Worrying about you? Only to find out you've been at it with some groupie?'

Time after time the truth hit home and the worse I began to feel. In my own selfishness to relieve myself of guilt, I had put onto Tess everything I was trying to prevent from happening. Indignity was one thing; outright humiliation was something completely different and altogether worse.

The drinks arrived with a clatter, the young Woods girl bending over just enough in front of me that I got an eye-full of eighteen year old arse. Tempting as she looked, and smelled, I wasn't in the mood. She exchanged flirty eye-contact with Jack and disappeared.

We sat in silence while the pub busied itself around us. It wasn't awkward or tense, if anything it was quite comforting. To know he was there and to be suddenly relieved of not one, but two major revelations that had been hanging over me like a bad smell. Was this what living like a normal person was really like? Heartache and guilt? What a waste of a life, really.

A few of the stragglers from the funeral party came into the bar to wish me all the condolences and mourning they could. Heavy breaths of coffee, wine and whatever was for dinner clung to me as uncles, aunts and everybody else hugged and kissed and cried on my shoulder.

68

The throng increased as they all began to shuffle out of the dining room and off towards home, their duty done for another short while. Wendy sauntered out with Dave beside her, arm draped over her shoulder, suit and tie still immaculately done up, where open necks and shirt tails were otherwise the order of the day.

They said nothing as they went, but I knew they were going back to the house to get up to all kinds of weird shit I wasn't interested in. Mindy and Gerry were the last to depart and my sister came into the bar to speak with me.

'We're off home now, Robert,' she always used my full name in company.

'Okay,' I said bluntly. She looked over my shoulder at Jack and then back to me, a scornful gaze of disapproval etched into her features.

'I see Jack Johnson showed up then.'

'Hi, Mindy!' Jack shouted from behind us, she ignored him.

'Don't get up to any mischief with him, Robert, you know what he's like.'

'Yes, Mother,' I said. Both of us winced at the same time, the wound still freshly opened and now dashed with vinegar. 'I'll be good,' I added, trying to smooth things over.

'Okay,' she conceded and headed for the door, Gerry close by her side, fishing out his car keys.

I turned back to the bar and slumped into my chair, a third round of drinks having arrived in my absence. I picked up the oldest pint and choked it down as quickly as I could, wiping away the excess on my shirt sleeve.

'Who was the shill I saw with Wendy?' Jack asked.

'That's Dave, her boyfriend.'

'Boyfriend?' Jack shouted. I smiled at his reaction and how

I had been the same. I nodded as I gulped more beer. 'Who is he?'

'Don't know, don't particularly care,' I said quickly. 'I think he works in the city, don't know what as, rent boy probably.'

Jack let out a sharp laugh and we descended into a fit of laughter. Laddish, immature behaviour had always been one of my favourite pasttimes but only Jack Johnson could understand it properly. Dick and fart jokes were always winners, as were toilet gags and general blue humour.

'What's his name?'

'I told you, Dave.'

'No, his last name, you idiot,' Jack tutted.

'Erm … Thatcher I think he said it was.'

'Thatcher,' Jack breathed, squinting his eyes.

'Why so interested? Do you know him?' I asked, patting my pockets for my cigarettes.

'No, no I don't think so. His face looked familiar though but I don't recognise the name,' said Jack. He was up to something but I didn't know, nor care what.

'Well, that's his name anyway, and it's about as much as I know about him. And quite frankly,' I said, pulling the old box out from my pocket, 'I'd rather keep it that way.'

'You're the boss,' said Jack, holding up his hands, palms flat towards me. 'So, are you out to play then?' he said in a Devilish tone.

'Maybe,' I replied with equal guile.

'You know if we're heading out you might want to invite your Mindy, I've always had a bit of a hard spot for her, if you know what I mean,' he said with a wink. I levelled my gaze as I sniffed my whisky, the fiery aroma igniting something altogether carnal inside me.

'Is that so?' I replied.

'Definitely,' said Jack, craning his neck to get a view of the car park. 'I imagine she has a pussy to die for.'

'Aye,' I said. He turned to look at me expectantly. 'But you'd have to cope with the fangs first of all.'

We both burst out laughing and clinked our glasses together. It was good to see my old friend again.

Chapter 9

With friends like Jacky Johnson, a man didn't need enemies. The trouble and strife caused when he is around is more than enough to make up for a lifetime of bad run-ins with others. And to make matters worse, the ensuing hangovers were usually a bitch, too.

When I awoke from my near coma state, it was only seven-thirty in the morning. The remnants of my ravaged memory were screaming that I'd only had two hours sleep, but it was impossible to get anymore. The blazing sunlight felt like concentrated evil and my head was fit to burst.

I pushed myself up from the bed, over the covers, not under them of course, and to my surprise found myself completely naked. More interestingly, my suit and shirt, socks and shoes were laid out perfectly on the floor beside me, done up and fastened as if I was still in them. The whole thing looked like I'd vanished and left my outfit behind, like some departed Jedi Knight.

There was a lingering smell, too. I couldn't put my finger on it, but I was sure I knew it from somewhere. Like an old balloon mixed with dust and sweat.

Everything hurt, but not in a way I could cope with, more like an irritating, under the skin type of feeling that would never go. My senses were numbed, my mouth tasted like the carpet of a junkie's flat, and I had the shakes worse than Michael J. Fox.

And, to make matters worse, I was being more creative than I had been in the past week and I couldn't find a pen. Bloody typical.

Standing up was a chore in itself, but I managed to stagger to the door and fish out a clean t-shirt and pair of pants from my bag. What should have taken ten seconds was more like a five-minute ordeal and I walked down the stairs very slowly, preparing for the worst when I reached the infamous kitchen.

To my surprise, and relief, I found it empty. The washing machine was on, humming away in the corner with a constant, throbbing pulse that soothed my aching head. The table was clean and clutter free and no dishes occupied the sink. In all, it was quite pleasant to be a part of, even the ice-cold tiles beneath my feet were cooling.

I was still too warm and decided to stick my head in the fridge. It was the first big mistake of the day. The smell of dry, stale food, the remnants of the chili, turned my already churning stomach into a full blown conga line that was making a reroute straight for my rectum. I slammed the door shut and raced to the downstairs toilet, hoping I'd make it in time before the exodus began.

One awful trip to the throne later and I fixed myself a mediocre breakfast of soggy cornflakes and burnt toast. As meagre as it was, it was just about all I could stomach in my sensitive state.

The kitchen clock ticked over and over as I stared blankly ahead at the empty bowl and plate. Try as I might, I couldn't remember a thing from the previous night. The sorrow and regret of the way things had turned out with Mother, that was still there. It would take more than a night of nicotine, alcohol, and God knows what else to eradicate that memory.

Yet I couldn't conjure anything up from the past twelve hours. I didn't even know if I still had my phone. Not that anybody would be calling me, I was hardly hot property.

I closed my eyes and tried hard to retrace my steps from the end of the dinner. Jack and I had finished our rounds and called a taxi to take us into town. We stopped off at a little rock bar on Union Street, the *Solid Rock,* that had been a favourite of mine since I was above legal age.

From there it got fuzzy and I was struggling to recall even the most basic of information, where did we go, how long was

I out for, how did I get home? All a mystery.

Resorting to my usual technique of letting sleeping dogs lie, I slowly moved towards the sink and dumped the dishes into some lukewarm water. I turned the tap to cold and dunked my head beneath the gushing stream. It felt so good that my headache almost cleared up immediately. I knew it wouldn't last.

'Good morning, Robbie,' Mindy's voice cut in above the water and I stood up with a startle. My hair left a streak of drops all over the worktop before slapping against my forehead with a clap.

'Mindy,' I stuttered.

She looked at me across the kitchen, her hands filled with shopping bags held up, waiting to be taken from her. Being in such a delicate frame of mind, I didn't have the intelligence to ignore her and dashed around the table to help.

'So, you're awake then,' she said.

'Barely,' I grunted.

'Was it a good night?'

'I wish I could remember.'

'That bad, then?'

'You know what it's like,' I knew she didn't, but I gave her her place anyway. She sucked on her tongue and shook her head.

'That Jack Johnson is trouble and you know it.'

'He's not bad, he's just ... full on, is all.' She was right, of course, Jack Johnson was bad for one's health, a bit like smoking but much louder, faster and altogether more expensive. I didn't know where my wallet was, but I was sure it would be empty when I did finally find it.

'Have you eaten?' she asked, emptying the shopping.

'Yes, although I think I'll be seeing it again sometime soon.'

'Tea?'

'I'd murder a cup.' She smiled and flipped the button of the kettle, the light burning orange and boring into my brain. This hangover carry on wasn't worth the effort; best left to young kids who had the energy to never feel it. Not washed up comedians with crippling social problems.

Mindy took care of the tea and sat down across the table from me, sipping from her steaming mug. She looked at me and smiled.

'What?' I asked.

'Nothing,' she replied, typically cryptic. I ignored her.

'Shouldn't you be at work or something,' I said, burning the roof of my mouth.

'Compassionate leave, off for the week.'

'Ah,' I pretended to care but found it increasingly difficult.

Silence fell over us, like it had done so many times in these situations. Both of us never wanted to admit it, but we'd strive to avoid these one-on-ones as much as possible, purely to save speaking to each other.

But something was different this time. I wasn't sure if it was just the booze leaving my system or something altogether deeper. My heart ached in my chest, I wanted to open up to Mindy, to say everything I should have always said, could have always said, but something stopped me. That animosity, all the tension over the years, still felt like an impenetrable barrier between the two of us.

'We were never good at talking, were we?' she said softly.

I looked up from my tea, surprised. Had the great Mindy, Queen of Sheba and all that she looked upon, just admitted to not being perfect? Not only that, that she came from a less than perfect family unit?

'No,' I laughed. 'We were always pretty shit at it, actually.'

To my relief she laughed, too. It was a genuine, tired chuckle that made the edges of her eyes wrinkle. She shook her head, pearl earrings twinkling in the bright morning sunshine that beamed in through the window, burning my retinas.

There were tears in her eyes, ready to tumble down her cheeks. A lump had formed in my throat and I struggled to swallow. For the first time in my life, I actually felt close to my older sister.

'I never wanted it to be like this, Robbie, never. We were just so very different, so different.'

'In almost every way,' I added. She nodded in agreement.

'But that's not an excuse, I know I should have tried a bit better, maybe even reached out to you. You're family, after all.' She sniffed.

Guilt was a normal feeling for me, but I'd rarely let it hit me quite as hard as this. I found it hard to breathe, my lungs feeling like they were shrivelling up, causing me to suffocate. My head was spinning and my heart was thumping, everything tingling from the top of my head all the way down to the ends of my fingers. When I finally found the energy to speak, a glob of snot dripped from my nose.

'Don't be silly,' I said, rubbing my eyes. 'I was hardly the most friendly of kids growing up ... or adults actually.'

The two of us sobbed a little and sat quietly. It wasn't a magic wand, nor was it an instant cure for thirty years of tension, but it felt good to speak with her. To know that the bridges weren't completely burned, to feel that there might still be connection enough there worth salvaging gave me the strangest of feelings.

It was hope, something I hadn't felt in a very, very long

time. I could argue I had never felt it, but there, in our old kitchen, my head throbbing, tears running down my face and looking generally worse for wear, one of the most powerful emotions there was came flooding into me. And it was uplifting, genuinely uplifting. I had never felt anything like it.

'Look at the two of us,' Mindy laughed, blowing her nose, eyes bloodshot within her rings of mascara, streaks running down her cheeks now.

I rounded the table and took her in my arms. We held each other, close and tight, and I never wanted to let go. There was no strangeness to it, nothing out of ordinary, she felt warm and dear and genuine. Like a sister should feel.

When we parted I looked at her and smiled. She returned the gesture and laughed a little again.

'About time,' I said, raising my eyebrows. She nodded in silent agreement and groaned, rubbing her forehead.

'Sorry, Robbie, breaking down and all that.'

'That's alright, don't think twice about it. I reckon we both needed it, don't you?'

'Yes.'

We stood silently for a minute and I felt breath enter my lungs again. The soothing calm was good, everything felt relaxed but something still gnawed away at the back of my mind.

'Mindy, is everything alright with you and Gerry?' She looked up at me with bloodshot eyes, her lips tight. I regretted the question immediately, why did I ask it?

'What have you heard?' she asked. There was no malice in the question, no sense of sharpness or accusation or even defensiveness.

'I don't know. Something he said at the funeral yesterday, it's been playing on my mind is all. Forget it, sorry, I shouldn't have said anything.' I moved to head back to my chair but she was holding onto my arm. Her grip tightened as I moved and I stared back at her.

For a woman who had prided herself on her stoic self-discipline, breaking down twice in ten minutes must have come as a total shock to the system. Yet here she was, sobbing uncontrollably and the only one around was me, her estranged brother of three decades and an emotional train wreck himself.

What was I supposed to do? Walk away and leave her? Maybe, it's certainly what I would have done the day before, the week, the month, the years that had preceded this conversation. Not now though.

Here was my chance to begin afresh. She had opened up to me enough to start the foundations of a new relationship. I couldn't turn my back on it already.

'What's wrong, tell me,' I said, taking her hand and moving her down to her chair beside the table.

Mindy paused for a second, a momentary lapse into hesitation that let me know I was onto something. I knew that my reservations had been right, but above all else, I knew that she needed somebody, anybody, more than ever in that moment. She stared at me with red ringed eyes.

'We're broke,' she said flatly.

'Broke?' I repeated, unsure what exactly she meant.

'Uh-huh, out of money, bankrupt for all intents and purposes.' I was confused, as always.

'I don't understand, Mind, you're pulling in a good salary, Gerry's got his own business.'

'*Had* his own business.' Her voice had a steely anger to it that shone through her sadness.

'What do you mean?' I asked, feeling foolish already for probing the obvious.

'It's done, down the drain. Finished.'

'How?'

'Bad investment, I should have seen it coming, shouldn't have encouraged him. Stupid, bloody stupid!' The anger built in her and she slammed a fist down onto the kitchen table, rattling the cups.

I sat numbly, unable to comprehend what exactly it was my sister was saying. I've never had a mind for business. One look at my bank account was enough to show I'd never be the next Alan Sugar. But even I knew the economy was a rich stomping ground for the likes of manual labour and unique skill sets.

Electricians like Gerry could go out in the morning and make their entire month's rent in a single working day. Hard work and toil it may be, but the rewards were excellent. Someone, somewhere always wanted an extension or conservatory or loft conversion. A jaunt around the suburbs would confirm it.

So how could his business be down the toilet? Something wasn't adding up.

'What happened?' I asked, doing my best Columbo impression.

'Stupid investment, pure and simple.' She sniffed and wiped her nose for the thousandth time, the end now red raw. 'We sank everything we had into setting him up, professional looking website, new tools, van, corporate logo, the works. We were trying to corner a market in localised, top quality electrical assistance, even took on two apprentices with the help of government grants. It was slick, really slick, we'd projected a six figure turnover in only five years.' I nodded and pretended I knew what government grants, turnovers and slick meant.

'But it was fool's gold, Robbie, too much too soon. We, I, underestimated the market. Scottish Power and the like, they're too big to compete with at any sort of mass profitable level. The company was haemorrhaging money from the off, even before Gerry got a phone call, it was an endless pit and we kept on trying to top it up with cash.'

Mindy explained the whole thing to me, throwing figures around that I wasn't sure was real money or just the Monopoly kind. One look at her face was enough to know these bank notes weren't used for little red hotels.

She talked about how the bank had issued a warrant to reclaim their house, how she had been working every hour she could as overtime at the firm to try and salvage enough for groceries. Maintaining a functioning family unit was hard enough when there was cash in the bank, it was nearly impossible when there was nothing.

On top of the financial strain, Mother fell ill and things became a whole lot worse. Like some clogged artery that was fit to burst, swollen from abuse, Mum's stroke had been the final nail in the coffin. Pardon the expression.

'I was at home when I got the call,' she explained. 'Gerry and I had decided we were going to sit in the garden and just enjoy the evening, something we hadn't done in so bloody long it felt almost criminal to do it.' She smiled a little and beneath the pain and toil I could see the young woman she had once been. Being sensible your whole life had a tendency to put years on you and for Mindy, who was nearing forty, she looked closer to a woman of seventy.

'Rob was out, playing a gig with his friends and Abi was in her room studying. Gerry and I sat watching the sun go down with a wee cheap bottle of wine.' A cheap bottle of wine for Mindy would have still been extortionate to me, although after what she had told me, I wasn't so sure.

'Then the phone rang. I went to get it and it was a nurse from the Victoria Infirmary. She said Mum had been found behind the door by one of her carers, the one who came to

80

tuck her in at night. Anyway, we went to see her straight away and she looked terrible, Robbie, bruises up the side of her face where she fell. She looked awful.' She cried again and I rubbed her arm.

I remembered hearing the news myself. Wendy had called. She was on some dig, or dive, or political movement in Manchester and winging her way back to Glasgow on a whim and a prayer. Even as she spoke to me, I remembered thinking of every excuse under the sun not to return home. What the hell was wrong with me? What a real piece of shit I was.

'The doctors told us she didn't have long to live but the old girl held on, kept fighting. Like she always did, Robbie, always. Twelve weeks exactly, to the day, almost to the hour when she was found and then she … she went.' Mindy's bottom lipped trembled and the muscles in her chin cramped with her sobbing.

I stood up and lifted her from the chair, pulling her close to me once again and letting her cry into my shoulder. I could feel her sadness, her frustration in every sob, the unhappy energy flowing through every pore in her body. This was a woman who was used to getting what she wanted, when and how. To have to deal with two massive failures in her life at once must have been devastating.

To me it was a normal occurrence, almost daily. When failure is more than just an option, it's an occupational hazard, you see the world in a completely different light. Or darkness, whichever you prefer.

Mindy stopped and pulled away from me, face red and lined and tired. She dotted her eyes with the sodden strip of tissue paper and shook her head, sighing loudly.

'I just … I just felt so helpless, Robbie, so utterly helpless, watching her in that bed. Going up, night after night, and watching her die, it was terrible. It was like I could see her slipping away, every time I looked at her. But it was still her, you know, still her. When I looked into her eyes I could see her, trapped behind them, aching to get out. It was just her body, you know, her body couldn't cope anymore.' She made a long, tired sigh.

I knew things had been difficult and I also knew that my cowardice was unacceptable. Hiding away, hundreds of miles from the action wasn't something I was proud of. Yet as I sat there and watched my sister break down, I knew I had made the right decision. If this was what it had done to a strong person, someone of determined grit and steely resolve, what would have happened to me?

I was weak and selfish and that was on a good day. I wasn't able to cope with that and now the remorse was chewing away at me, relentlessly, like a cancer.

'Anyway, need to push on,' Mindy said.

'We'll sort it out,' I said. She looked at me and tilted her head.

'I never thought we'd be like this, Robbie,' she smiled. 'Never in a million years.'

I laughed a little and shrugged my shoulders.

'You'll find I'm full of surprises.'

Chapter 10

To my surprise, my hangover cleared up in record time. Not since the heady days of my youth, eighteen and nineteen years young, had I been able to feel vaguely human so quickly.

The gut busting, rocket powered, nuclear explosion of emotion that had smashed its way into my head had gone a long way to banishing the spirits, Johnny Walker and Jim Beam. Regardless of how it happened, I felt pretty good about myself and wasn't about to dissect things enough that it would change my mood.

A shower, shave and two rounds of toothpaste and Listerine had me back in the land of the living and ready to put myself to good use. I even splashed on some aftershave, the smell much nicer than the one still plaguing my room. I opened the window to let in some fresh air, still unable to place what was causing such a stink.

Mindy had emptied the shopping bags and returned home sans Gerry, who I assumed, was working. It was a pretty miserable state of affairs for the two of them and I felt bad for Gerry in particular.

This was a terrible world and even worse if you were genuine. Nice guys didn't just finish last, they were stamped on by the Gucci loafers of the slime bags and weasels who would clamber on their own grandmother just to get that little bit further in life.

The comedy circuit was the same. Like most industries, everybody thinks they have it the worst, but in stand-up there was a premium of arseholes. I was hardly the king of the castle, or even a knave, but I knew I had some drawing power. For some guys, and gals, having their name on a gig poster was enough recognition, no matter how small the print.

For others they wouldn't stop until it was just their face, on fifty-foot billboards that dominated the skylines of every major city in the country. Sure, they were popular but it wasn't because of their act. It was their marketing team and ability to sell themselves to a wider audience.

That's why Billy Connolly still filled out theatres and venues around the world. On paper he was a foul mouthed, aggressive, opinionated Glaswegian with little-to-no education and an act that was bluer than Margaret Thatcher's knickers.

Yet, he was a millionaire ten times over, with a brace of celebrity friends, a legion of loyal fans, both hardcore and casual, and boasted one of the best acting CVs of any actor Scotland has ever produced. And why? Because he was marketable.

Purple beard, long hair, distinctive voice, it all lent itself to how well he could be sold and crammed down the public's throats. Granted it was a different public then to the one now, but it still worked. He was like cigarettes. If smokes came out today, they would be banned in a heartbeat. But, like so many other things in this world, they were a relic from a time long gone that had never gone away.

For every superstar comic, there were thousands left in their wake, trying to get a foot on the bottom rung of the ladder by performing their arses off night in, night out to no crowds at all. Even the Edinburgh Fringe had lost its 'wow' factor, its launching pad status for careers.

TV was the best outlet to get into, but getting there was about as impossible as a real hair follicle on Cheryl Cole's head. Now, there was a zinger.

To cut a very long point short, guys like Gerry Dawkins were always going to be the doormat that the rest of the world wiped its feet on. And that made me damn angry.

Despite the diversion in my train of thought I was still upset by what was happening to my sister and her husband. Sure, it was easy to get caught up in the good vibes of patching things up with her, but I felt a genuine remorse for their situation.

Maybe all this empathy would blow over and things would revert back. But until then, I was going to give it my best shot at lending a hand.

To my surprise, the house was still empty when I headed back down stairs. The world outside was bright and airy, but I could stomach it now, the dregs of the headache now banished.

Wanting to do something but unsure what, I paced around the living room. Every lap threw up a trinket from the past, ghosts of History, or something altogether forgotten about that made me jump a little.

Mother had always been one for photos and the living room was the centre of her collection. All along the mantelpiece, in every corner of the room, piled on top of shelves and cabinets, little moments from our lives growing up were immortalised in frames and dust. One caught my eye in particular and I picked it up with trembling fingers.

Taken on a summer trip to Arran, in the west of Scotland, the three kids were lined up in a row, ankle deep in the browny water of the north Atlantic. Mindy was holding her bucket and spade up to the camera, Wendy was barely old enough to stand and I was sandwiched between them, fist in mouth and holding a small fishing net. Oh the irony.

Mindy wasn't much older than twelve, which would have made me seven and Wendy a toddler. I couldn't recall much of the trip, but I did remember the photo being taken. The water was freezing and even in my infancy I knew what a bloody stupid idea it was to go looking for fish.

Mother had taken it, Dad was lost somewhere back on the shore. She had insisted that we all huddle together like that, a nice picture for Granny back home. Against my better wishes I'd gone along with it and now, nearly twenty-five years later, I was looking at it again.

The impact of time hit me then and caught me a little

off guard. A quarter century was a long time, by anybody's standards, and I thought of how much had gone. The round faced, ruddy cheeked little boy in the picture was now a man in his thirties. Tired, ravaged, rail thin, and addicted to nicotine, alcohol and everything else that was bad for me.

My regrets were done, finished, but I wasn't prepared for the impact of knowing how much time had passed. As if I needed reminding of my own mortality, here it was staring back at me.

I put the picture back down on top of the old TV and took a deep breath. I figured I'd do something more creative before I ripped off Sylvester Stallone from the first Rocky movie any more.

With that I pulled out my phone and rang my agent, as hard as it was to believe I did indeed have an agent, of sorts. Booking my own gigs was something I'd much rather do, but in a world of celebrity stand-ups and rock and roll comics, an agent wasn't just a necessity, they were a status symbol.

Fitting then, that mine was only part-time. Although what he did with the rest of his time I hardly knew. I wondered, more often than not, what he actually did with the time he *was* meant to be my agent.

'Rabbie, how good to hear from you,' came Terry's snake-oil tones from the speaker. 'Turbo' Terry Starr, his actual name and not made up, was the type of person you couldn't trust as far as you could throw. And at a plump twenty-two stone of sweating, oozing fat, that was never going to be very far.

With a name like Terry Starr, young Terrance, as his parents still called him, had limited options in what he could do for a living. Show business seemed like the obvious choice. But, to Terry, musical talent, singing ability, sporting prowess and political ambition, were something he could only dream of.

Like the old phrase goes, those who can't do, teach. Terry moved into the world of 'executive representation' as his business card said. I cursed the day I ever bothered to ring him up.

'I'm not too bad, Terry, all things considered,' I said, feeling my energy begin to wane already. Turbo Terry had that effect on me. He was like a more corpulent, greedier Kryptonite to my weedy, less than heroic Superman.

'Yeah, yeah, triffico, triffico. So, what can I do for ya?' Some papers rustled in the background but I was sure it was the remnants of a McDonalds.

'I want you to get me a gig,' I said bluntly.

'A gig?' he asked, like it was the last thing he was expecting.

'Yes, Terry, a gig, you know, a stage, a light, a mic and me telling jokes. Remember what those are?'

'Yeah, I know what they are,' the sarcasm was lost on him, of course. 'But are you sure you want to head back on stage so soon?'

I had been sure until he asked. Maybe he was right, maybe it wasn't good for me to tread the boards so soon. What if this was just me riding the wave of positive thinking I'd had for the last hour. Or even the remainder of the booze being broken down.

Either way, I didn't care anymore. I stuck to my guns.

'Yes, no, I mean, get me a gig, Terry, I want to go on.'

'Alright,' Terry said sucking his gums. 'When do you want it for?'

'Soon, soon as possible eh … ' I paused, trying to think, a difficult enough task when I was sober. I needed time to help the others; I needed time to help myself. But I wanted to get on with things, maybe even jump-start my career somehow.

'How about a fortnight?' I asked hopefully.

There was another rustle of papers. The sound of chewing

came from the other end of the phone, but I wasn't sure it was Terry eating or just one of his unusual habits. I looked at myself in the mirror above the fireplace and found that I was biting my nails.

'There's an opening on a bill in a little club in Whopping in the second week of December if you're interested,' Terry said flatly.

That was over two weeks away, would it be enough time? It was something and that was all I needed.

'Book me.'

'You got it, Rabbie boy.'

'Thanks, Terry, I'll be in touch when I'm back down South.'

'Oi wait a minute, don't you know how much its worth, what the rate is?'

'I trust you, Terry, I'll be down when I'm down.' I smiled.

'Alright,' he said with a groan. 'I don't know what's happened to you up in Jock-land, but all that roamin' in the gloamin' better not have gone to your 'ed.'

'Like you'll never believe,' I said with a laugh and hung up on my agent.

I shoved the phone back into my pocket and rubbed my hands together. Not a bad morning's work. I could get used to this efficiency lark.

Did I know everything was about to change? Did I hell.

Chapter 11

The flat, lingering smell still filled my room as I tried to scrawl down some changes to my act. Sitting at my desk, window fully open in front of me, I put together what I thought would be the bare bones of something worth talking about. Much to my surprise, I found it easier and more therapeutic than I had suspected.

I stared down at the sheets of paper with terrible handwriting on them and realised that something had changed inside of me. Ordinarily I would have taken the positivity, messed around with it a little then become bored and sodded off to the pub.

Yet, here I was, still scratching away almost an hour later and I was still going strong. Whether what I was writing was any good or not was a completely different issue. The public would decide that, the venomous critics they were.

A gust of chilled wind blew in through my window and scattered some of my notes like some Hammer Horror movie. I picked them up and looked out at the street beyond the sill.

More light flakes of snow were falling from the sky, resting on each of the flat, stone surfaces of the street, the cars and the pavement. The old gravel pathway was dark with the wetness of the moisture in the air and soon it would be beneath a sheet of white. Covered up and forgotten about until the frost melted, the snow would be purifying enough for those who walked past.

I was digressing, I could feel myself slipping into the usual tropes that had plagued my career from the off. They had cursed my whole life in fact, exams, homework, anything that needed done. Distraction was something I actively encouraged and, yes I admit, actively sought.

I remembered a particularly bad report card that came through at the end of a first term. Christmas decorations, festive cheer and the delights of jolly old Santa Claus were lost that weekend in the Argyll household.

'The preliminary exams we conducted have yielded a particularly poor set of results for Robert' said the year tutor's comments, 'He will procrastinate at any and all opportunities and is seriously distracted by anything and everything'.

I was defiant to the last. In fairness to my teachers and the curriculum, I really should have performed better. Laziness in its purest form, and a penchant for comics and masturbation, had contributed their fair share. But the rest of the blame was laid at the door of my attitude. Plain and simple, it stunk.

The report showed off my bad marks in all of their glory, neatly written out with not only the class average, but also the year average noted beside it. Something I had always disagreed with, even in my infancy as a student of academia.

Why would you publicise to paying parents how terrible their child was? And ruin my weekend in the process. The bloody barefaced cheek.

This rap sheet was probably my worst and, coming to an age where exam results were beginning to mean something, I really had no excuses. Mother had gone ballistic, moving through the full spectrum of anger and approaches to reprimanding a bad child. First came the shouting, then came the tears and eventually, and most potent of all, the silent treatment.

Dad, on the other hand, was more distant to the whole thing. In hindsight, he was probably thinking about doing his secretary, or the intern, or the work experience girl fresh out of school. Anybody to take his mind off our family. Off the record, I could hardly blame him. Who needed to think about pointless exam results when you could be 'up to your guts in sluts', as I'd heard on the TV before I'd left for Euston station. However, if I was being quoted, he was a total shithead.

At the time though, I saw it as a blessing in disguise. Dealing with one angry parent was bad enough; a double act was nearly impossible. No matter, I was out of my depth with just Mother.

I was grounded, of course, and as a condition of my imprisonment, was to make a start on next term's reading which Mother secured from the school that Monday morning. I was given Christmas and Boxing Day off, but other than that I was locked away in my room; at the desk I was sat at now, revising. The only shame was, studying was the last thing I was doing.

A smile crept across my face and I scribbled down some notes that I hoped would yield something to work with. Reflective humour was selling big these days and the mob loved nothing better than a relatable tale.

The heavy thud of car doors closing distracted me and I snapped out of my creative bubble. I leaned over the desk and saw the rear of a Range Rover poking out from the old red sandstone of the house.

'Dave,' I sneered to myself.

'Hi, Robbie!' shouted Wendy from the drive and I remembered the window was open. My younger sister waved at me from the driveway.

I waved back meekly and resolved that work was finished for the afternoon at least. The front door clicked open and I heard footsteps in the hall.

When I walked down the stairs, my heart boomed in my chest and my throat dried up in an instant.

Wendy and Dave were in the small hallway shaking off the snow from their coats, Angela, my sister's timid flatmate, stood behind them. She wore a look of feigned shyness that belied something altogether more alluring. It was at that single moment I realised what the terrible smell in my room was.

It was the unmistakable scent of sperm and latex, specifically the two of them mixed together in a condom. And I suspected that Angela's crotch would smell exactly the same way.

91

'Hi, big bruvver, how are you today?' Wendy asked, extending her arms wide. She hugged me, but I kept my eyes on Angela who was smirking a little in the doorway.

'You weren't up when we left this morning, thought we'd leave you be. Big night and all that. How was it? Did you pull?' she nudged me in the ribs.

'Eh … ' I stammered, looking between her and Angela and trying to give nothing away. 'Yes, yes, I did actually,' I said.

'Oh really? You dog. What age was she? Sixteen?' Wendy giggled, Dave moving to her side and putting his arm around her bony shoulders.

'Eh … no, no bit older.'

The two of them laughed and jostled each other. Dave looked down at my sister beneath him and leered a shark's grin.

'Remember when we were like that, darling?' he said.

'No, we were never like that,' she said, faking a frown.

'That must have been another Wendy then,' he said, looking away and arching his eyebrows. Wendy pulled away and weakly punched his arm.

The bastard, that was a great line. Something I'd say. God, I hated this prick.

He would have to stew for the moment; I had bigger things to worry about. Like the fact that I'd slept with one of Wendy's classmates and how I could prevent Wendy from ever finding out.

'I'm parched, who's for tea?' my sister asked, heading into the kitchen.

'I'd love a cup, darling,' Dave agreed and followed her in. Angela walked up to me, dangerously close, and gave a frisky smile. I'd be lying if I said I wasn't just a little bit turned on, I

92

am human after all, even though I sometimes didn't act like it.

'What do you say we forget about the tea?' she whispered, tugging on my t-shirt.

Her hot breath lapped against my freshly shaven cheek and made me tingle. Where had this woman been the other night in the kitchen, locked away beneath her baggy t-shirt and shapeless jeans? Suddenly she was a sexual predator and I was the main course, served up on a platter.

'Eh, I'll take a cup!' I shouted and slid past the banister, contorting my lanky frame enough that I didn't have to touch the smouldering vixen in front of me.

I scurried into the kitchen and hoped she wouldn't follow. She did, of course, and I was thrown back into the frying pan without any time to think.

'So, where did you guys go last night?' Wendy asked, pouring the cups.

'Do you know something, I can't remember,' I said in haste, one eye watching the door for Angela.

She came strolling in, long red hair draped over her shoulders, eyes shining like two emerald orbs beneath a pale brow that was speckled with light freckles. She didn't take her eyes off of me and I daren't lose sight of her.

This was a nightmare. How could I have been so bloody stupid? What was wrong with me? Was nothing sacred anymore? Had it ever been? Just when I figured I was getting back on my feet, I go and pull a boner, pardon the expression, that sets me back almost immediately.

I wasn't worried about Angela, I doubted she was in any way, shape, or form, in love with me or anything like that. It was Wendy I was more concerned about.

She had always been protective of her friends around the rest of the family, for reasons that she never admitted. Ever since she moved onto solids, Wendy had been different. Not in a bad way, just a little edgier, a little more fringed, always on a different side of the fence to everyone else.

I was no Son of the Year, and Wendy's rebellion was a little easier to stomach than mine, but she still retained the fierce sense of independence that we all shared. Perhaps it was being the youngest of three children that had cultured her very different attitude towards life. By the time she rolled around, our parents had already gone through the whole process twice and were undoubtedly fed up with the whole raising kids adventure.

Yet, for somebody so unique and confident in her own ability and beliefs, she had always maintained a level of distance between her family and her friends. A fact that worried Mother to no end, especially when long-haired, hemp-smelling weirdos called Moon-Fountain turned up at the door looking for her. Maybe it wasn't quite as xenophobic as that, but the principle was still the same.

Despite the seemingly distant void between her personal and home life, Wendy had wanted for nothing growing up. An advantage of having a sister so much older in Mindy meant that she had effectively grown up with three main parents. Picked up, dropped off, given anything she wanted at a second's notice, Wendy was the classic spoiled youngest child.

And if she didn't get her way, she would quickly let everybody know it. I remembered being out with Mother one afternoon, shopping in Glasgow. It was just her, myself and Wendy and we were out looking for summer clothes or new school uniforms.

To keep us happy and onboard, Mother had taken us for a stroll around a department store with a hefty toy department. Wendy had taken particular delight in some robotic dog that did backflips, a snip at almost fifty quid. Being told she couldn't have it sent her into a huff so bad that she stood in the aisle and stamped her feet so many times, the soles of her Hush Puppies fell to bits.

I remember watching her get madder and madder until eventually Mother caved in and bought the damn dog. Not fully appreciating the complexities of overprotective parenting, I put it down to Wendy being a pain in the arse.

For my own worth, I never engaged in such vulgar displays. I just did really badly in school exams as my form of protest. Much worse of course, but at least it could be kept behind closed doors.

I wasn't quite sure how close she was to Angela, but I knew if she found out I had slept with her, there would be hell, with lashings of fire and brimstone, to pay.

Then again, maybe I was being completely unfounded with the whole thing. A quick look at the facts was hardly conclusive and I may have been making the whole thing up.

All there was really was the clinging smell of sex in my room, the amorous approaches of a woman I barely knew, and the dreadful sense of guilt building up in my stomach. Not concrete evidence entirely, but more than enough to make it a plausible reality. I sometimes cursed living so relentlessly in reality.

To top it off Angela was still giving me 'the eye' across the kitchen. I had never been one to command the attentions of women like some men could, Dave I imagined was a prime example of this. So, when one became so interested in me within a three-day turnover, I sensed it was more lustful than anything else.

Shit.

'How's Jack anyway, I didn't see him at the service?' thankfully Wendy was still blabbing on.

'He's fine, still the same.'

'Oh God, that's trouble then,' she laughed. 'Is he still with that woman, the artist, what was her name … Betsy?'

'It wasn't Betsy,' I said, now completely avoiding eye contact with Angela.

'Yes it was, she was a painter, had a couple of exhibitions I remember, in Park Circus. All pomp and bluster but with very little talent.' Wendy snorted. 'Typical really, she'd sink her talons into somebody like Jack.'

'Yeah,' I said. I felt like my head was about to explode. On the one hand, I wanted to crawl into a hole and disappear forever. On the other, I wanted this mundane chitchat to last for all eternity. Talk about between a rock and a hard place.

I resolved for the latter and sipped at my tea. Angela was still floating around my periphery, but I didn't dare see if she was still making those eyes at me. The ones that said my genitals were the only thing between her and the end of the world.

'Who's Jack?' Dave chimed in from the corner. Wendy moved to answer, I certainly wasn't going to.

'He's Robbie's old school friend. Made a fortune, now lives out his days in his own little fantasy world.'

'How did he make his money?' Dave asked, typically.

'I don't know really, computers was it?' she replied, launching the question in my direction.

'Internet company,' I said, trying to keep tight lipped. When it came to money I had a suspicion that Dave wasn't the type to throw insider secrets about easily. Not for free anyway.

'What kind of company?' he asked, eyes lighting up. I could have sworn I saw pound signs flash in them. I should have expected better of my own judgement and known he wouldn't let it drop.

'Something, I can't remember what,' it was a feeble

response and made me look even weaker than I felt.

He made a low hum, nodding with his big, bullish head, hair still immaculately slicked back over his scalp. His arms were crossed enough that biceps bulged from beneath the washed out rugby top that barely covered his massive shoulders. Collar upturned of course, the hint of glistening chest hair poking out from beneath the last button.

'Anyway, I best be making a move,' I said, slapping my hands loudly on the table.

I slid the chair from under me, clumsily scraping it along the floor with a screech, and headed for the door. It was like my limbs weren't responding to my brain. Every little signature of my body language was screaming shame. A neon sign above my head that read 'Guilty as Sin,' would have been more subtle.

'Where are you going?' Wendy asked.

'Working on some new material,' I felt better saying it. 'I've got a gig at the start of December, going to get cracking on it right away.'

'December?' she said, looking between myself and Dave. 'Are you going to be here for Christmas?'

Christmas, everybody's favourite time of the year, when we pretend that the world is a wonderful place and everything in it works. Dogs loving cats, political harmony, the end of human suffering, all for two days of the year. Then it's followed by the biggest, messiest binge drinking week most people are ever likely to take part in. The Roman Empire had been reduced to dust a long time ago and it was probably for the better. They wouldn't have been able to keep up with a Scottish Hogmanay.

'Eh … ' I stammered.

In truth I hadn't actually thought that far ahead. For years the family had been trying to coax me back up to Glasgow for the festivities. And every year I had either excused myself politely, forgotten about the whole thing, or blatantly refused. This time though, I didn't feel quite the same.

'Feels different this time,' the immortal final words of Peter Davison, the fifth Doctor Who, as he lay dying in the TARDIS. It was a show I loved as a child and still harboured a healthy enthusiasm for.

If only I had Nicola Bryant's sweaty cleavage hanging over me, I would have felt much better. It reminded me of a short section I'd put in my act on my first trip to the Edinburgh Fringe.

'I love *Doctor Who*, can't get enough of it. But I'd always felt for Pete Davison.' I had started, hoping that it wasn't a lost reference on the festival crowd. The show was off the air at that point and confined to nostalgia. 'He had a few great years on the show, had to talk to men in rubber suits and cardboard baddies, but when it comes to his last story, he's handed something Shakespeare could have written.' To my surprise, there had been a few laughs. 'Anyway, he's dying … '

'From spectrox poisoning,' one of the punters shouted from the crowd. I gave a wink towards that part of the audience and suddenly felt right at home. We Whovians are a tight bunch.

'So, he's lying on the floor of some draughty BBC studio, acting his *arse* off only for his co-star, the lovely Nicola Bryant, to be wearing a low cut top with her Leicester cities hanging out!' The room erupted, claps and coughs and everything in between.

'I mean, honestly, if I were him I'd have been raging, who's going to pay attention to you when there's a soft pay-per-view going on above your head? But there you go.'

The memory made me smile. Like a dying Time Lord, I felt like I was regenerating and Christmas would prove to be my first trip in a new body.

'I'll be home for Christmas,' I said, and that was it done.

'Really?' Wendy was beaming. 'That's fantastic news, Robbie, I'm so happy,' she clapped her hands together and came to give me a hug.

'I know, sis, I know.' I said gently, quiet enough that only she could hear.

It's been said that behaving in a relatively human manner can give you a warm glow inside. For almost all of my life I didn't believe it, palming it off as some romantic bullshit that Hallmark had trademarked.

But not this time. Maybe this regeneration thing was an actuality.

I did feel good about myself, I did feel confident and for the first time in a long time I had the sensation of not being a selfish arsehole. A simple gesture like this was cleansing, good for the soul. But above all else, it was genuine. I did want to be with the others at Christmas, why not.

'Right, I need to go,' I said hastily, trying not to ruin the Hallmark wet dream.

'Okay, you go up and do your thing and I'll shout on you when dinner is ready. Mindy and Gerry are coming over, too.'

'Okay,' I turned for the door.

'And, Robbie,' Wendy said after me. 'Thank you.' I smiled at her and headed for the stairs.

Back in my room, I shut the door and lay down on my bed. I put my hands beneath my head and stared blankly up at the ceiling, tracing lines through the artex and counting the cracks around the light fitting.

What a day. On reflection, I didn't think I'd ever had one quite like it. From the doldrums of a hangover, to reconciling with not one, but both of my sisters, and finally accepting a Christmas invitation to be with my family. At this rate I'd be free from booze, fags and all the bad things in my life by the end of the week. Turned to religion before the month was out, and next year be living amongst tribes in deepest, darkest Peru teaching them how to speak English. Well, maybe not that far.

I sat up and moved to the desk, hoping that my good vibrations would translate into some usable material. The door opening and then closing behind me stopped me.

'Thought you could escape me, did you?' came Angela's sultry tones.

I turned to face her. She was standing by my bed, unfastening the buttons of her tight, plaid shirt to reveal her pallid flesh and a black lacy bra beneath. She finished and took two paces towards me.

'Erm ... ' I managed, wishing the growing erection in my pants would stop.

'You seem pleased to see me,' she said, placing her hand on my crotch. I was surprised and let out a little groan.

'Angela, sweetheart,' I started. 'I don't quite know what you think is going on here but ... '

She leaned in close to me and kissed my lips. Her tongue probed at mine until it was halfway down my throat, free hand grasping my head, nails digging into the back of my neck. She pulled away and stripped her top off.

With one expert movement, she unclasped her bra and it dropped to the floor with a gentle thump. Her breasts stood pert and proud, areola barely darker than her skin, nipples pert and pokey.

She ran her hands over them and down her tight abdomen until she came to the lip of her jeans. She unfastened her belt and dropped them to reveal a small, black G-string that matched her bra. I stopped gawping and tried to remember when, why, how and where we were.

'Angela ... ' I said again, but she stopped me, putting one

finger on my lips, pulling herself closer.

'Why don't we talk about it later, when we're a little less flustered, hmm?' she smiled a look of sheer Devilment that made the blood pump faster in my veins. One vein in particular.

From bookish mouse to smoking-hot sex kitten, I wasn't sure how this transformation had come about in my sister's friend. Nor did I know exactly what part I had played in the whole thing, if any.

But when the push came to shove, I had always believed that a good opportunity wasn't one to be wasted. I pulled her into me and kissed her once again as my hand ran across her tight, fresh skin. When in Glasgow, do as the Romans do, or rather *did*.

Chapter 12

I wasn't expecting all my Christmases rolled into one and that's certainly not what I got. Sex was a dreadful business at the best of times, but doing it with a complete stranger, for the second time in twelve hours, or thereabouts, was absolutely awful.

The blame sat squarely with me of course. Lust was never a substitute for love and it showed during my appalling efforts to conjure up some enjoyment for her. And for me.

I was hardly James Bond in between the sheets; James Blunt would have sufficed. But it seemed I wasn't even getting that much dignity.

Four minutes was all it took, from start to finish, and I was bloody glad it was so short. A final thrust, a surge of reality through my mind and the whole ordeal came to a short, sharp, if not slightly elated, end.

Now we lay silently beside each other, sweating and panting for breath. To her credit, Angela at least pretended she had found some fulfilment from the whole thing. I doubted she had been satisfied in the way that she deserved but her acting was top notch.

'That was good,' she said, laying an arm across my chest, almost on cue.

'Glad you liked it,' I said, cringing inside.

Another prolonged silence between us as I stared out of the open window. The sun was already setting; a Scottish winter was a dark and dank thing to behold. The air was glowing with a sodden dampness, the snow having turned to rain in the middle of the afternoon, making the place look like one big, slush-filled smudge.

In truth, I had quite enjoyed the sex. Just having somebody so close to you that you can feel and smell and move with them as one was a treat I hadn't felt in a long while. Things between Tess and I had deteriorated to the point where we hadn't been intimate in almost three months before she threw me out.

Even my mistress, the term still strange in my ears that I should ever have one, had closed all passionate doors in my face. I was the last person to ever have the beck and call of women who were willing to take their knickers off.

My past relationship misadventures were a well-documented part of my life that I reserved for only my set list. To have slept with two different women, now three, in the past twelve months was something altogether unheard of, a new personal best.

Perhaps it was the celebrity. Any fame, no matter how small or insignificant, could act as an aphrodisiac. Somehow I doubted it was the case with me. My brush with the limelight had been too short for it to be given consideration. She would have to be addicted to cable TV shows and repeats to even vaguely know about my lone credit.

And above all else, I was an ugly bastard. High cheekbones were about all I had going for me.

'When are you going back to London?' Angela asked, nuzzling into my shoulder.

'That's a strange question.'

'Is it?' she replied, quickly.

'Well, I thought you were at university with Wendy.'

She pushed herself up from the bed and looked at me, stray strands of blazing red hair dropping over her eyes. She pushed them out of the way to reveal a look of mild hurt, bordering on anger. Shit.

'I am. Why would you ask that?' she squinted, her eyebrows arched. 'Did you think I was planning on coming with you?' There was poison in the question.

'No, yes, what? No, I was just saying.' This was bad.

Not only had I embarrassed myself in the bedroom department, I was now effectively spewing verbal vomit in this young woman's face. Still, it was better than actual vomit.

'So you're saying you don't want me to come with you to London, then?' she sneered.

'That's not what I'm saying at all, Jesus Christ,' what had been a bicker, was now a fight. This wasn't right, surely? We didn't even know each other, but we were arguing like a married couple.

'You know something, Robert?' She pushed herself out of the bed, pulling my duvet with her. 'You're a real piece of shit.' She picked her things up and hastily threw them on.

'Wait a minute here, darlin', I'm not the one to blame,' I got up, my nether regions still tender and sensitive.

'Excuse me?' she said.

'Well, it's not like I had to try very hard to get your knickers off, was it?' What was I saying? I wasn't Mick Jagger or Rod Stewart. I couldn't treat women like shit and expect to get away with it. I was terrified of them.

'Oh, really? Well that's not what you were saying last night.' Oh shit, here it came. I knew whatever had happened was going to bite me in the backside. I would have preferred to be wearing something when it did though. I cupped my genitals in preparation, feeling them retract as I did so.

'I love you, Angela, you're everything to me, I have done since we first laid eyes on each other,' she said in a mocking voice, pulling on her shoes.

Those lines did sound like something I would say, especially if I was trying to get her into the sack. They had worked on Tess, they had worked on my mistress, and now they had come up trumps with Angela. Three in one year, I should have been elated to be keeping the match ball. As it happened, I wanted to boot it away as hard as I could. Or better yet, replaced my head with the thing and have it kicked by a set-piece specialist.

'Yeah, well. I'm sorry,' I said, sounding only a little apologetic. I was probably more sorry than I wanted to admit, but the heat of the argument had gotten my hackles up.

Angela let out an exasperated laugh and shook her head, long ginger hair swaying as she did so, streaks of it clumped and matted with sweat and God knows what else. She picked up her bag and slung it around her shoulders before moving to the door.

I stood and watched her, hands still clasping my vitals, my thirty-two year old body feeling old and used in the brisk draught coming from the window. Seemed wholly appropriate, her leaving, me staying behind, not a shred of clothes, or dignity intact. I could have laughed.

'You know something, Robert,' she said before she left. 'You're a real piece of shit.'

Not bad going, I thought, could have been much worse. She stormed out of the door and poked her head back in.

'And you're shit in bed, too.' The door slammed shut with a bang and I flinched.

I heard her leave through the front door, crunch up the pathway and disappear into the growing darkness. I didn't move, instead I stood staring blankly ahead. Was it bad I was feeling strangely better about the whole thing?

She was right of course. I *was* a piece of shit and I *was* shit in bed. No use denying the obvious. The blatantly obvious at that.

Maybe if I did it more, I might find a bit of success. Take one look at the garbage on TV and you could blatantly see an army of people living in self-denial about their ability, their 'talent'. Hell, there were whole shows dedicated to them on

Saturday nights. On prime time, no less.

But I was trying. Fair enough, Angela didn't know much about my sudden turning over of a new leaf. I was still getting used to the notion myself and would have been further down the road with it if she hadn't wanted to knock boots. It wasn't her fault she was still seeing me in that light. There was still plenty of it left.

I didn't blame her, and in truth she had done me a favour. Leaving in such uncertain terms meant she wouldn't want any further amorous attention from me. Not ever, which got me off the hook a little. I only hoped that she would keep tight-lipped around Wendy. Otherwise my ass would be grass, as the Americans say.

I unclasped my hands from around my cock and balls and smiled down at them. The cold had shrunken them to a fraction of their size, a luxury I could barely afford.

'Don't worry, little guy,' I said. 'Daddy still loves you.'

'Robbie!' came Wendy's voice from downstairs.

'Yeah?' I shouted back.

'I was just checking who'd gone out the front door. Angela said she was away for a smoke about twenty minutes ago. Was that her leaving?' she asked.

'Yeah, must've been,' I said.

'Oh, she didn't say goodbye.'

I don't know where it came from, but I started to laugh uncontrollably. My ribs hurt and tears began to run down my cheeks as I chuckled away, lost in the hilarity of the whole situation.

'She did,' I managed to get out between fits. 'Oh, she did alright.'

Chapter 13

'You're wrong in the head,' I laughed, having to put down my carrots and mashed potatoes as I wiped away some stray roast beef from my chin.

'It's true, would I lie about something like that?' Gerry pleaded at the other end of the table. He was smiling, a broad, beaming grin that lit up the whole kitchen.

'There I was, in the middle of the restaurant when Barry says "Here I know how we can get out of this without paying." Next thing I know he's on all fours, crawling between the tables and heading for the door.'

Another wave of laughter rippled around the table, everybody enjoying the story tremendously. Everybody but Mindy who looked distinctly sour. I knew this was hardly her type of conversation but it was still funny as hell. If there was one thing Gerry Dawkins could do, it was tell a great story.

'When he reached the door, he stood up, bold as brass, and shouted back to me and the lads. "The coast is clear, come on!"'

I lost it at that point, almost laughing water out through my nose. I slammed my hand down on the table a couple of times as the rest of the family chortled along to the tale. When the painful encounter passed, I gulped for air and rubbed at my sides.

Wendy and Dave, the shill, were laughing and smiling and I even thought I caught a glimpse of a smile from Mindy. It hardly mattered I didn't know who this Barry character was, all that I was sure about was how much of a family we all seemed to be. Who cared if it wouldn't last, I was proud to have people's lives be a part of mine and, for my small part in proceedings, to be a part of theirs.

In hindsight, it was probably the happiest I had felt in close to three decades.

'But I tell you, no more nights out with Barry, he's too much,' Gerry said, filling his fork.

'Amen to that,' said Mindy agreeing. She sipped at her wine, a gift from Dave, and offered more veg around the table.

'I agree, completely,' I added and I really did.

The roast beef was tremendous, the trimmings delicious and the gravy so pure that I could have drank it by the gallon. Living on the road, or even living on my own, meant that cooked meals were a particular luxury that I could neither afford nor be bothered to do.

I had always likened my attitude towards food to that of a survivalist or an SAS operative stuck behind enemy lines. As dramatic as it seemed, it helped me keep my sanity when it came to defrosting a two-year old lasagne from the depths of my freezer. When I did venture out to restaurants or bars, it was on the cheap, anything to avoid paying full price. I wasn't hard up, not for my lifestyle, but I refused to hand over good money for something I could do for a fraction of the price at home.

Tight-arse or not, I was happy with my lot. That was until I tasted a meal as good as this. Family cooking is something everybody should enjoy, or at least have access to. You don't quite realise how much you miss it until you savour the flavours, juices and even ambience around the table after a long absence.

Bloody hell, all this romantic nonsense, I was turning into a fop. What would the neighbours say?

'What were the neighbours saying, Wendy, when you came in this afternoon?' Mindy asked.

'Nothing, not to me anyway, they were speaking to Dave about business.'

'What kind of business?' Mindy pressed. I kept my head low but my ears wide open.

'Just talking about doing some investments in the commodities market,' Dave answered, voice booming about the small kitchen.

'Commodities market?' I blurted. I couldn't help myself.

The family stopped and looked at me in turn. I choked down the remnants of the beef in my mouth and quickly tried to make amends.

'The Waltons next door are moving into the commodities market?' I tried to make it sound like a question. Mr and Mrs Walton were about two hundred years old, even back when I was growing up. A pair of retired doctors, the extent of their risk taking came when they went for extra mushrooms in their Bolognese sauce. They weren't the market hotshot type.

'Yeah, I was speaking to Eric about it this afternoon.' Dave continued coolly. 'His son plays squash at my gym in town, I've seen him about, didn't know his folks lived up here, though. He seems keen.'

Gym, squash, keen, who did this arse-twat think he was impressing with all of these terms? I wanted to stand up and clock him over the head with the fridge door, or fillet him with one of the fish knives in the drawer. Why couldn't my aim with the chili pot had been better? Lucky bastard.

'Oh,' I said.

'Dave has some insider secrets,' Wendy chimed in. There was a smug pride in her voice that I resented, but I wasn't going to cause a fuss. New leaf and all of that jazz.

'Really?' said Mindy. 'Well, fire some our way, always good to know,' she smiled awkwardly. Gerry said nothing. I tried to avoid them altogether.

Since she had opened up to me, I felt bad that I hadn't given

Mindy and Gerry's plight more thought. I could hardly have expected what happened to, well, happen but it still gnawed away at me. There had to be something I could do to try and ease the pressure. Gerry didn't deserve that type of life and neither did Mindy. Even if I was getting used to thinking that way.

'Oh,' said Mindy. 'A letter arrived this morning from Mum's lawyer.'

'Really?' said Wendy.

'What did it say?' asked Dave. I felt a little behind on the whole thing, legality was never my strong point.

'Apparently, she left explicit instructions about her will, said that we were all to be present when the envelope was opened.'

I cracked a smile and looked about the table. Nobody else was joining in on my hilarity.

'What?' I said, still nothing. 'Don't any of you find it just a little bit funny?'

'Funny how?' asked Wendy, doing a poor Joe Pesci impression.

'That we're all to be in the room when the envelope is opened. It's all a bit Agatha Christie, is it not?' I breathed another laugh, but still nothing.

I didn't take it personally and waved it off, scoffing the last of the broccoli. I tell you, don't get no respect.

'Anyway, moving on,' said Mindy, playing the headmistress again. 'We've all to be in attendance when it's opened.'

'When's it getting opened?' Wendy probed.

'Tomorrow lunchtime, at the offices.'

'Where are the offices?'

'Victoria Road, just up from the old school house that's got

110

the McDonald's outside of it.'

'Will you be able to get time off?' Wendy turned to Dave who steepled his fingers.

Every word of the question burned my insides like boiling hot acid. Not only had he muscled in on my family, he had disrespected me from the get-go with his smarmy attitude and know-it-all antics. Now, he was being coerced, by Wendy of all people, into attending a will reading for the children of a departed woman now no finer than fag ash.

I moved to say something but was pleasantly surprised that somebody got in there before I did.

'Why does he need time off?' asked Mindy. Her voice was cold and full of accusation. She had her lawyer's hat on and that spelled trouble.

Despite our differences over the years, I never doubted for one moment that Mindy wasn't a brilliant solicitor. While I may have always taken jibes at her frostiness, her lack of feeling and general prickly demeanour, they were the key ingredients to being the cold-hearted bitch it required to operate in the law racket.

Of course, I always thought she should have been good at what she did. She sacrificed having a good time during her best years to learn and learn and learn again the ins and outs of the game. But dedication isn't always enough to be great, it takes an attitude shift and want to become a leader in the field. Law wasn't just her job, it was her passion.

And for the first time I felt like I was on the winning team. It was bloody brilliant.

'Well, I thought … Dave's part of the family now, too.' Wendy pleaded but I could tell by her whimpers she knew she was fighting a losing battle. Mindy stared at her, dark eyes icy cold like a wolf ready for the kill. Not unlike Dave's, I noted.

'It's alright, Wend,' said the shark, putting one of his hands on my sister's shoulder. 'It's a personal thing, I'll catch up with you guys outside.'

This was brilliant, he was absolutely furious. Subtle shifts in his body language were enough to let me know. I never claimed to be an expert at anything really, but I did know how to read people. You can't become an observational comedian without good people watching skills.

As obvious as it sounded, some comics thought they could get away with it. And some have, but they always lack that extra spark, the little bite of viciousness needed to make you truly funny.

His shoulders had tensed, his hands were now clasped around each other in a ball and a vein had begun to protrude from his neck. There was even a tiny change in his complexion, his skin turning that little bit redder around the cheeks.

He might not have been showing it to the untrained eye, but for the first time since I'd known him, Dave wasn't in complete control. In my crueller days I would have kicked him when he was down. As it happened, Mindy was doing all the legwork for me.

'Well, it's immediate family, Dave,' she said. 'And I'm sure you can appreciate that you've not been part of our little group long enough to be considered that quite, yet. I'm sure you agree.' Goodnight, sweet prince, there was the headshot, no coming back from that. I loved my big sister.

I sat smirking, pushing about the remnants of my mash and a stringy piece of roast beef. The rest of the family finished theirs off in silence and Gerry cleared everybody's plates into the sink.

We moved into the living room and stretched out on the couches, the best of Tuesday night television on, but nobody was really watching it. There were a few comments on the scantily clad women that dominated the viewing, even on a school night. Gerry made the big mistake of commenting on one of their derrières to which the Argyll sisters proceeded to rip him to shreds.

The news came on and with it brought fresh political debate and opinions from all parties. I threw my own into the mix just to be polite, but in truth I hardly cared. It was just nice to have somebody to talk to.

Dave stewed for the whole evening, sitting in the single chair over by the bay window, never talking, always watching. I thought he might have come out of his huff but he remained defiant, petulant even. He didn't strike me as the type who took failure or rejection well. One day in my shoes and he'd become a natural.

When the late movie started, it was time to go to bed. John Hughes' *The Breakfast Club* was worth the attention, but I could barely keep my eyes open. A hangover, two rounds of pitiful sex and the reconciliation with the rest of the family could take it out of a guy.

'Right,' I said, pulling myself up from the couch with an exhausted groan. 'I'm off to bed.'

'Night, Robbie,' Mindy said with a yawn, the others following suit.

'Night night, big brother,' said Wendy, giving me another hug.

'Goodnight,' said Dave, not even bothering to look at me.

'Night, pal,' said Gerry.

'Goodnight, John Boy,' I said with a titter. Again nothing. Tough crowd, toughest I'd ever faced.

'*The Waltons* innit.' I nodded out the window to where the actual Waltons stayed. 'I give up.'

With that, I left the rest of the family and traipsed up the long stairway and towards my bed. I was so tired I didn't even bother with my ablutions, even though the lingering taste of

113

booze still clung to my furry tongue. I figured I'd get away with one night's worth of laziness. There had been plenty of others after all.

I climbed into bed and lay perfectly still, eyelids heavy and the droning echo of my mild tinnitus. I thought back on the events of the day, just like I had done before Angela broke my concentration earlier.

There was a rather overwhelming sense of emotion and importance about the whole thing. Of course it was important, I had patched things up, or at least begun to, with the remainder of my family. That was about as important as life got, was it not?

Maybe I was being too dramatic. Although, when I reviewed things, I didn't think I was. I had spent the majority of my teenage and adult life trying to run away from the people who, when it's all said and done, are the only ones who matter half a damn. Despite my problems, my difficulties and, as a result, me being difficult, they had still stood by me. They weren't perfect, not by a long stretch of the imagination, but then again who was?

The outward nonsense, painting a picture for the rest of the world, that didn't mean anything when the doors were closed. And yet, for reasons I would never understand, they all continued to welcome me back with open arms.

The death of our mother shouldn't have been the catalyst to get us all in the same room, it shouldn't have needed to take such a landmark moment in our lives. Yet, it was what I needed, personally, to jump-start my own sense of family ties. There was plenty of work left to do, and I knew it had to be done. As first days went, however, I was surprised and, above all else, happy, that we were going in the right direction.

My throat was dry from all of the thinking. I slid out from the duvet and headed out into the hall. Everything was dark and quiet and I was reminded of the times I had snuck home late at night after a boozy bender on the tiles. Creeping around the shadows, pretending I was Jason Bourne when in reality I was being as subtle as a herd of elephants.

To the credit and patience of the rest of the family, they never seemed to mind or say anything. Even if they did find me the next morning passed out cold in a pool of my own saliva, begging for mercy from a wretched hangover. A glass of orange juice and bacon sandwich were my saviours.

There was no sign of the others, the whole place was quiet. I couldn't have been in bed that long, but I had been so lost in my own little dream world that I had missed Mindy and Gerry leave. Wendy and Dave were staying over, they had been for the duration.

But now they were all gone, leaving Robert out in the cold. Boohoo for me, I thought flippantly.

I skipped into the kitchen and took a can of juice from the fridge. Half of it was gone in one gulp and I could feel the syrupy fizz coat my teeth. Feeling that my change in attitude should probably extend to healthier eating and living, I finished it off and ran the tap for a cold glass of water.

The house was too warm, a thick heat hanging in the air even this late at night. Although I felt more part of the family than I had in decades, I still wasn't sure if my jurisdiction allowed for tampering with the thermostat. People, or men in particular, could be quite sensitive about that, a long documented joke, one of the classics.

I rounded the hall and headed for the stairs. As my foot went to fall on the noisy third step, I heard a muffled voice coming from the living room. I stopped and looked back towards the closed door.

Everything appeared quiet, no light shining underneath the chipped and battered door. As far as I could make out I was on my own in the hall.

I looked about the place, still nothing. Long shadows were cast along the ancient carpet near the front door, the sickly orange glow of the streetlights outside bleeding through the stained and frosted glass of the porch. A wave of panic engulfed me as I hoped, and prayed, that whoever had left last had locked the door behind them.

My eyes had adjusted to the dark and I could make out the individual lines and edges of the umbrella stand, the coat hooks mounted on the wall, and the sharp right angles of the telephone table.

All was silent and I began to feel stupid. Maybe I had imagined the sound, a wave of paranoia sweeping through me, a sharp chill running up my spine. When I was a little boy, I had been terrified of the dark. Not because of monsters or ghosts or any of that supernatural nonsense. Robbers, thieves, murderers, and rapists were what kept me awake for hours. The thought of somebody entering into the house after hours with nothing but badness on their mind was so terrifying, I had insisted on the hall light being left on until I was eight. Well, all right then, eighteen.

Ironically, when I got older and realised the motives behind such break-ins and illicit behaviour, the fear seemed to vanish. Perhaps it was a familiarity I had built up, staying out to all hours at pubs and clubs, that had eventually vanquished my terror.

I had built up a healthy respect for the darkness. I took a sip of my water, scanned the scene one more time and started up the stairs. No sooner had my foot landed on the first step and I heard the sound again. This time I knew I wasn't imagining things.

I moved away from the stairs and crept up to the living room door. It was slightly ajar and I nudged it open just a little bit further, hoping that whatever was on the other side wouldn't be frightened off by my presence.

It was then I heard the voices fully and knew instantly who they were.

'This is brilliant,' said one, deep and hoarse. It was Dave, obviously.

'I know, isn't it,' came Wendy's. I straightened myself from my hunched position of stealth, like a hunchbacked spy, and went to go in. Then I stopped, again, and thought it might not be the best plan.

Maybe they were about to have sex. As much as the thought repulsed me, she was my baby sister after all, I did unhappily concede they were two consenting adults and could take responsibility for their own actions.

My thinking made me frown and I felt myself making a sneer of disgust. I figured I'd leave them to it and headed to bed.

'You realise what we'll be able to do with the money, don't you?' followed Dave's voice.

'I know, it's just fantastic. Just like we'd said when Mum was in hospital. All that money, I can't believe it,' Wendy agreed.

My ears pricked up, the sound of cash always did that to me. Living just half a step above a squatter on the social ladder made me astute to all things financial.

I was confused. I didn't know what they were talking about, but it seemed strangely odd. Wendy had never been one to be so keen on money; Dad had always said she'd never learned the value of a pound. Now she was talking like a regular Gordon Gekko. I listened on.

'What are we going to do with your share?' Dave asked.

'Whatever I get I'm pumping into the trip. Upgrades in travel, expenses, hotels, food, you name it. It'll be like we're going on a freebie.' Wendy giggled. I still didn't know what they were talking about.

'And we can sink some of the extras into the firm, get it off the ground. No risk, free money after all,' Dave made a scoffing laugh, the type I imagined he reserved to rugby club dinners and events at the said firm. Prick.

'Oh, definitely, I mean, who would want to stay in an old dump like this anyway?'

A twang went off in my head. I could feel it, like breaking a guitar string or an elastic band stretched beyond its limit. I understood then, in a blood-chilling moment, they were talking about Mother's will.

They were dissecting what Wendy would do with her share even before they knew what exactly it would be. Mum wasn't cooling down in her urn yet and already they were spending the money and, by the sounds of it, selling the house.

Then it came to me, a second right hook of reality that would have scared Mike Tyson. This was my sister, my own flesh and blood, talking about our family home like some cast off acquaintance. She had never been like this, the complete opposite in fact, never bothered at all about assets, investments, luxury travel.

This was the same girl who had spent the last ten years struggling to glide a brush through her tangled, matted mass of hair. She was no more an economist or executive zealot than I was the next King of England.

She might not have been a cold, ruthless businesswoman, but I knew exactly who would be goading her on. Dave, the corporate shill, the shark in human clothing. He was poisoning her mind, infecting it with his charming wit and guile. Like some Charlotte Brontë pulp, the lady of the house was being snared by a cad. I never pictured us as the *Pride & Prejudice* lot, but it's always the ones you least suspect.

I was mad again. I wanted to storm into the living room and

knock that prick out with a well-aimed jab between the eyes. I wanted to stand over him while his nose bled all over the rug and tell him to keep his hands off my sister, stay away from our inheritance and leave town forever.

Two things kept me cowering in the dark. The first was the physical difference between the two of us. While I wasn't wretchedly weak by any stretch of the imagination, I was much better suited to long distance running than brawling and fisticuffs. Not that I did either of those on a regular basis of course, this was all a product of my imagination.

Secondly, to beat out somebody with as much manipulation as this guy, the all guns blazing approach wasn't going to get me anywhere. It would take a long game, a cunning plan, a method of genius so diabolical it would be brilliant.

As those schemes went, I was a bit short. I resolved to listen in for any more details I could and think of the best course of action.

The pair chatted for another while, but never mentioned the will or Wendy's inheritance again. My muscles started to cramp from standing still for too long, the creaking of my joints filling my head every time I tried to move.

The small clock that sat on a table beside the stairs chimed, signalling one in the morning and I heard them start to shuffle beyond the door. That was my cue to exit, any plan I came up with would need the element of surprise. I had to make sure they didn't know that I knew what they didn't want me to know. I skipped up the stairs and reached the top landing as the door swung open behind me, the two of them plodding up the steps as I slid into bed.

I pulled the duvet over my head, hoping they wouldn't come in. They didn't, heading into Mother's old room and closing the door behind them with a quiet click.

My head hurt and my throat was like a desert again. The water was finished and I wasn't heading back downstairs for a second time. Instead, I muscled it out and tried to go to sleep. Things had taken on a different light tonight, a strange way to cap off what had already been one of the most upside down, topsy-turvy days of my life.

Things would look different in the morning. They always did.

Chapter 14

Things didn't look any better in the morning. They never did.

By the time I had woken up, hauled myself out of bed and was sitting in a much more civilised state, Dave and Wendy had joined me for breakfast.

I couldn't look at either of them. Instead, I opted for staying quiet and sullen as I mulled over my toast and mug of tea. I must have chewed the same piece over a thousand times until it was little more than a sodden ball of wheat and saliva stuck to the roof of my mouth.

'You all set for the big will reading then, Robbie?' asked Wendy. I swallowed the glob and burned my tongue with the tea.

'Yeah, I suppose so,' I managed.

'Good, Mindy and Gerry are coming round at around ten to pick us up, it's not a long drive.' She was making polite conversation. Could she tell how angry I was?

It probably wasn't that difficult to see, I'd never been devious enough to hide my emotions very well. For all of our sakes, son hadn't taken after his father in the Argyll household. A small mercy I had been afforded in the genetics department.

'Right well, best get moving then, it's gone nine,' she fussed a little then dumped the plates in the sink without any water.

This was altogether weird and if I wasn't so sure of myself, I could have sworn I was having a bad trip. My sister was acting, talking, even smelling exactly like she always did, but I knew what secret she was harbouring within that weed-addled mind of hers.

Something was very, very wrong here and I didn't know what it was. Just when I thought I was getting to grips with things, another spanner was thrown into the works and I was back to feeling helpless.

'I'm going to have a shower,' said Dave, sitting at the head of the table. 'You going in first, Rob, or shall I?'

A shiver went down my spine and I was suddenly reminded of the muddy, rainy days of school rugby. Pricks like Dave were ten a penny at my school and they all seemed to relish the whole changing in front of other boys. Then again, I suppose I would have been the same if I had hair sprouting everywhere and dangly bits worth showing.

Instead, I had about as much muscle as a skeleton and spots the size of golf balls. Only Jack Johnson's ever present, always acidic tongue kept me sane throughout those tedious sports lessons.

'I'm fine, be my guest,' I said with as much grace and manner as I could muster. In short, it wasn't very much and he thudded out the room like a brooding silverback.

That left Wendy and myself alone for the first time since I had overheard her plotting. Once again, I was caught between a rock and a hard place; did I confront her about it or just let it slide? After all, I still wasn't entirely sure if what I had overheard was at all malicious. Could I have been mistaken in reading between the lines? Where there even any lines to read between?

'You want another cup of tea?' she asked, peeling back the lid of a yoghurt pot and licking the excess from the underside.

'No I'm fine, look, Wendy I need to … '

The front doorbell went and she hurried out of the room to get it. I clenched my fist and punched the tabletop lightly, knowing if I was ever going to bring it up, that was my only chance to do it. I would have to let the whole thing simmer for a while, or as long as could be afforded.

Wendy came back into the kitchen with two hands filled

with white, brown, and multicoloured envelopes. She dumped them down on the table and let out a sigh.

'The postman,' she said with a shrug. I nodded and sifted through the letters that had arrived.

Mother's name was all over them. No reason it shouldn't be of course, how would the world of Personal Protection Insurance, phone bills, and every other junk mail under the sun know that she had died? It was still strange to see that the world was still moving on, despite our loss.

She had passed away almost a week ago now, but everything else continued. If I was being philosophical, I could have looked upon the arrival of the mail as something to relish, a little chip away at the grieving process. Life did go on, there was no stopping it and we, as a family and as people, should too.

Things weren't that simple though and I felt a crushing sense of unhappiness bearing down on my shoulders. I was frowning, more scowling, as I pawed through each of the letters in turn, looking at my mother's name over and over again.

Every time I moved an envelope, another one was there to take its place. And each time the name looked back at me, hammering the point home.

I felt sick and sat back, dropping the letters and wanting to burn them. Wendy sensed I was upset and stared at me across the table.

'You alright?' she asked suspiciously.

'Yeah, fine.' I lied. 'Probably need to let these folk know that Mum isn't with us,' I tapped the top of the pile. God knows where this sudden sense of bureaucracy came from. Maybe it was the last vestment of my Britishness finally being released. If there was one thing we Brits loved, it was a bit of administration. And forms, we all loved forms, we went

123

mad for them. Mad enough that there was a whole government department set up for them, called the DVLA.

'Yeah, I suppose so,' shrugged Wendy.

She furrowed her brow for a moment, attempted to run a hand through her frizzy, matted hair, pulled something out of it and began to mouth some words. When she was sure about what she was going to say, she asked it.

'How … how would I go about doing that?' she said.

I laughed and shook my head. She looked at me with a forced frown.

'Seriously?' I said.

'What?'

'You're seriously going to phone and write to all of these people to tell them Mum's died?' I sounded more pointed than I perhaps intended.

'Yeah, why?'

I shook my head and pursed my lips, crossing my arms in front of me. Wendy remained stoic, staring at me with her big, butter-wouldn't-melt eyes.

'I'm just surprised is all,' I said with a smirk.

'Why?'

'Well, you've never been one to take the bull by the horns, Wend. Even you would admit that.'

She pretended to look surprised, then miffed, but I saw right through the act. I had known her all of her life, a strange fact that few people can ever say about anybody else. It was a privilege reserved for parents and older siblings.

'I know but I'm trying to change,' she answered and immediately, like that elusive right hook that had levelled me the night before, I felt guilty as hell.

Why should change be exclusively mine? Why should I be the one who hogged all of the new leaf to be turned over? Surely one aspect of my new found direction was to be less of a selfish prick. Maybe Wendy had been going through the same soul-searching that I had over the past few days. Highly doubtful, but I could dream.

I nodded, a little defeated, and opened my hands up to her. She smiled softly and winked.

'Be my guest,' I said. 'Although watch out for Mindy, you know how she loves a good argument with an automated phone system.'

'Like a Dalek fighting a Cyberman.'

'Excellent reference,' I said, not quite having the heart to tell her she was way off with her *Doctor Who* monsters.

She got up and gathered the mail, shoving it into a plastic bag she grabbed from the pile behind the door. She gave me a kiss on the top of the head as she headed out the kitchen and back into the house.

I sat for a minute listening to the quiet stillness of the world. A few winter birds chirped outside, the faintest chorus of light rain pattering against an already soaked ground making for quite a pleasant soundtrack. I certainly enjoyed it; noise wasn't something I coped with well.

As odd as that may seem to a man who made his living by making people laugh, I had never been one for loudness or deafening sound. Living in London it was nearly impossible to find a place that didn't come with its own soundtrack of honking horns, broken catalytic converters, and the endless drone of emergency service sirens.

There were parks aplenty and the suburbs themselves could offer a sanctuary of sorts, but I always had to go back.

I hadn't realised how starkly different my home had been from where I lived now. Noise had always featured prominently in our house, whether it was shouting matches, screaming contests or the always favourite raised voice stand-off. The competitors were always different, but I was always World Champion.

But in actuality, it was a very quiet, serene place to be. Glasgow itself could be a loud, brash place but twenty minutes, ten on the motorway, and you could be forgiven for thinking you were in the middle of nowhere. A gentler, softer way of life, time stretched out much longer here.

It felt like a lifetime since I had received that fateful phone call after my show. So long in fact, that I had completely forgotten all about my phone, my e-mails, my connection to the rest of the universe.

I sat for a moment and listened to nothing in particular but conceded I had the idea in my head now. With a grunt, I pushed myself up from the table and headed into the living room to find my mobile.

As much as I was part of the great world spanning grid of communication, I very rarely used it. My call to Terry had been the first time I had had any desire to make contact with anybody. Before that, I was sure it had been the call I got to say Mother had died.

Mobile phones weren't my favourite item in the world, far from it. Indeed, my unhappiness with them was so bad that they had made it into the act around the time they were beginning to get very popular.

'What's with these iPhones?' I had started, doing my best Jerry Seinfeld impression. I wasn't a fan of Seinfeld, the man or the show, but he certainly knew how to start a set.

'These things, I don't know, they're like little computers in your pocket. Suddenly you can check your e-mails, your messages, the internet, everything except make a fucking phone call!' that had raised a few laughs, a cheap gag really, but it got the job done. 'But no, I can't get my head around how people can spend so long going around with their faces buried in these things. I mean, what's the big attraction anyway. You can be contacted anywhere, everywhere, in the car, on holiday, when you're taking a shit. What's next?!'

I rummaged around the sofas and found my own ball and chain. To my surprise there were less than ten messages. I scrolled through them but there was nothing even remotely interesting. A few circular e-mails about phone bills, changes to my tariff, a begging message from a charity I donated to once. But other than that it was quiet.

I moved onto my text messages, and found there was one waiting unread. I opened it but didn't recognise the number.

Just to let you know you're

a real piece of shit Robert

Argyll!!!!!!

One quick glance, and then a second read, I was sure who it was from. She could have at least added a kiss at the end.

I hit the delete button and threw the phone back down onto the couch and sighed. Gone were the days of me getting upset over a woman.

The door opened behind me and I turned to face a dripping, even slicker Dave. His towel was wrapped around his waist, a fine dew of shower water still clinging to his rippling shoulders and heaving chest.

'Shower's free,' he said.

'Thanks, Dave,' I replied, it was easier to be polite than rebellious.

He left without responding, thankfully, and I gave him a minute to clear the hallway. When I was convinced the coast was clear, I skipped upstairs and headed for the shower, a nasty

127

little headache brewing across my forehead that I knew would cause nothing but misery for the rest of the day.

Another shower, another shave and another shit later, we were outside the porch waiting for the others to arrive and pick us up. The street was empty, a cold wind blowing up from the South, that made the bare tree branches shudder and shake.

The three of us stood about in silence, Dave occasionally mumbling something to my sister but on the whole kept his mouth shut. Wendy looked ill, like the weight of the world was pressing down on her skull. I was glad. If her intentions were as bad as I thought they were then she deserved as much misery as possible. So much for my compassionate streak.

She darted me a look of suspicion, like she could read my thoughts. Maybe she could, maybe they all could. I would have to invest in some sort of psychic protection device, anti-virus software. The internet is full of bollocks like that.

'Wendy!' came a shrill voice from behind us. We all swivelled around at the same time to see the neon brilliance of Philippa Campbell striding down the pavement, dog leash in hand, dog itself being dragged by the neck a few paces behind.

'Oh, God,' Wendy Mumbled to me from the corner of her mouth.

Philippa Campbell was the eldest of the four Campbell kids, who lived across the street. She was about the age of Mindy and was as obnoxious, domineering and snobbish as the middle classes got.

I had always harboured a small, reluctant crush on Philippa, I think it had been the older woman syndrome. She had always been fairly kind to me, never going out of her way to make my life a misery on the few occasions we spent in each other's company. I did know, however, that both Mindy and Wendy had a healthy distaste for her and anything she did.

One look at her and it was easy to see why. Tall and prim,

she was always as popular as Mindy in school. Although they weren't in the same year, they still shared many friends across groups and there could only be one winner. Philippa took the title: she was blonde, after all.

In my mind Mindy may have lost the battle, but she definitely won the war. While she had been driven enough to pursue a career, a credible, successful career, Philippa had married into money and remained a buttoned-down housewife to raise her own kids. A difficult enough task, of course, there had always been the lingering disappointment around her and the rest of the Campbells, who felt she should have done more with herself.

Where Wendy's animosity came from I had always been unsure. Maybe it was how close she was to Mindy, monkey see monkey do.

'Hi, Philippa,' she said with a broad, painfully obvious smile.

Philippa strode up to us and batted her large, brightly coloured puffer jacket down, her little dog gasping for air by her snow boots.

'Good to see you, very sad news about your Mum,' she tutted and leaned in for a hug. I couldn't help but smile at the familiarity of the situation.

'We were going to come to the funeral, but little Stephen has been ill the last couple of nights, off school and everything. How did it go?' she spoke like a machine gun. I was convinced some of her words could be deadlier.

'Yeah, it was fine, had a massive turnout, which was good. Even Robbie's set went down well.'

Oh shit, here it came. The only thing worse than being recognised by a member of the public was being spotted by somebody you hadn't seen in years.

'Robbie?' Philippa said, staring in false disbelief between

myself and Wendy. 'This isn't little Robbie, is it? Robert Argyll?' she threw her arms around me and pressed herself against my stomach. I could smell her hair, clean and fruity with a hint of expensive perfume. Was it bad I had a little jolt of excitement run through my penis?

'How are you, darling?' she asked, pulling away. I was grateful for my long coat covering my crotch.

'I'm alright, Philippa,' I wheezed. 'All things considered.'

'I understand you're a big superstar comedian now, or that's what Mindy tells me. I'm across the road in the old house, so I've been seeing her a lot recently. You must tell me all about it.' She patted my arm and, in my imagination at least, let her hand linger a little longer than necessary.

I smiled, thinking that despite all of our troubles and strife, Mindy was still flying my flag to the neighbours. That was true dedication, no matter if it was for her own ends.

'Yeah, that would be good,' I could feel Wendy's eyes burning a hole in the back of my neck.

'Definitely, how long are you up for?'

'Probably another week or so, I've got a show in December, so I'll have to head back down for that but, yeah, should be lurking about.' I clapped my hands together and rocked a little on my heels. Smooth Argyll, real smooth.

'Excellent, it's a date. And who is this lovely young man?' Philippa asked, moving towards Dave.

'This is Dave, my partner,' Wendy said, slipping her own arm through the crease in Dave's elbow.

'Pleased to meet you,' he said with a smarmy smile.

'And you, I'm an old friend of the Argyll's,' she shook Dave's hand politely. I got a hug and a boner; he got a measly shake of the paw. Take that, you shill.

'We all went to school together. Two big happy families.' There was a silence.

Thankfully Philippa's dog had the good sense to make some noise. A yap and a skip and it was ready to be punished all over again. Being choked by Philippa Campbell with a collar and leash, that was many a man's fantasy. The lucky mutt.

'Behave Baxter, honestly this dog,' she pulled the lead and it made a small yelp. 'Right, anyway, must be off, places to go, people to see. You know what it's like. I'll speak to you all later, be safe and keep your chins up. Say hello to Mindy for me, bye.' Our orders were issued and she tottered off across the road towards her house.

When she was out of earshot, I noticed both Wendy and myself let out a gust of air, like we had both been holding in our stomachs. I laughed a little and looked at my sister.

'Blimey,' I said.

'Blimey is right, Robbie, I can't stand that woman.'

'I thought she was alright,' I replied.

'Seemed perfectly nice,' Dave agreed.

Wendy looked at us both and twisted her lips. She shook her head adamantly before pointing an accusing finger at me.

'I thought better of you, Mr Argyll,' she said.

'What?' I laughed.

'Mr 'I'm a big shot comedian when it suits me' fluttering your eyes. You make me sick.'

She threw a soft punch at my shoulder and I feigned a knockout blow, rubbing at the impact zone. We laughed, all except Dave, who looked on oblivious, lost to the less than subtle humour of the whole scenario.

A loud honk broke the quiet suburban stillness and Gerry's old BMW came rolling up the pavement beside us, rocking like a boat. Mindy was in the passenger seat and dressed to the nines by the looks of things. My plaid shirt, tie and jeans suddenly didn't feel quite as tidy as I had thought it was when I threw it on. I was never going to match Dave for sharp dressing and Wendy had a style all of her own, but Mindy and Gerry were putting us to shame.

'Good morning, my darlings,' she said as we climbed into the back of the car, Wendy first, me next and Dave close behind.

I sat in the middle like a rocket, my face taking up the whole rear-view mirror. Dave shut the door with a thump and we all tried to fasten our seatbelts, shoulders rubbing, knees touching, everybody feeling awkward and cramped.

'Are your belts on?' Mindy asked, leaning around from the front passenger seat.

'Yes,' Wendy and Dave chimed together. This was getting ridiculous.

'Robert?' she asked, staring at me.

'Yes,' I said, irritated and feeling altogether too warm to be treated like a five-year-old.

I saw Gerry look in the mirror and choke down a laugh. He shook his head and held the back of his hand up to his mouth as he tried to hide his hilarity.

'Thanks, Gerry,' I said sarcastically.

'Any time,' he chortled.

'We all set?' Mindy asked. She took our silence as a confirmation and signalled to Gerry to set sail the good ship Dawkins.

The mid-morning traffic was light, the roads resting after their daily dose of rush-hour blitz. The sun was blazing down from the wispy blue sky, bathing the whole city in a cool, pale light. There was a sad melancholy to the place, the spindly trees, the dirty puddles, and the washed out faces of the punters on the street.

Only Scotland, and specifically Glasgow, could look so unhappy in relatively nice weather. That was an attitude problem, a selfish paranoia, that overruled all logical thinking. I sometimes thought the good old Glaswegians relished in this attitude. They had to, otherwise it could never have lasted so long.

Back in the car though, I had my own problems to deal with. Dave was a fidgeter; I found that out quite quickly. He couldn't seem to keep his feet together or hands rested for any longer than three microseconds. In fact, he couldn't keep them steady for any time at all. We were all uncomfortable; let's not try and make it any worse by constantly moving and readjusting ourselves.

Wendy didn't seem to mind at all, instead choosing to distract herself with the buildings and scenery passing by the window. I tried to see what she was looking at, craning my neck to get a glimpse out of the window, but all I got was an eye-full of concrete whizzing past.

'There's the new shopping centre, Robert, was it here last time you were up?' Mindy asked, playing improvised tour guide. 'We've got a new entertainment venue opening up on the Clydeside, too, going to be huge.'

'The Hydro,' Gerry finished.

'Yes, the Hydro, Rod Stewart is playing there.'

'I thought it burnt down,' I added, remembering hearing something along those lines.

'Did it?' asked Mindy. I rolled my eyes.

'No, just a bit of it,' chimed Dave.

'Well, what bit, it's rather important?' Wendy asked.

'I think it was the roof,' said Gerry.

133

'No, Rob said it was the main arena,'

'No, I didn't,' I defended myself.

'No, Rob, your nephew, our son,' Mindy quickly rectified.

This went on for the remainder of the journey and by the time we found a space and spilled out of the car, I was glad to get some fresh air. Gerry fumbled with his loose change and poured coins into the meter as I produced the old, battered packet of cigarettes from my pocket.

So far on the trip I had been good and not popped out for any on the sly. Granted I couldn't remember if, or indeed, how many I'd smoked on the night out with Jack, so I decided to pretend that it didn't count. A Mulligan, whatever that was.

Other than that little foray on the wild side, I couldn't remember smoking once since I left London. That was quite an achievement when it was said out loud.

I had a love and hate relationship with cigarettes. I loved to smoke them and I hated anybody telling me that I couldn't. As selfish as I acknowledged that was, and no doubt there were whole campaign groups set up to crucify people like me, it was one of the few beliefs that I would defend vigorously in conversation.

Passive smoking was a killer, of course I knew that and I would be, and often was, the first to not recommend taking it up as a pastime. But I had made peace with the fact that these little sticks of chemicals were probably going to kill me. Therefore, as a responsible human being, I should be allowed to smoke them when, where and how I like, free from the casting judgement of society.

But above all the self-righteous crap, I thought I looked pretty damn cool doing it. A rare achievement for me.

It was a hot topic amongst comedians, it always had been. From Bill Hicks' famous monologues to Denis Leary's rants of the same, ripped-off, material, comics simply loved to smoke and tell their audiences they were doing it. When the 'no smoking indoors' ban had come into effect, it changed the way comedy clubs and the people in them viewed these acts forever.

Suddenly you could see the comic through crystal clear air, high definition eyes. And in turn, they could see you in the audience. From a performer's point of view it was a total shift in perspective and preparation. The lack of smoke went much deeper than a simple addiction.

When I was younger and just starting out, I knew some stand ups who used their cigarettes as a shield from stage fright. Knowing they could do something with their hands other than hold the mic was a blessing in disguise for them. Harold Wilson had been told to start smoking a pipe for the same reason and he had been elected Prime Minister.

When that defence mechanism was taken away, they found it hard to cope. In the first month after the ban came into effect, I must have counted ten or so comics who had previously seemed invincible onstage, cancel last minute because they had lost their nerve.

And now the same comedians gather in a group outside the back door of the building, shivering, sweating and congregating, rain or shine, sleet or snow, as they puff away before going on. I always felt sorry for those who didn't smoke, the dressing room could be a pretty lonely place.

Even the clubs themselves had changed. I remembered my first set after the great exorcism of tobacco and nicotine Devils. The smell almost knocked me out cold.

A vile mixture of cheap perfume, aftershave, old smoke and stale air mixed with the cleaning products and air fresheners brought in en masse to make the place smell better. The taste stuck in the back of my throat for two whole days afterwards. Not even a full twenty pack of Lucky Strikes could make it go away. Disgusting.

I popped the unlit ciggy between my lips and patted my pockets for a lighter. I realised then that I'd thrown it away in a fit of anger just a few nights before. As I moved to ask a passer-by, Mindy's voice barked from the car.

'Robert Argyll!' she shouted. Both names, now I knew I was in trouble.

'Yes,' I said, squinting in the sunlight and taking the cigarette from my mouth.

'You're not thinking of smoking that, are you?' the question was rhetorical, but I felt I should answer anyway.

'Well actually, big sister, I was.' I smiled, it wasn't returned. 'Is there a problem with that?'

Mindy stepped forward, heels clacking on the pavement, and snatched the cigarette from my hand. She snapped it in half, dropped the pieces into a nearby bin and held her hand out expectantly.

Ordinarily I would have been angry, offended even, that somebody would have the nerve to break a man's smoke in front of him. And had it been a week ago I probably would have been even angrier that it was my older sister doing it. But as a testimony to how far I was willing to go to patch things up between us, a calmness had taken over and I actually thought very little of her actions.

'And the rest,' she said. Boy, was I being tested. I wasn't a religious man by any means but if there was a God, he was certainly stretching me to breaking point this morning.

Reluctantly, I fished the old packet out from my pocket and handed them over. Like a headmistress confiscating sweets, or marbles or, as for kids today, knives, guns and drugs, because they grow up so fast now, she took them and threw the packet into the bin.

'There we go, now come on,' she said with satisfaction. Dusting her hands off, she stretched out her hand to take mine.

And like the chastised schoolboy I took it as we walked to join the others, who had made their way up the street. I half expected her to tell me to tuck my shirt in, comb my hair, wash my neck and behind my ears. But she didn't and I was grateful, obviously.

Chapter 15

Gratitude for having my dignity, or what was left of it, intact was one thing. Preparing for a legal onslaught was something altogether harder and more confusing. Times like these were when having somebody like Mindy in the family to take us simpletons through the whole process was a bonus. Otherwise I knew I'd be ripped off something terrible.

No doubt it was happening anyway, but at least a family member was doing it to me. There was something oddly comforting about that.

We joined the rest of the party at the door of the solicitors. I could tell already we were about to step through a time portal into a world that had barely changed in the past forty years.

Everything about the place screamed seventies redevelopment. The faux marble façade, the font of the name above the door, even the coffee coloured glass that shielded just enough light from the inside to make it look permanently closed.

I held my breath and prepared for a blast from the past. I wasn't disappointed, either.

Brown was the overall feeling of the place: brown carpets, walls, ceiling, and furniture. Cramped and stuffy, the lingering odour of sweat and stale air hung about the place like, well, a bad smell. Puddles of dust and lint lingered in the pools of light beaming in through the brown windows, the pedestrians outside little more than dark brown blobs.

The people weren't much different. Two women sat at ancient computers, perched on even more historic desks. They didn't look up when the five of us entered, instead droning away at their workstations, getting older, and wrinklier, by the second.

Mindy was the first to speak.

'Excuse me,' she said, no gentle throat clearing for her.

'Yes,' said one of the women, her breasts hanging like two massive melons wrapped in shopping bags and resting just below her keyboard.

'We have an appointment with Mr Fraser, for eleven,' Mindy nodded towards the ancient clock on the back wall.

'Mr Fraser,' the woman said to herself, clicking her mouse to what I suspected was a totally blank screen. The other drone didn't look up, her eyes glazed over and square behind her relatively fashionable spectacles.

'Ah, yes, here we go. The Argylls,' she said.

Only in a lawyer's office could our name sound sinister. For all of its Scottish heritage, I had always viewed the family handle as being quite soft, even pleasant to the ear. But amongst this dreary, flower-powered throwback of a place, we sounded like a bunch of serial killers. Or worse, a family band, all ruffles and bell-bottoms. Carpenters eat your heart out.

'If you would like to follow me, I'll take you through to the back room.' She forced herself up from her chair and began to waddle towards the rear of the office.

We shuffled after her in single file, Mindy at the head of the expedition, Dave playing rear-end Charlie. I was lost somewhere in the middle, suddenly desperate for the smoke that had been so cruelly snatched away. In a place like this it would have been inappropriate not to smoke. The whole building seemed to be held together by the oozed out nicotine of a million Jack Regans, Theo Kojaks and Gene Hunts.

The back office was almost as cramped as Gerry's car. The secretary who led us in waited at the door and smiled at me as we piled into the tiny box like sardines in a can.

There were three seats laid out in front of an even older desk than the ones outside. Mindy, Wendy and Gerry took them up, Dave and I shuffled in behind them, squeezing past old filing cabinets and stacks of folders stuffed with documents. Sitting at the head of the cupboard was Fraser himself.

A soft spoken, placid man, I remembered him from Dad's demise. Looking at him, it was almost impossible to believe he had been to university to study the same subject as Mindy. As two people went, they were about as far apart on the spectrum as was possible.

Receding hairline, thick glasses and a shirt that looked as creased as his ashen white skin, Fraser sat amongst a pile of folders and papers that almost reached the roof. The king of his own chaos, he stood up and greeted us all individually with a firm handshake.

'Welcome everybody,' he said, voice smooth and throaty and barely above a whisper. 'Thank you all for coming in, as you know your late mother left instructions that you all be present at the reading.'

I looked about at the others. Nobody seemed to be protesting that Dave was still amongst our company. I could have made objection but the pressing heat and claustrophobia of the tiny little office were making me feel dizzy.

'Thank you, Mr Fraser,' said Mindy.

'Yes, thank you,' Gerry agreed. A few more thanks were voiced by the rest of the party.

'Well, without further ado, I suggest we crack on with things,' he unclasped his hands and fiddled with an old cardboard folder that was sitting on the only spare space of his desk. He pulled out a pile of white sheets, held tentatively together by paper clips, and proceeded to hand them around, one for each of the children.

'These are copies of the actual binding contract, will, and testament of your mother that I'm required to show you and get you to sign. Now, feel free to read these yourselves, or I can go through them with you as a group or individually if you

140

like.'

Mindy made some agreeable noises, Wendy handed hers straight to Dave. I glanced over the front sheet and got an instant headache from the jargon and sheer amount of words. It looked like Leo Tolstoy had taken a shotgun pen to a piece of paper. War and Peace didn't have as many words. It probably wasn't as funny, either. A zinger I knew every pseudo-intellectual would appreciate.

'Sorry, Mr Fraser,' I started, waving my will about and almost knocking over a pile of stray papers. 'I'm not quite so technically minded with these things. Would you mind going through it for me?' I expected the usual groans of frustration, but the others remained silent.

'Yes, of course, Robert, I'm required to read it aloud to you anyway.' He smiled, but it vanished almost immediately.

'Ah, excellent.' The others looked at me. 'Was just checking,' I smiled.

Fraser recomposed himself and removed his specs from his long, pointed nose. He breathed on one lens and cleaned it on his tie, repeating the action for the other before replacing them. He cleared his throat and looked at his audience.

'Are we ready?' he asked.

'Yes,' we said.

'Good.' He licked his lips and lifted his copy of the will, preparing for his speech like some tragic hero of old.

'I hereby leave all of my worldly possessions, assets, and finances to my three children, in equal share.'

Fraser placed the will back down on the desk, cupped his hands together and peered out across his desk. We all remained silent, although shocked would have been a better description.

I could feel something strange brewing in my belly. It wasn't a discomfort or a feeling of sickness, not this time.

More like a sense of injustice.

'That's it?' I asked.

The old lawyer fixed his gaze on me and pursed his lips. He passed his hands over the will and shrugged a little.

'That's all your mother left in her will.' He said. There was no apology in his voice, but there didn't have to be. He got his fee either way.

I was in a state of shock. To be handed a pile of papers that made *Les Miserables* look like a *Mr Men* book only to be read out one sentence, this was an outrage. An almost tragically funny one, granted, but still outrageous.

I let out a gust of air and looked at the others, hoping for some help. Of course, there was none.

'Is he serious?' I asked them. 'Mindy, that's all Mum put in her will, we're each left a third of her *assets*. I mean, what does that even mean?'

Mindy looked embarrassed. Why wouldn't she, she was a lawyer after all, she knew that something as vague as this stood about as little hope of legal challenge and clarity as a house of cards in a tornado. Only when she stood up, nudged past the others and rubbed my arm did I realise she was embarrassed of me and not the will.

'Robert, why don't we step outside for a minute,' she said softly.

'What? Why?' I protested.

'Come on, I'll explain.' She was forcing me out the door.

'Wait, hold on a minute, what's going on here, what's this all about?' I felt like a protestor being huckled out of a busy summit with lots of politicians. Need to know basis and I didn't need to know.

'Thank you, Mr Fraser, if you want to carry on with the

others I'll be back in a minute,' Mindy said, closing the door behind her.

She spun around and held a finger up to her lips, eyes wide in a sort of angry expectation. I moved to say something, but she wagged her finger.

'Not a word until we're outside,' she said, composed but most definitely irritated.

I was frogmarched through the front of the office, past the human robots and out onto the street. Catching my breath, I turned to my sister.

'Mindy … '

'Don't start, Robert,' she cut me off.

'Mindy, I … '

'I know what you're going to say.'

'How can you know what I'm going to say? I'm not even sure *I* know what I'm going to say.' She cocked an eyebrow.

'Well, you better say it then, hadn't you?'

Now that I had the floor, I wasn't sure what I was going to do with it. I decided to start at the beginning.

'Well, first off, I thought Dave the Rave wasn't supposed to be in the will reading, but I can let that slide.' I felt the need to get that off my chest. 'But my main issue is the will itself. I mean, maybe it's just me being simple, but isn't a will and testament meant to outline, in no uncertain terms, *exactly* what everybody gets. That in there,' I pointed raggedly towards the lawyers'. 'That, *that*, was barely a sentence. I don't even think there was a fucking verb in it!'

A few of the passers-by trying to enjoy their morning shopping looked around but remained quiet. There was nothing worse than a ranting lunatic in the middle of the street. I know, I tried to avoid them.

While I gesticulated and threw my hands up in the air like a bad actor, Mindy was the image of collected calm. She stood patiently and quiet, watching my every move with a stern silence. I knew I wasn't going to break that down and in the end stopped trying.

'Are you finished?' she asked.

'No. Yes, oh I don't know.' I slumped my shoulders and shook my head. I wanted to scream and shout and tear up and down the high street like the Hulk on steroids. Worse still, I wasn't even sure why.

'Do I take it from your reaction that you're a bit pissed off?' my sister asked.

'Yeah, you could say that,' I managed a breath that sounded like a laugh.

'Why don't you come in and we'll go through it together.'

'No, definitely not, nuh-uh,' I shook my head. I even held my hands up, I was that adamant I wasn't going in. 'I'm not heading anywhere near that office until you tell me what all of this means.'

I crossed my arms and thought about adding a stomp for good measure. Easy to see why Mindy treated me like a child, I was barely out of nappies.

'Well, what do you want to know?' she asked.

'Where do I begin? First off, erm, why is the will so damn short. I thought these things were meant to be full of jargon, loads of pages, written on a goat skin, for God's sake.' I was getting uptight again, but I forced it down into my chest where it burned.

'We've moved on a bit since the days of *sheep* skins, Robert but I know what you mean. I do know what you mean.' Mindy sounded confident. She should be, she was a lawyer after all. But more than that, she sounded reassuring, like she

144

understood what I was going through.

In my rush to escape the room, or be thrown out of it, I hadn't seen anybody else's reaction. From what I recalled, they were all perfectly calm. Anything would have been, compared to my reaction, though. I was starting to feel the pressing pang of regret creeping into the back of my mind. Ah old friend, how I hadn't missed you.

'Wills these days are very little more than a formality,' Mindy continued. 'Although granted, Mum's was a little short.'

'A little,' I raised my eyebrows in unison. 'I've taken pisses longer.'

'Robert,' she tutted. 'The fact is, she formalised her wishes in a last will and testament, with the view to having us all be there when it was read aloud. You didn't expect anything different from the outcome anyway, did you?'

'Seems I was the only one,' it slipped out before I knew what I was saying.

'What?' Mindy asked.

I felt a rather large rush of blood fill my head, making my cheeks flush. A cold sweat formed on my brow and the back of my neck. I'd dropped myself in it here and now faced a difficult decision. Did I tell Mindy about Wendy's plans, spill the beans on my eavesdropping and be done with it? On the other hand, I could stay quiet until I thought of something else. This was a class A, triple-decker, no holds barred nightmare.

'Erm ... nothing,' was about all I could get out.

Mindy gave me an unconvinced look and closed her eyes until they were nothing more than slits. She knew I was hiding something. Hardly a difficult deduction, I probably looked as guilty as I felt.

'Anyway, that's that, then. You're getting a third of the

house, the cash left in her account, and proceeds we get from any future sales. It's what she wanted and we'll respect that.' There was a finality to her tone and I didn't disagree.

'Now, will you please come back in and listen to Mr Fraser. He's been with the family for a long time and I don't want us letting ourselves down.' Again, very sound logic. 'Or Mum and Dad,' there was the stinger. One of Mindy's dressing downs always had that venomous bite that zipped straight for the nerve.

I didn't dance to the tune of others often, but when it came to the family, they were still on my side. The least I could do was to be on theirs.

'Okay,' I said, unfastening the top button of my shirt and loosening off my tie.

We headed back into the stuffy old office and through the back to Fraser's lair of paper and files. The old lawyer was droning on about some long winded service when we got back in.

'Ah, welcome back, you two,' he said. I wasn't sure if he was being sarcastic or not. I didn't really care. 'Can we continue?'

'Yes, please, Mr Fraser,' said Mindy, straightening her dress once she sat down.

He nodded at her, then to me, and started up one more time, like an old engine that refused to die. I leaned against the wall and tried to stay awake.

The lecture only went on for an hour, but it felt like days. Minutes seemed to tick by slower than normal and every word from Fraser dragged on and on and on. I also swore I saw the second hand tick backwards at one point on the clock beside his computer.

When he was finished, he insisted we sign our copies of the will and hand them back. I didn't bother reading mine;

sure, that all the important stuff like that would be done by somebody else. Irresponsible, I know but the room was simply crushing. I doubt even Hitler's bunker was as depressing as this place.

Fraser thanked us and said we were free to go, at least that's what I thought he said, as I high-tailed it out of the office and back onto the street. I searched up and down the busy road for a convenience store, some heavy-duty tobacco would be a nice little treat. There was none, only pound shops, tanning salons and about twenty Greggs bakeries.

I remembered this street from when we were all growing up. It used to house a host of small business. Butchers, barbers, local produce, a great place to shop without venturing into the centre of the city.

By the time we were kids it was already on the decline, but I had never imagined it would deteriorate quite so badly. Or quickly. I hadn't been gone all that long. Not relatively, anyway.

Now I couldn't even get a newsagents to buy a packet of smokes. What was this country coming to?

'We all set?' Mindy asked coming out from the lawyers. She had stayed behind to talk shop presumably.

'What's the plan?' Wendy asked.

'I need to stop off at the firm, tidy up a few loose ends,' said Dave. 'I'll get the train though, so don't worry.' The classic line of somebody fishing for a lift. The bait was set.

'Don't be silly, we'll run you in,' and there was the hook, courtesy of Mindy.

'Are you sure, I don't want to be a bother.' Stop doing my little sister and sod off, then you won't be a bother, I thought.

'Of course, where's your office?'

'Waterloo Street, should be quiet enough around this time,

147

you can head straight onto the motorway afterwards.'

'Sounds fine. Everybody coming?' Mindy looked about. Gerry nodded obediently, Wendy seemed indifferent as usual and I remained silent. Of course I was going, I was barely allowed out in public, let alone trusted to get home on my own. And for good reason, the last time it had happened I was out of control.

'Right then, let's all go.'

We headed back to the car and crammed ourselves in one more time. I tried to process the events of the will and what they meant, but there were still far too many questions and not enough answers. I resolved to bite the bullet again.

'Do you guys get Rock Radio up here?' I asked.

'Yup,' said Gerry quickly.

'Can we have it on, please?'

'Sure,' Gerry jumped in first again, pressing the number two button on the dashboard presets.

I could tell he was keen, even before he got over-enthused. It was no doubt a guilty little pleasure of his when Mindy wasn't in the car and a definite no-no when she was. But he was in company and could get away with it this time. Her manners were too impeccable to call him out in front of us. I liked his thinking.

The flailing guitar shreds of AC/DC's *Hells Bells* blasted out of the speakers and I tapped along. When we hit the chorus, Gerry and I started singing at the same time. He was a good sort, and not a bad singer, either.

Chapter 16

Stage performance left a lot to be desired. Or at least it did in my case. Going to a theatre or venue used to ensure punters a ripping good show that would feature dancing, singing and a dollop of comedy thrown in for good measure.

Now, it was just one or nothing at all. The art of the show had been lost and, in my mind, that was a bad thing. Old school entertainers like Bruce Forsyth and Bob Dole were things of the past. Sure Brucey still got a run out on a Saturday night, but he was getting on a bit. His routine was almost as old as he was.

In a world that needed entertainment quick, hard, and straight to the point, a lot of the heart had been lost. Making people laugh with fart and dick jokes was all well and good, but it didn't mean anything. Not really.

I could hardly be counted as a great protestor to this. My act consisted of anywhere between twenty minutes and an hour and a half of blue language, adult oriented themes and a good, unhealthy dose of foul-mouthed ranting. If I were a CD, I'd have a Parental Guidance sticker slapped on my front.

Because I didn't follow suit, didn't mean I didn't care. Using myself as an example, it could be said that I was being punished for being too crude and rude. Success was hardly knocking my door down, after all.

But there were plenty of big name comics making a fortune, literally millions a year from just swearing and talking about sex. The same went for the music business, and to a lesser degree, the movies. Long gone were the days of hearty, good-natured fun films that didn't take a lot of effort to enjoy.

My sad lament to the days of old had only come on me once we got home. I sat watching Danny Kaye leap and lunge about the stage in *Wonder Man*, an old musical from 1945. Looking at it so long after it first came out was a strange, almost surreal experience. Just thinking about the difference in audience expectation in the short decades between its first release and the present day.

Granted there was probably a lot more positivity in the air back then. The Nazi threat had just been crushed and the world was breathing a sigh of relief as things tried to return to normality. It would be difficult to pitch a film like *Oldboy* or *Silence of the Lambs* to producers back then.

Big smiles, bright colours and a score to keep you tapping your feet all the way through, it was giving me a headache. Changed times, brave new world and all of that old rope.

I flipped through the channels but there was nothing on. I knew I should have been writing, working on the act, but I just couldn't muster the energy. The will had been a big shock and I hadn't quite gotten my head around what any of it meant. Mindy had promised to take me through it later, but I couldn't have cared less.

Then there was the issue of Wendy and her plotting. Was this what she had been planning all along? Even Mindy said that she had expected all of mother's belongings to be divided up three ways.

I had never given much thought to it, personally. As tight as money was for me I didn't exactly rub my hands with glee at the prospect of a big payout. Or any payout for that matter. Things had been rocky with Mother, but I certainly never wished her any harm or, indeed, the suffering I had been told she had gone through towards the end.

As surprising as that sounded, and nobody was more surprised than me, it was the truth. Mum's death was a massive shock to me and I was starting to think I might be getting a handle on coping with it. These new revelations about my young sister were confusing to the point of losing the plot altogether.

'Too much,' I said aloud to the empty room. The young,

'cheek of tan' faces of the family looked back at me from the gallery of pictures dotted about the place. None of them replied, I wasn't expecting them to. I probably would have shit myself if they did.

I slapped my knees and headed into the kitchen, thirsty. There was very little there by way of juice, or milk or anything non-alcoholic. A fresh six pack of Miller sat twinkling at me, little beads of water trickling from their necks in as tempting a way as any advert could make them.

I leaned around the door and checked the time. Half-past four on a Tuesday afternoon.

'It's five-o'clock somewhere,' I said aloud, again to nobody, and cracked open a bottle.

The first drink after a big night out is usually a fifty-fifty affair. Either it tastes great and puts you back in the mood. Or it makes you want to throw up all over again. Or 'whitey' as the kids so colourfully put it.

This one was definitely the former and I felt it take effect immediately. My neck was sore and stiff, shoulders tight and taut but they began to loosen up. I swigged half of the bottle down in one gulp and looked at it.

Alcohol and I had always enjoyed a strange relationship. Strange in the sense that I loved to drink but hated the effects it had on me, both before, during, and after a lengthy binge. I wasn't a rowdy drunk or a belligerent one, but I knew I wasn't a saint either.

The hangovers were always killers and I detested them enough to always swear I was never doing it again. Empty promises from a weak-minded idiot, I thought. There was some truth in it, too. Self-discipline and regulation weren't my strong points, the bottle in my hand a testament to that.

I grabbed a bag of nuts from the cupboard near the back door and glided back into the living room to settle in for the rest of the day. There were a few unpleasant twitches of guilt somewhere in the back of my mind, the rest of the world hard at work, toiling away while I jollied things up at home. I actively chose to ignore them.

I sat and drank and ate and watched TV. When one beer was finished, I opened another and polished off the rest of the nuts, crisps and other snacks that were loitering about the kitchen. I wasn't particularly hungry, only grazing out of boredom. And where boredom reigned, something else was sure to follow.

It didn't take much to set me off, then again, it very rarely did. An advert for a woman's razor was enough to get a twinge from the depths of my boxers. Long, smooth legs that shimmered in the false sunlight of the advert, a gentle caress along the length of them to show how glossy they were. Bloody Hellfire I never stood a chance.

Much like my pubescent days, even the slightest hint of anything remotely sexual would get me going. To the point where I couldn't think of anything else. More importantly, I wouldn't be able to think of anything else until I was suitably relieved.

The situation was all too perfect, which didn't help my guilt. Wendy had left with Dave to go shopping in town, although I suspected she was scoring weed from a dealer somewhere. Mindy and Gerry had gone to pick up Rob, their son, from university, leaving me with little more than myself for company. Or, indeed, myself to play with.

I thought through the possibilities, all the eventualities that might come about. The art of masturbation when nobody was around, and I had practised enough that it was an art, was to make sure it stayed that way. At the height of my teenage sessions, I would carefully plan ahead by half an hour, sometimes whole hour slots, to make sure there would be no chance of getting caught.

For the most part it had worked, the only blot on my record

was when the Campbell girl had walked past the front gate. And even then, twenty years later, I was still convinced she hadn't seen anything.

Thinking of the Campbells brought Philippa back into perspective and my mind was made up. I lifted myself off of the couch, crumbs spilling over the rug, and headed into the small study Dad had kept at the back of the house.

I hadn't been in that room in years, but it may as well have been hours. The whole place was exactly the same. Books lined the walls, untidy files and folders poking out between copies of Keats, Wordsworth and Scott. A whole collection of Agatha Christie pulp took up most of the far wall, surrounding the window like a murderous frame.

The writing desk and small couch were in the same position they always were, flanking both sides of the study, locked in an eternal staring match. Another desk was beneath the window and on top of it a newish computer.

Dad had never been one for computers, but he had been forced to invest for work. On the rare occasions he spent working at home, or so he said, he would spend hours on the machine mumbling to himself. It took him twice as long to do anything on it because of his technophobia, ironic really when you counted the vast volumes of sci-fi novels he used to read.

I sat down at the desk and swore I could smell his aftershave, Old Spice or some such pungent cologne, lingering even after all of this time. I pushed it from my head; there was business to be getting on with. The scent of my late, bastard father wasn't a great aphrodisiac.

The computer hummed into life and I quickly navigated the desktop. Internet browser open, zip undone, I was ready to rock and roll. Or shake and bake, depending on how you looked at it.

I found the whole thing completely bizarre, of course, and had made light of it in my act over the years. While I may have lamented the death of light entertainment and showmen like Danny Kaye, even they couldn't have imagined the wealth of free material at the fingertips of modern man. Or woman.

'That's the thing about internet porno,' I remember starting one particularly racy routine. 'It's just so easy to get a hold of these days you know? I remember when I was growing up, all you could get was a dirty magazine from the newsagents. And even then you had to be eighteen, or at least look like it. "I'll have one of these please, Mister." I put on an obviously faked deep voice. "And a copy of the Beano, while you're at it."' That one got a huge laugh I remembered. One of my best.

'But now it's two clicks and here we go. Dogs, cats, horses, Muppets, you name it. I was on it the other day there and they've even got full blown cartoons of all your favourites. Fred Flintstone doing George Jetson, Scooby Do having a quickie with her from Wacked-Off races, it's unreal.' The dirty stuff always drew the biggest laughs. I always believed it was something to do with the spotlight being taken away from people's sordid little lives and shone on me instead. Projection, I think psychiatrists called it, anything to hide away their dirty secrets. And we all had them, of course.

'So, the next time you fancy a wank to Mickey Mouse and Bugs Bunny going at it in a vice den, just check out my hard drive,' I lost it towards the end, falling into a fit of laughter as the sweat poured out of me. The punters loved it, though. That was one of the better nights I remembered.

Even now, as I sat trolling through the depths of humanity for something even remotely arousing, I was smiling. If dirt and filth were the way to go, give the people what they want.

The people would have to wait for half an hour or so as I took some personal time out of my otherwise hectic schedule. Settling on a website creatively titled *Hardcore Knockers* I got down to business.

Some cultures viewed masturbation as illicit and evil,

others looked at it as a necessary part of everyday life. For us Brits, and more locally Scots, it was something altogether sordid and not spoken about. From a personal point of view I couldn't care less. I did it, was happy to admit doing it and that was final.

The videos were streaming quickly through the internet and I was beginning to settle into a nice rhythm when I thought I heard something outside. I stopped and held my breath for a moment, fully expecting to hear a door open or voices from beyond the window. A good stealthy masturbator learns to be paranoid for every microsecond of their willy rubbing ways.

My heart was racing. There was a genuine nervousness to the whole thing, my breath loud, filling the room like a stereotyped pervert's. I looked about the study, checking that the door was still open a crack before resolving that there was nobody else about.

I started again and could feel things build up. I lost myself in the fantasy unfolding on the screen, putting myself in the place of the steroid fuelled stud who was being paid a fraction of what his partner was. Union law hadn't quite stretched to the adult entertainment industry, yet.

But I didn't care, I was on a roll. I could worry about the left wing politics of the San Fernando Valley another time. With every thrust on screen I mimicked it with my own hand. My toes began to curl and muscles clenched all over my body. I could feel my eyelids twitch and my lips dry as I panted for breath, short and sharp, pushing myself further and further.

I thought of Angela, naked beneath me, Tess on top of me, my mistress, pressed against me in the shower, lips touching, breasts warm and wet against mine. I thought of Philippa across the road, the smell of her hair, her gorgeous body, stripping her out of that outfit and finding nothing beneath but her delicious flesh that I'd kiss and lick and bite all over.

The sensation kept growing and I got faster and faster.

Everything became blurry as I pressed on and on until, until, until Wendy walked past the study window.

Everything stopped in a heartbeat. The fantasy was destroyed by cold, hard, relentless reality that came charging out of the blissful nowhere like an out of control bulldozer. I froze, like I did all those years ago, and felt the colour drain from my face.

My hand was jammed down the front of my jeans, my cock poking out from the top of my boxers, a little wet and sticky. I heard the back door in the kitchen click open and footsteps shuffle in.

'Hello!' came Wendy's voice from the other room.

'Eh … ' I said, sounding like a dying cat.

'Anybody in? Robbie?' I could hear her approaching.

I pulled my hand out of my trousers and crossed my legs at the computer. It was then I realised that the couple on the screen were still ploughing away at each other good and proper. I panicked, the door creeping open behind me.

I dropped to my knees and yanked the power cable out from the cluster of sockets on the floor and prayed to God, Buddha, Mohammed and SpongeBob that the computer had been killed.

Wendy entered the study behind me and came over. I looked around from beneath the desk.

'What are you up to?' she asked. She sounded genuine enough, not accusing in any way. Was there a chance she hadn't seen me in full flight?

'Erm … ' I couldn't think, my brain still reeling from all its stimulation. 'The computer wasn't working, I was trying to fix it,' I said.

'Not working? It was fine last night,' she clicked on the mouse above. I half expected it to come away with her hand,

156

but it remained flat on the desk.

'Yeah, no. I'll have a fiddle with it,' I replied, looking at her from below.

She leaned over and frowned. Oh shit, this could be it.

'You alright?' she asked. 'You look a little flushed.'

'I'm fine,' I squeaked, clearing my throat. 'Just a bit warm. Could you get me a beer from the fridge, that would be great, sis.' I didn't sound like myself, she was bound to notice.

'Okay, fine.' She shrugged with a smile and headed for the door. I breathed a sigh of relief but sucked it back in when she stopped. 'Oh, and I'm heading out for a pint with some friends later if you want to come, might be good craic.'

'Yeah, sure, no probs. Sounds good.' I would have said anything to get her out of the study.

'Alright, cool, cool. I'll join you with the beer, then.' She left and I was alone once again.

I pulled out from underneath the desk and untangled myself from my shirt. I looked down at my jeans; the open zip, button and belt yawning back at me like a mouth. A little dark spot had formed above where my now flaccid penis sat in my boxers.

I looked at the dark screen of the computer with a great relief and let out a little laugh. So much for my big comeback into the ever-glamorous world of professional masturbation. Legend? I was more like a puny rookie, still learning the ropes. Stupid as it was, I was still a little sad about that realisation.

Chapter 17

Sadness wasn't allowed in bars, pubs and clubs. There should have been a sign above every door that read, 'If you're sad, you're not getting in.' As it was, the political correctness police had made sure there wasn't. Just as well, really, as the majority of people I knew who went to the pub were deeply unhappy.

Sitting amongst a bunch of twenty-something students, however, it was difficult to think of anybody ever knowing sadness. There were a dozen of us grouped around a long, scratched, beer stained table and the conversation was free flowing. Pints were the order of the day, cider and cheap lager for the most part. I felt out of place and a bit cheeky for ordering a Guinness.

That decision had only come when I realised that Angela wouldn't be joining us. My exploits earlier had forced my hand into coming along without thinking through the consequences. Only after dinner did I realise she might be with the group.

The train journey into town had been spent in quiet, nervous contemplation. A thousand scenarios raced through my head on how to get out of it but none seemed to work. Wendy didn't have a clue, thankfully, so I kept it under my hat.

When we headed into the bar on Glasgow's Bath Street, the hub of reasonable entertainment at low cost pricing, I held my breath and scanned all of the faces. None registered and I breathed a sigh of relief. The pint was making things go a bit smoother, but I was still keeping an eye on the door.

Chat was the usual student fare: politics and academics for the most part, usually a combination of the two. There were some heated views on the government, both national and the devolved Scottish parliament, with the general consensus being that of unhappiness.

I had to chuckle to myself. Students were never happy. They

thrived on being contrarians, always on the outside looking in. No matter who was in the hot seat, the student classes always felt like they should oppose them in some way.

Most of them grew out of this habit by their mid-twenties, but not all of them. Those remaining grew up to be readers of the Guardian or worse still, its editor. I should have written that one down, but I was short on pens.

'So, that bastard Cameron is doing the same as Thatcher in the eighties, shitting on the poor and lining the pockets of the mega-rich. It's terrible,' one of them piped up.

He was sitting next to Wendy, long shaggy hair that was receding enough to make him bald within the next two years. A dirty beard and even filthier clothes hung around his chubby shoulders. Max, or Alex, I couldn't remember his name.

'And then he turns around and expects us to vote for him next year. Well, I say rats to that,' he took a big gulp of his pint to a murmur of approval.

'And what about Salmond?' came another of the group.

'Don't get me started on Salmond,' said Max-Alex. 'He's just as crooked as the rest of them, but at least he talks a good game. About time we were separated from that lot down there anyway, I reckon.' Another chorus of agreeable chatter from the group.

The Scottish independence debate had sort of passed me by. Living in London the general consensus was there wasn't a consensus. Scotland had played an important part in the British history, but it had been so long since we were all separated, nobody knew, or cared, what it would be like to be apart.

Even when I was with English colleagues or friends I didn't get asked about it. Admittedly I didn't have the strongest of Glaswegian accents and I was sure I had lost some of the brogue over the years. But I was still unmistakably Scottish to the ear. Except for one woman who thought I was Canadian.

God knows where that came from.

Listening to these grotty, spotty students talk government shop was amusing. But it did drone on after a while.

'So, Rob, Wendy says you're a comedian,' said Max-Alex, turning the group's attention onto me.

'Well,' I started. 'So I'm told.' A couple of laughs from the less powerful players in the company. A cheap gag but they were the ticket buying public after all.

'How did you get into that then?' he said. I tried to pick something up from his tone, but it seemed clean enough.

He didn't strike me as the quiet type, this Max-Alex. Confrontation was etched across every crag on his face, the fire of a rebellious youth still burning in his adult eyes. I had possessed that same look once, but it was long gone now. Crushed under a mountain of scepticism and fatigue.

I didn't feel uncomfortable talking to him, or the others. I was simply cautious and aware he would be making mental notes of everything I said.

'Wasn't much of a choice really, I sort of fell into it.'

'Really? How?' he pressed.

'Well, I wasn't very good at school, barely scraped into uni and had always thought I was quite funny.' A couple more laughs, but I wasn't looking for them. It was the truth. 'Then I got the chance to write some stuff and perform it around local bars in the South Side before deciding that it was the gig for me. And here I am,' I spread my hands out across the table to a bunch of smiles. Everybody but Max-Alex.

'Interesting.' He mused, scratching his chin.

I couldn't put an age on him, but he was under thirty certainly, just. He was the type of guy who wanted to be so much older than he was but was unsure why. I was certain he was also used to being the centre of this little group. My

160

presence must have been killing him a little. I quite liked that thought.

'So, how do you go about it then?' he asked.

'Go about what?' I took a sip.

'The act, how does it come together? You know what I mean, when you're watching *Live at the Apollo* or *Mock the Week*, the guys just seem so natural. Frankie Boyle, Chris Addison, it's like so natural to them. Is that what it's like?'

He was digging his heels in, determined to make this into something it really wasn't. I could talk all night about the secrets of performance but I wasn't going to. Not to anybody and certainly not to a jumped up little twerp like this. I needed to bury it before it got out of control.

'It's hard to explain, just sort of happens. I'll show you.' I rose to my feet and looked out across the table, every pair of eyes now on me.

A little switch was flicked in the depths of my mind. It wasn't subconscious; I could feel it turn on. The same thing happened when I was about to go on stage. Call it a sixth sense or something much less dramatic, I was on and it was game time.

'So, normally I start with something loose like, good evening ladies and gentlemen, glad you could all make it tonight. Nice to see you're not waiting around for the DVD of this show to come out,' I could hear the difference in my voice. I was confident, cocky and self-assured. My onstage character wasn't much different to reality, the only thing was, he didn't have a family to worry about, an ex-girlfriend who despised him and all the other bullshit that came along with being alive.

'I'm back up here in Glasgow, great city, wonderful city. Doesn't deserve the bad reputation it gets. When you're the capital city of Europe for heart-disease and strokes, you deserve a little more respect, you know?' The group loved it

161

and I could see Wendy smiling wryly. Max-Alex remained perfectly stoic.

They were set up perfectly, laughing and smiling. All I needed now was a killer line to bow out on and I could enjoy the rest of my evening.

'But that's just what happens when you consume so many deep friend Mars bars. I've never had one myself, never tried one. But I suppose the next time I want something yellow and veiny with a black centre I'll ask your man Alex here to give me a quickie in the gents.'

Claps and thumps on the tabletop and a few whoops from the others. I took a gamble with his name but I didn't care, the joke was in the ending not the detail. I gave a small bow and sat back down for a drink, the two lads either side of me patting my back as the applause rang on.

I looked up at Wendy, who was smiling and laughing. Alex sat beside her and raised his pint glass, a little smile across his mouth that showed he was gracious in defeat. I did the same and we left it at that, the best of enemies.

When the laughter died down and my limelight faded, the group splintered into pairs and trios. After another few rounds we had left our table/life raft and were mixing quite amicably.

I got chatting to a couple of Wendy's PhD friends and colleagues, who shone a little intrigue on my younger sister. Nothing devastating or scandalous, just little character quirks that I never expected of her. She was apparently quite vocal in class, always questioning the tutors' beliefs and long standing theories. Philosophy was a subject like that, or at least that's what I had always thought. But apparently, even the soundest of thinking and well oiled theories were no match for Wendy Argyll.

She also had a reputation as a ball-breaker with her own students. Part of her course required Wendy to take weekly student groups and research marking to help undergraduates.

She was paid a small salary for it and it helped her overall learning curve. So I was told.

But apparently, she was strict and gruff with her pupils. Throughout the department she was known to be the one the students didn't want to get every year. Late assignments were a no go; even worse would be failure to turn up to classes. I couldn't help but smile a little at the thought. Mindy's influence hadn't been completely eradicated.

I was joshing around about how different she was growing up when I felt a tap on my shoulder. It was Wendy, with a fresh pint.

'Everything alright?' she said, rocking on her heels.

'Yeah, yeah, smashing,' I said, draining my glass and taking the new one.

'They're not boring you, are they?' she asked.

'No, no not at all. Just getting told about the fearsome Miss Argyll and her iron fisted rule.' I smiled.

Wendy gawped and then looked embarrassed. Her cheeks went a little redder in the dim light of the bar. She shook it off and returned my smile, flashing her teeth and pushing a clump of hair back behind her studded ear.

'You fancy a smoke, Robbie?' she said.

'I would love a smoke, Wendy.'

'Good, walk with me, talk with me,' she straightened and offered her arm. I hooked mine into her elbow and we skipped out of the pub in a fit of hysterics.

The outside world was cold, damp and busy. A long, sheltered smoking section ran along the length of the bar. The street was a level above, tall railings acting like barriers to keep people from falling into the long trough. Or to stop drunks from climbing up, I wasn't too sure.

The flat paving stones shimmered with the glow of the streetlights above, giving everything a weird, night-time glow. Cars raced past and sent a light mist of spray down into the smoking section, coating the walls in a fresh dampness every few seconds.

Wendy commandeered an old, weather beaten bench and sat on its back, feet on the seat. I sat down the traditional way and took one of her cigarettes. She lit hers, then mine and pulled the hood of her sweater over her head so she looked like an older, greyer E.T.

We sat in silence for a while, listening to the conversations that floated about us and the thumping sound of the music from the bar. Our initial hilarity had worn off, replaced by a quiet contemplation.

'So,' I said, taking the lead, 'your friends seem nice.' Hardly prime conversation fodder but it would do.

Wendy sucked on her cigarette and nodded. She blew out a ring of smoke and tapped the ash into a puddle by the bench. Something was wrong, I could tell. She wasn't acting in her normal, self-assured self. She had asked me to come out for a smoke wanting to talk, about something. Now that we were here, she must have lost her nerve.

'Wendy,' I started, not sure where I was going with it. 'Is everything alright?'

Sometimes simply asking the obvious was the best way to go. Not always but when you're stuck for other options, keeping it simple was always a good plan.

'Yeah, fine. Why do you ask?' she replied.

'I don't know. Just, something seems a bit off. You sure everything's all right? You can tell me, you know.' I didn't want to come on too strong, I knew what she was like. Helpless and selfish for the most part.

While Wendy had always been closer to Mindy, the two of

164

us had still enjoyed a relationship better than I had with the rest of the family. Kindred spirits I would have called it, if I were in any way, shape or form romantic. The two of us had always shared a similar humour, the same view on life. Never to take it too seriously was the order of the day.

My regrets with my sisters, as if my mother and even my father weren't bad enough, had always harboured a special shame. I felt particularly bad about my ignorance of Wendy. She was young when I left; barely a teenager and she had grown up during her most important years without me being around. Without any of her siblings around for that matter.

Little details like that could shape the very future of a person. While Mindy had gone off to become a lawyer and I had started my self-imposed exile, she had been effectively raised as an only child. The others flew the nest and she received all of the projected attention of our parents. Well, one of our parents anyway.

I had been glad, then, when I first came home that we had slipped back into our old familiarity without a second's hesitation. It was like I had never left. Things were difficult enough with the situation, I needed to know that she was still the little sister I loved.

Sure, things had changed with her; things had changed with us all. I didn't exactly approve of Dave and his intentions, whatever they were. But if it meant Wendy was happy then of course I would give them my blessing.

That was a strange thought, giving my blessing. I hadn't realised it, but I was the senior man of the family. I had been since Dad had died choking on a bra strap or whatever it was. There was even a reasonable argument for before then, his head of the family ticket stamped with a 'void'. I took a long draw of my cigarette and choked down a gulp of fizzy beer. Real mind bending stuff.

'Anyway,' I said. 'If you don't want to tell me, that's fine.

165

I won't force it. But you know you can always talk to me.' I finished my ciggy and flicked it onto the ground.

I stood up and cracked my back with a groan, draining the last of my pint. I pointed a finger at Wendy's, silently asking if she fancied another. I wasn't expecting the answer I got.

'Dave wants me to marry him,' she said.

There weren't many moments in life where every emotion comes onto a person at once. Having this sudden flurry of change injected into you, you would expect a spectrum of actions, gestures, shouts and tears. I was surprised at how I reacted. A rather strange calmness started in the pit of my stomach and slowly oozed out to the farthest reaches of my toes, fingers and head.

I hoped it was the sudden discharge of every emotion possible. Either that or I had a bleeding ulcer. Knowing my luck, it was a mixture of the two.

So, Dave had asked Wendy to marry him. I couldn't say I was surprised, the way he was fawning over her in his own, leering way. I didn't know how long they had been dating, but I sensed it wasn't the joyous occasion it perhaps should have been. I decided to delve deeper.

'What did you say?' I asked bluntly.

Wendy didn't meet my stare, instead choosing to swirl all of the gas from her half full pint. She bit on her bottom lip and frowned a little, her brow narrowing.

'I'm not sure,' she said. 'Really, I'm not. I told him I needed a bit of time before I gave him an answer.'

'And how did he take that?' I asked, sitting down beside her. She didn't answer me, which meant it had gone down like Judas Priest at Sunday Mass.

She shivered a little and forked out another cigarette from her pocket. She offered me one but I refused, the taste had

166

gone off me and I had sobered up almost instantly.

'I don't know,' she said lighting it. 'I love the guy.'

'You love him?' I prodded, sounding a bit miffed.

'Yeah, I do, he's great. He's successful, he's handsome, he's got a future. It all makes sense and I do love him. Truly, I do.'

'But?'

Wendy sneered a little and shook her head. She rubbed her eyes, a smear of wetness coming away on her fingers.

'I don't know. I didn't ever think I was the marrying type, you know, Rob? I can't see me being the buttoned-down wifey that looks after the kids while he's away at work. I just don't think I'm ... I'm ... '

'Mum?' I asked.

She looked at me as a stray tear ran down the inside of her nose. She sniffed and tried her best not to start sobbing, her bottom lip wobbling. I reached over to her and took her hand.

'Look at me,' I said. She forced herself to meet my line of sight. 'You don't have to do anything you don't want to, Wendy. You've got a loving family who only wants the best for you and we'll stand by your decision, whatever that may be.' I tried to sound as reassuring as I could without appearing to be insincere. I was aware of how patronising I could sound at times, even when I wasn't intending to be. But this was important, I needed to let her know she wasn't alone.

'Whatever you decide, we'll be behind you. I'll be behind you. I know I haven't been around all that much for the last couple of years, but that's all going to change, I promise.'

A lump had formed in my throat and I could feel myself starting to slip. I took a deep, quivering breath and tried to hold it together.

'Alright, kiddo?' I said.

Wendy nodded at me and leaned in for a hug. We held each other warmly, tenderly, for a long moment and I could feel her crying into my shoulder. I wrapped my arms around her and squeezed as hard as I could. Whatever happened with us, whatever Dave's intentions or, indeed, Wendy's were with her share of the inheritance, her happiness was still paramount to me. That and her safety, along with the rest of my family's.

She pulled away from me and wiped her face clear. So far this trip had seen more crying, sobbing, shedding of tears that I had experienced in the past thirty-years. Between the funeral and my own sense of familial duty, I had effectively made everybody I ran into cry uncontrollably. Not to mention myself, I was the worst.

There was a joke in there somewhere, but I couldn't think of it. Wendy sniffed, rubbed her nose and smiled a tired grin at me.

'You alright?' I asked. She nodded.

'I will be. Thanks, Robbie.'

'Don't thank me, lil' sis.' I said, poking her shoulder with my finger. 'That's what I'm here for … What I'm going to be here for.'

'Look at the state of me,' she said. 'Blubbing like this. It won't do, you know.' She laughed, sounding exactly like Mindy. 'What would Mum think?'

'She'd probably think you were mad, but then again, she thought that about us all,' I tried to sound reassuring.

'Except for Mindy,' she laughed.

'Yeah, except for Mindy,' I agreed. 'Come on, then,' I said, reaching out for her hand. 'Let's go inside and you can buy your big brother a drink and tell me all about your trip.' It was out before I knew I was saying it. I stopped flat and hesitated

168

before looking around; I could already tell that the reaction wasn't going to be good. Excuses flooded through my head, every way possible of getting out of this with a shred of family harmony intact.

The truth was there wasn't a way out. I had put my size tens right in it and was now wishing I'd booted my own teeth out with them instead.

When I did pluck up the courage, I looked around at Wendy who stood perfectly still by the side of the bench. Her eyes were wide and bloodshot, ringed with red skin that matched the end of her nose. She wore an expression of blind surprise. Not good surprise, more annoyed that bordered with white, hot rage. I had really done it now.

'How do you know about my trip?' she said, voice flat.

'Nothing, come on, let's go inside, it's freezing out ... '

'Robert,' she said firmly. 'How do you know about my trip? I haven't told anybody about it yet.'

Being there for one's sister was all well and good. Coaxing her into telling you her problems was also something that was encouraged. Dropping yourself hip deep in shit by saying the wrong thing, that came under the sheer bloody stupid folder.

I swallowed, throat dry and rasping, the lingering taste of warm smoke and warmer lager still very much present. Taste buds were shot, head was racing, I was going down worse than a felled Luftwaffe bomber.

'I'm not asking you again, Robert.' She was getting louder and something told me she wasn't going to keep her voice down. I was never one for public scenes, they always seemed to thrive on spectacle. I was even less keen on ones that involved me.

'Nothing, honestly.' I straightened up and faced her.

'What do you know?' she said firmly.

This was my chance to wriggle out of things and pretend nothing had happened. I could protest complete innocence, play the dumb guy who crashed the party with the wrong saying and maybe hoped to salvage the night. But I wasn't going to do that, I was never going to do that.

It may not have been the way I would have liked to bring the subject up. Indeed it was nothing like the way I wanted to discuss this delicate matter. But cometh the man, cometh the hour as some famous historical figure had once said. Although I suspected they were talking about a war less vicious than the type fought within families.

'The other night, in the house,' I sighed. 'I overheard you talking to Dave about money. About the house and what you were getting in Mum's will.' Wendy remained silent, making me even more uneasy. 'I heard that you were planning on selling up, putting the money towards some trip so you could eat better, sleep better, something along those lines. I wasn't noseying, honest, it just sort of happened.'

My sister remained perfectly silent while I listed off my ill-gotten knowledge. The tendons in her cheek twitched and I could tell she was mad. But I was going to carry on, get it all off my chest. In for a penny, in for a pound. Where were these old terms coming from?

'I don't want you to make a mistake. You and Mindy are all I've got left and I know I've been a shit brother up until now, but you have to believe me when I say I'm trying to change. I don't want to see you stung by Dave, or anybody else for that matter. I think it would tear you ... tear us apart.'

When I was finished she was still quiet, looking at me with a gaze of disgust. I stared back at her and prepared to defend my case. Before I could, she stormed off down the smoking section, heading for the exit.

'Wendy!' I shouted after her but she quickened her pace, reaching the stairs and bounding up them towards the street.

'Wendy, come back here!' A hard shoulder barged into my chest and I shuffled back a little. Dazed, I recomposed myself and saw a thickset student type looking at me.

'Watch where you're going, eh?' he said, accent from the Lothians by my estimation.

'Get out of my way,' I said, pushing him to one side.

I moved after Wendy but was pulled back by the arm. I looked around and saw Lothian holding me back. Without thinking, I took a swing at him.

Fighting was certainly not a strong point in the Argyll family. Dad had always remained the 'think before you leap' type, scrawny little arms and bony body dictated that. Mother always encouraged words instead of violence, too, like all responsible adults should. A perfectly reasonable way to raise children, of course, it had resulted in a lack of first hand brawling action for us all.

In all of my years of going out, partying and walking home late from places, I had been fortunate enough to only witness two fights. Three if you counted a mass brawl with police but two actual, proper battles between men in the street. But witnessing and being in one were two radically different worlds and I don't know what possessed me to strike first.

Strike would have been a fair to generous summary of the punch. My aim was bad at the best of times, it seemed punching wasn't going to better that fact. The loop came around and I grazed Lothian's shoulder, sending my fist off target and brushing against his neck and chin.

He recoiled a little, more in surprise than anything else. It didn't take him long to steady himself and take aim for my face. I should have expected it, but then again, nothing can ever quite prepare you for a full-on fist to the gob.

I remembered seeing it come speeding towards me, every muscle around my mouth and forehead cramping tight to absorb the blow. He caught me just beneath the eye and I staggered back, hitting the wall and tumbling over a decorative shrub.

Before I could begin to start breathing, he was on me again. Two strikes to my ribs made me wheeze, already a tingling numbness stretching out across my face. I tried to fight him off, flailing mindlessly like a dog in a swimming pool.

Everything was dark and I could hear him grunt. Flecks of spit flew from his mouth as he continued his assault. I was about to give up when I remembered I had a pair of legs that had gone unused. Without much thought, I brought my right one up as quickly as I could, hoping for the best.

My shin thudded to a stop and I felt something squish. Lothian made a muffled wheeze and lurched over to one side, the world filling with light again as he rolled off of me and collapsed in a pile on the wet concrete tiles.

I pulled myself up and tried to breathe, but it was almost impossible. I looked at my attacker and realised exactly what had happened. A lucky shot, I had mashed his private parts with my leg, felling him instantly.

'Shit,' I slurred in disbelief, half of my face now completely numb.

My victory was short lived as two sets of calloused hands grabbed my shoulders and yanked me backwards towards the staircase. I tried to protest my innocence but knew I would be fighting a losing battle. Instead, I let the security staff do as they wished, which they promptly and efficiently did, throwing me out onto the street.

I assumed Lothian would be next on their target list and I wasn't willing to enter round two. I picked myself up and began running down Bath Street, heading for home. I got halfway towards a waiting taxi when I realised I was crying.

Chapter 18

I had really messed things up, that much was certain. Just how badly, I wasn't entirely sure. Perhaps that was why I had sobbed like a baby the whole journey home.

In the end, the taxi option hadn't been an option at all. By the time I managed to flag one down I remembered I didn't have a penny to my name. All of my cash had been spent on cheap booze and even cheaper conversation and now I was stuck.

Strangely the prospect of walking all the way home didn't feel like a bad one. I started the long trek to the south side at a sprint, but by the time I had reached the river, I was reduced to a jog, then a trot and finally a walk. The lungs of a smoker weren't built for running, they weren't much good for anything other than dying, really.

I reached the front door at a princely five o'clock in the morning, roughly three hours after my expedition had first started. Walking through a city like Glasgow at night was as close to a zombie apocalypse as anybody could ever get.

The whole place shuts down at three, with the last remnants of humanity properly scattered by no later than four. All of the roads clear by then too meaning the empty chip boxes, tipped over bins and seagulls are all that's left to show of any life having ever been present.

It makes for a rather eerie walk. The South Side and West End were the only real places you could properly walk to without coming across a big chunk of motorway or endless countryside.

They were also, ironically, some of the safer places to venture at night. Although staggering home, tears running down my face and struggling to remember if I was going the right way, I could have sworn they were as dangerous as any viper's nest on earth.

When I got in, after ten minutes fumbling with my keys, I shut the door and made sure it was locked multiple times. My brief flurry of OCD completed, I went about trying to find my sister.

'Wendy!' I shouted, not caring what time it was. This was important; I had to explain my actions, my intentions, my sheer nosiness.

'Wendy! Wendy, are you in here! We need to talk!' There was no answer and I was left in the darkness, on my own.

Sweat made my shirt and jumper stick to me. The temperature outside couldn't have been much above zero but I was far too warm. It was then I realised that I didn't have my coat. I'd left the damn thing in a rolled up ball amongst the others at our table. Maybe somebody would pick it up and realise, not much help when I would probably never see them again.

I headed for the kitchen, the first port of call. The place was quiet and dark, the garden rolling away into shadow beyond the windows. I hurried into the study, same scenario, then finally to the living room.

The whole house was deserted on the bottom floor, no sign of life anywhere. Even our faces in the old photos seemed to vanish in the darkness, lost amongst the gloom.

I raced upstairs and headed straight for Wendy's room. I knocked on the door, thumped it with my fist.

'Wendy!' I said, upping my rattles. The door gave way a little, its lock dislodged. I pushed it open and stepped inside.

The last time I had been in Wendy's room was the day I left home. I remembered her crying, sobbing because I was going away. In a better mood I would have laughed at how things very rarely changed. Only this time I had made her weep for completely different reasons.

She had lined up with my parents at the front door ready

to bid me farewell as I stretched my wings and prepared to take flight. When I loaded up the car, an old 1995 VW Polo Harlequin, oh the irony, I had saved from scrap at the very last minute with a display of pathetic pleading with the owner, I stood in front of them all and prepared my goodbyes.

Mother gave me a warm hug and told me not be a stranger. She kissed me on the cheek and hugged me again, keeping control of herself, well-practised already when Mindy had left a few years before.

Dad was the complete opposite, a tired boredom hanging about his limp shoulders. He gave me a wet fish of a handshake and wished me good luck. More fool me that I took it as a sincere gesture. That prick had never been sincere in his whole life.

Then, when it came to Wendy, she had leapt forward and clung onto my waist tightly. I could hear her whispering something as she held onto my middle, her twelve-year-old body strong with the pains of puberty. I moved her away so I could look at her face, all red and smeared with snot.

I forget what I said to her, but she tried to smile and failed miserably. She dashed up the stairs and into her room. I had been ready to go, but Mother had insisted I go and speak to her and level things out.

Selfishly, I had huffed but I knew it had to be done. I traipsed upstairs and into her room, sitting on her bed while she cried into her pillow. We talked for a while and eventually she stopped her sobbing as I reassured her I wouldn't ever be far away.

Standing now, in the same room, staring at where her bed used to be, the guilt was so unimaginably bad that I felt like I was dying. I slumped down onto the carpet, mouth wide open, hoping air would come in as I had forgotten how to breathe.

Pain stretched from my head to my toes, tearing with it every atom and fibre along the way. My head thumped with

175

the memories, the unquestionable selfishness and the fact that I was a complete waste of a human being.

Who had I been kidding all of these years? Everybody knew that I was a self-absorbed prick but they didn't know just how deep it went.

Mindy had an excuse, she had gotten married, had a family, grown up. What had I done? Pissed away all of my money, skulked about the country from north to south like it was my own personal back garden and tried to make a go of comedy. The only funny thing about me was how deluded I had been. And that wasn't a rib buster of a joke. Far from it.

No, I thought I could change, I wanted to change. I had to start somewhere. But being in Wendy's room, I realised something much more important. If I were to change, truly to change, I would have to acknowledge how bad my behaviour had been.

No more delusions, no more excuses. I had to start being honest with myself and with the others. It was the only way I could save what little we had left.

My moment of revelation had lasted long enough that the sun had begun to poke above the chimneystacks and terraced roofs of the suburbs. My slouched, defeated form began to cast a shadow across the floor that I watched until the end disappeared beneath Wendy's old cupboard.

I rolled my head, feeling my neck creak, and looked into the bright sun. A faint warmth lapped against my cheeks and I closed my eyes, a thick blanket of tiredness now hanging over me. I could sleep, I wanted to sleep, but there was far too much to be done.

I needed to find Wendy first and foremost, to apologise for everything, to reassure her that I would never be the same man I had been for so long in our lives. I needed to tell her, to tell Mindy and the rest of the family that they were all I had, ever had, or likely to have, and that they meant everything to me.

Without them I would be nothing, without their support and help and knowledge of just being there, I would have been dead a long time ago. And that only now did I realise that.

Making amends for over thirty years of bad behaviour wasn't going to be an overnight, quick fix. It would take time and effort, but I knew exactly how much now. I knew that, to properly amend things between us all, I would have to commit myself entirely to them and hope that, in time, they would learn to trust and rely on me. That would be my salvation.

Mustering what energy I had left, I lifted myself up from the floor and headed for the bathroom. There was no time to sleep, I needed breakfast and a shower and to make a phone call or two.

When I stepped into the searing hot water, the steam engulfing my pain ravaged body, I had the beginnings of a plan formulating in my head. My only hope was that I was clever enough and not too late to see it through to the end. An end that might just save us all.

I needed some answers, though. Every great plan couldn't start without at least knowing the limits. My own limits had been tested and found, I needed to know everybody else's.

Chapter 19

My search for answers started in the logical place, Mindy's house. After a quick search in the phone book, a jump online to find out where the hell it was, I set about my quest. All drama and over the top indulgence aside, I felt like the great heroes of old. The Arthurian legends, the Tolkien warriors, the John Waynes out on the prairie, searching for the lost gold or village girl.

With a rough idea in my head as to where it was, I set off from the house, locked the door with my spare key and started for the main road. Nobody bothered me on my journey, I forgot how early it still was. A few neighbourly faces looked up and then away as I passed, returning to their windscreen scraping, the great suburban morning routine.

I reached Fenwick Road, the lifeline that connected the city centre and the outer most parts of the southern side of Glasgow. There were plenty of busses and taxis whizzing by, the road heading south quiet compared to across the street.

Bumper to bumper, honking horns, angry rat racers getting their blood pressure up already, miles from the office. My mother had cursed and sworn more than I ever knew her to during the morning school run in this traffic. That's what it could do to a person; change them from middle class suburbanites to snarling monsters.

I didn't envy the small army making that journey this morning, but I didn't feel much sympathy for them, either. If they wanted the real commuter experience, they would try driving in any other major city in the world at the same time. London, New York, Rome; they were all ten times worse. Watching rush hour in those cities made me glad I couldn't drive.

I reached the nearest bus stop and waited patiently. The internet had very kindly mapped out my entire journey, beginning to end, even telling me what bus to get, where to get it and when to get off. I wondered, silently, how in a world of complete guidance, a wealth of knowledge at your fingertips, how anybody could ever get lost.

Pride, I supposed, and not wanting to be seen to have to ask for directions. The staple of a thousand generations of female comics' routines right there.

A small, single decked number four bus came charging up the road and I stuck my thumb out. It came to a stop and after a deposit of some spare change I found in my other trousers, the driver gave me a grunt and a ticket. I took a seat near the back, facing the window and watched the world go by beyond the glass.

It was cold, damp, dreary and depressing, the usual fare for a public bus. No matter where in the world you got on a bus, you could be guaranteed of two things: the gritty smell of soot and petrol lingering in the air and a permanent puddle gathered at the front near the door.

I leaned over the edge of the seats in front of me to check. There it was, sloshing around and looking particularly filthy. Manky, as the Glaswegians so delicately put it.

We ploughed our way through the morning traffic, leaving it far behind us as the houses got bigger. A few school children jumped on and quickly hopped off again a few stops up the road. I tried to tune them out when they sat behind me, but they were altogether too loud. Not that it mattered much anyway; I couldn't understand a bloody word they were saying.

The bus reached the huge, sprawling Eastwood Toll roundabout that I remembered from my youth. At Christmas time the local council would erect a huge tree and douse it in tiny little lights, usually too little to cover the whole thing.

I looked about the busy junction as we whirled around it, every sight rekindling memories from days out to the nearby park and visits to friends and relatives. A colleague of my father used to live in the red brick block of flats that looked out over the roundabout.

Space age and modern when they were built, disaster had struck in the early nineties when a helicopter had crashed into the front of one of the buildings. A policeman had been killed and the building required extensive reworking.

I remembered speaking with friends years later about the incident, but none of them could remember it. I had championed the case, kept on pressing home how I wasn't barking mad. Still they denied it, dismissing the story as little more than an urban myth. I had given up telling the story after that.

As the bus began to climb up and away from the roundabout, it occurred to me of where we were. Affluent areas of cities don't like to be reminded of the bad times. Bad memories can have a crimp on the resale values of a property. Business was business. That was more than likely why the story hadn't been bigger, had a longer lasting effect. Or maybe people just forgot, stranger things had happened.

My stop was a little way up the Ayr Road and I unfolded myself from the seat. Pressing the little bell to stop the bus, I stepped in the puddle as I made my way off and into the cold air.

Mindy's house was on the borderline between Whitecraigs and Newton Mearns, two of the city's most sought after postcodes. This was the territory of lawyers, doctors, accountants, and drug dealers. There was a healthy mix in this part of the woods.

I counted the house numbers as I made my way up the street, almost slipping twice on the icy pavement. In that great suburban style, trees erupted every fifteen yards, breaking the age-old concrete. Beautiful in the summer and autumn months, deadly in the winter.

My traversing of the deadly side walk came to an end when I reached the number I was looking for. I came to the front gates at last and had to sigh loudly to relieve some frustration.

A long, winding pathway of dirty red chippings weaved up to the front door. The famous BMW and Gerry's work van were still parked near the house, meaning they were in at least. A small victory and one I hardly celebrated.

Clambering up the driveway, I eventually reached the summit, out of breath and sweating. I could see the steam rising off of my bare hands and through my jumper, any regrets at not having my coat now long banished.

I rang the doorbell and tried to pull myself together. There was thumping from within until Mindy appeared at the other end of the hallway. I waved at her through the window in the door as she hurried to open it.

'Robert!' she screamed. 'What happened to your face?'

'My face?' I asked. I touched my cheek and was reminded of my scuffle the night before. In all the confusion, soul searching and beginning of a nervous breakdown, I had completely forgotten about the thump I had taken.

Even in the bathroom, when I was getting ready, I hadn't bothered to look at myself in the mirror. Steam had covered the glass and I had no reason to stare at myself. I rubbed my cheek and felt it sting, suddenly curious.

'What happened?' Mindy asked, ushering me into the house.

'I was in a fight last night.'

'A fight?' she sounded almost as surprised as I was to say it aloud. Fighting wasn't an Argyll thing to do, what had I been thinking?

'With whom?' she pressed.

'Nobody, nothing. Look, it doesn't matter. I need to speak with Wendy. Do you know where she is?' We were in the kitchen. Quite a bit different to the one in our parents' house, all new and shiny.

Mindy raced straight for the freezer and dug out a bag of frozen peas. She wrapped them in a towel and ushered them into my hands.

'Here,' she said, obviously worried. 'That'll bring the swelling down.'

'Swelling?' I asked, looking for confirmation. Was it really that bad? Had I been walking about looking like Joseph Merrick all morning? Or an extra from *The Hunchback of Notre-Dame*?

'Why do you need Wendy?' she asked.

'I … I said some things last night that I shouldn't have,' I answered. Mindy looked at me, her brow narrowed, mouth already shaping her next words. She was in full lawyer mode now.

'What did you say?' she said, half expecting the answer already.

'Nothing, it's nothing. I need to speak to her, where will she be?'

'Have you tried her mobile?' Mindy answered. Was it possible I had gotten away with it so easily?

'I don't have her mobile number.'

'You don't have her mobile number?'

'I barely know my own, Mindy,' I said, feeling the freezing cold sting of the peas finally penetrate through the dishtowel.

'Here, I've got it, hold on,' she said, leaping for her handbag. She pulled out her phone and began tapping away faster than I could follow. 'Here it is, give her a call.' She came back over to me and held out the phone.

As I went to take it, she snatched it back into her hands. She was quick, too quick for a tired, hung-over, guilty me, anyway.

Who was I kidding, she was faster than me when I was at the peak of my powers, all those decades ago now.

'I'll give you it as soon as you tell me what's wrong,' she said. Damn, I thought I'd get away with it. More fool me.

'I can't … ' I said weakly.

My sister raised her eyebrows and tilted her head a little. She cocked her hip and rolled her tongue around the inside of her mouth, waving the phone back and forth and looking at it with an almost teasing glare.

'You know I could just give her a call myself and find out.'

'No!' I leapt forward and almost tripped over my own feet. Mindy's eyes were like saucers, as she looked at me, more than a little surprised.

I cleared my throat and sighed again, this was becoming a nasty little habit. I pressed the cold peas closer onto my wounded cheek and thought carefully about what I was going to say.

'Last night, when we went out, I may have overstepped the mark a bit,' I started.

'How so?' questioned Mindy immediately.

'Well, the other night there, and understand I'm only telling you this on the provision that you don't get angry.'

'Robert, when have I ever not gotten angry when you've said something like that?' I thought for a moment and couldn't think of any one time that she had kept her head. I wasn't sure what made me think that this time was going to be any different.

'I was downstairs, in the house the other night, there, minding my own business, all perfectly innocent like.'

'Uh-huh,' Mindy groaned.

'And I overheard Wendy talking to Dave.' I twisted the

183

corner of my mouth into a frown and could feel my eyebrows wrinkling.

'And?'

'Well, they were talking about money.'

'Money?' something sparked into life in Mindy. I shouldn't have been so surprised.

'Yeah, money. Specifically what they, or she, was going to do with her share of Mother's inheritance.'

'But they didn't know what that inheritance was going to be,' Mindy butted in, sharp as ever.

'No, that's what I thought, too. But you said outside the solicitors' that we all had a fairly good idea.'

'Ahh,' said Mindy, crossing her arms and nodding slowly. She had pieced things together. 'That's what you meant when you said you were the only one who didn't know.' She smirked.

I nodded helplessly. My clued up knowledge, or lack of it, was infamous, I was surprised it had taken her this long to work it out.

'So why is she upset then?'

I swallowed, my mouth dry, throat red raw. I needed a cigarette, I needed a drink, I needed a bit of time to get my head together. Was I missing something here? Should I be spilling my guts like this, dropping Wendy in it?

'When we were out, she … ' I hesitated. I knew I had come too far to stop now, Mindy would get it out of me eventually. God, I hated all of this. When I was on my own it was simple, only myself to worry about. If I was going to change, I needed to adapt to these scenarios.

'What?' asked Mindy.

'She said that Dave had asked her to marry him,' I said it all in one breath.

'He did what!' Mindy shouted, hands shooting down to her sides. 'He's what!'

My sister stomped about her kitchen, breathing hard and fast and looking a little lost. I watched her dart from one corner to the room, wondering if what I had done was the right thing.

'She can't, no way. She's too young. He's done what now?' she kept on saying, repeating it over and over and over again. When she had paced enough she stopped and stared at me. 'What did you tell her to do, Robert?' she asked.

I knew my sister and I knew she only had our family's best intentions at heart. But there were times where I could throttle her for thinking that she was the ruler of clan Argyll. On another day I probably would have stormed out of the house, cursing and swearing and ruing the fact that I had tried to help. As it was, I had to try harder than that.

'I said that whatever decision she made we would all be behind her,' I shrugged. Saying it again reaffirmed that I had done the right thing with my younger sister.

Even in her rage I could tell that Mindy knew that too. She moved to say something but caught herself before any noise could come out.

We stood for a moment in silence, letting the news set in. I bowed my head and looked at the mud stains that had spattered my boots from the hike up to the front door. I knew I should probably take them off, Mindy was fiercely house proud, but we had bigger fish to fry at the moment.

'So, why is she upset with you?' Mindy asked, breaking the silence.

'I sort of let it slip, last night, after she had told me about Dave's proposal, that I had overheard their conversation about the money.'

'Robert,' Mindy said disapprovingly. 'You were eavesdropping on them?'

'I know, I know I shouldn't have been listening in. It just sort of happened, an accident, I was only getting a glass of water and some juice and … '

'It's not that,' she interrupted. Mindy sauntered over to me and handed me the phone. 'First rule of bartering, never show your hand too early.' She cocked her head and smiled.

She was good, she was very, very good. Sometimes I forgot just how ruthless my sister could be when it came to business and dirty dealings. She was more her father's son than I ever would be.

'Call her, she'll pick up if she sees it's my number.'

'And then what?' I asked, taking the phone.

'Invite her over for dinner, tell her you're cooking us all a big meal to make amends.'

'Me, cook?' I asked, voice cracking a little. The limits of my culinary prowess came to an end with burnt toast and cold beans.

'I'll do the cooking,' Mindy said tiredly. 'Tell her to bring Dave over and say that we're all going to be there. A big family meal, I'll bring the kids and it'll be a nice, relaxing family night in.'

'She's never going to fall for that,' I said.

'Try her,' Mindy pressed.

I held the phone up and looked at Wendy's name glowing on the screen. Taking all things into account, the next phone call would be arguably the most important I was ever likely to make. If I could get my younger sister to this dinner, a summit of the Argylls from all across the land, there was a good chance that things might get resolved.

If I failed then there would be serious repercussions that we might never recover from. No pressure, I thought, as Mindy urged me on. I took a deep breath and pressed the call button and heard the dial tone change to a ring.

After a couple of drones, it clicked into life on the other end and I started my pitch.

'Hi, Wendy? It's Robert, look please don't hang up, I'm phoning with a peace offering. I'm sorry about last night and you know I would never, ever try to cause you any harm or pain. I'm so, so very sorry about what I said and I want you to understand that I've changed. I'm trying to be a better person and a better brother to you and Mindy. I want things to be different in the future and I have to know that you're at least willing to let me be a part of your life, both of our lives, it's important to me. So please forgive me, I know I don't deserve it, but I'm asking for another chance. We're having a big family dinner tonight at the house and would love you and Dave to come over and be part of it. I'm cooking, would you believe? So please, little sister, please come back and let me say sorry.'

I choked back some air and hoped it had been enough. Mindy flashed a thumbs-up, waiting for the response. There was silence on the other end until I heard something shuffle.

'This is Angela, Rob, Wendy's in the other room,' my heart sank and balls tightened at the same time. I didn't know if I was going up or down.

'Oh, could you put her on, please,' I looked at Mindy, who rolled her eyes so much I thought they were going to fall out of her head.

'Fine,' said Angela.

'Thank you,' but she was gone.

'Hello,' said Wendy.

'Wendy? It's Robert, look, please don't hang up, I'm phoning with a peace offering...'

Chapter 20

Making peace with people did wonders for your self-esteem. The positive energy it created was so strong that I felt better about myself than I had done in a very, very long time. So much, in fact, that I began to regret not having tried it out sooner.

There was still a lot of work to be done and the feast tonight would be a huge challenge. But in the interim period I was feeling positively dandy.

Wendy hadn't taken much convincing to come around. She accepted my apologies, all of my grovelling included, and agreed to join the rest of us at our parents' house. Mindy had set about getting the actual meal ready with her usual, military styled precision and planning.

I very foolishly offered to help gather in the stock. One trip around a supermarket with Mindy Dawkins was enough to frighten any man straight. She was ruthlessly efficient, had a propensity to bash old ladies in their ankles with the trolley and a built-in nose that could sniff out bargains better than a bloodhound. I would have marvelled at the whole thing, if I wasn't having orders barked at me every second of the trip.

She had dropped me off at the house with strict instructions about slow cooking the meats that would make up the backbone of the dinner. I duly followed her instructions, despite her constant protests I wasn't listening. This wasn't a meal I wanted to mess up in any way, shape or form. And I certainly wasn't going to let dry roast beef or burned to a crisp ham spoil the proceedings.

My views on cooking weren't the best. To my mind, spending hours delicately preparing a dish was a waste of time. Whether it was haute cuisine or a microwavable ready meal, it still took the average person less than ten minutes to finish. The effort to reward ratio just didn't add up to me.

When done properly I, of course, tipped my hat to the master chefs. Undoubtedly an art form in its own right, unfortunately I had missed the boat when it came to appreciating the finer points of the effort and toil over a swelteringly hot stove.

But I was pulling my socks up for this one. Everything had to be perfect and I followed my instructions to the last detail as Mindy left me alone to get ready. I kept going back to the oven to make sure everything was coming along nicely.

I felt like I did as I was about to go onstage before a big gig. The same nervousness and excitement making my stomach churn and flip more times than a Blue Peter pancake. I couldn't put a ratio on what was stronger, all I kept thinking about were the implications, the stakes that were loading the whole night. Gambling was never my forte, but I had wagered big on this one.

Trying to take my mind off of it I resorted to a little writing. A couple of things were coming together and by the time the sun had begun to set I had what looked like the bare bones of a set. The isolation had helped greatly, the only human contact that afternoon coming from the kids who walked past the front gate on their way home from school.

I resolved to watch some humdrum afternoon TV before I had to get ready. Some quiz I had never heard of was on before *Deal or No Deal* dominated the viewing, Noel Edmonds leering back at me in his crisp, prim, multicoloured shirt. I had always harboured a healthy respect for Noel, he was a man born to be on TV or radio. When *House Party* had gone down the toilet he was left in a netherworld that alienated him slightly from the rest of society.

Several failed comebacks had pushed him further out and he had resorted to the law of attraction theory promoted by positive thinking book *The Secret*. I had never read it myself, but, if it was to be believed, Noel Edmonds stood as a living testimony to its practises.

When he was finished with the so-called *Dream Factory*, perennial favourite *Countdown* came on. I was just about to switch it off when I noticed the guest star in Dictionary Corner.

It was none other than Morton Roll, at least, that was his stage name. I knew him as Jim Currie, a fellow comedian who had started out at the same time as myself on the Glasgow circuit.

His use of a stage name had always baffled me; the opportunities you got with a name like Currie were almost endless. The fart jokes alone wrote themselves.

Jim and I had first met when we both attended an improv workshop at Strathclyde University's adult learning centre. It was an awful experience that the uni had the cheek to charge for. My patience was well and truly frayed by the other classmates, though. One of them, a stressed out accountant type, tried to run with a gag of the tutor's and made a real mess of it. I looked at Jim and we decided, then and there, that we would make the most of things, taking the piss at every turn. Call it cruel, we found it hilarious.

We were thrown out, of course, and spent the remainder of the evening in the union bar, chatting up students and generally talking shit. He was a funny guy, one of the few naturally humorous people who could make me laugh. As a serious comic, I very rarely got the chuckles from the usual rubbish most TV stand-ups spouted. But Jim, or Morton as he started calling himself not long after, was a very rare exception.

Rotund, little spectacles and with a shock of hair that curled around and around his dumpy little head, he was made for a career on TV. Either comedy or kids entertainment, Jim had the drive and commitment that was needed to make a go of life in show business.

His family were from the East end of Glasgow, a notoriously tough part of the city. Jim had grown up with two brothers and three sisters; all of varying ages and with him stuck right in the middle. From opposite ends of the social, and economical scale, on paper the two of us wouldn't have ordinarily gotten on. However, we quickly became friends, doing gigs and sharing rides and rooms on the road all over Scotland and the north of England.

A true professional and as dedicated a student of comedy as you would ever meet in the game, Jim was always on course for the big time. His natural charm and wit were unmatched, certainly by anybody I knew, and I would have killed for some of his bits.

He was also one of the dirtiest little buggers I had ever known. Not in his act, that was all above board and vaguely respectable. Or as respectable as a mainstream comic can get. But off stage and as a person, there was nothing Jim wouldn't sink to.

Not in a devious sense, he just liked to have sex. Hardly the best looking bloke in Christendom, Jim had the gift of the gab like no other man I've ever known. Not even Jack Johnson could compare.

He would systematically drop himself into any conversation and immediately take over. And with women as diverse and wide ranging as you could possibly get.

I remembered being out with him one booze fuelled afternoon that had gone on too long. We resolved that it was too late to go home but too early for all the decent hangouts or 'Pussy dens', as Jim like to call them. So we headed to Glasgow's famous School of Art, looking to drop in for one quick light ale to pass the time.

Once in there he proceeded to chat up any and every woman he could lay his beady little eyes on. Blondes, brunettes, red heads, no hair, the Art School was the only place that provided a cattle market with a range big enough to satisfy his cravings.

'I'm a film director and my mate here's an actor,' I heard him say to two girls who giggled as I quietly groaned.

191

That was Jim though, always had a line for the ladies. What made things more staggering though, was the ladies always seemed to like him in return. The old phrase 'he's shagged more birds than Mick Jagger,' was usually overrated, in Jim's case it was the truth.

We had fallen out of touch when I moved to London, for my shame. It wasn't because I thought I was better than him, far from it, I just needed to 'find myself' as so many bullshitters claim.

The last I had heard of him he was doing very well for himself, regular appearances as a talking head on 'Best Of' shows. It was the perfect outlet for his type of humour, very reactionary and great for an opinion. His stand up always let him down a little as he constantly needed to feed himself with lines. In a room full of hecklers however, Jim Currie was in a league of his own.

And now it appeared he had scored a slot on Countdown. I turned up the volume and listened to him do his little intro. He was plugging a new radio show he had on Radio 4 at the weekends. From what I knew these gigs paid, it was a cushy little number that would probably pay for my next five years in one month.

I wasn't jealous, not with Jim. He was a good sort and a great guy. I liked to see him getting on, God knows there were plenty worse than him who were richer, more popular and certainly less talented.

I watched him battle away with the dictionary and laughed at the story he told before the break. Nothing racy or even remotely risqué, it was a tale about when he was growing up and how he used to steal the caps from the air valve of expensive cars who parked in his neighbourhood. The way he told it on Countdown was vastly different to how he had shared the story with me.

'If I got a hundred of those little caps,' he had said during one heavy drinking session, typical. 'I would have had enough to shove up my sisters' noses while they slept at night until they'd have a head full of them. I was a little bastard so I was,' he had cackled. That same laugh spouted from the TV as I thought about him.

I wasn't a great believer in fate, but something made me think that I was meant to tune into that episode. A shiver went down my spine as I reclined on the sofa and played along.

By the time the final round came about I was bored out of my mind. Daytime TV had that effect on me; I couldn't concentrate enough during its humdrum mentality. When the closing credits rolled I felt like I'd been released from prison, a fresh start all over again.

I looked at the clock on my phone and remembered to adjust the heat of the meats in the oven. When my culinary practise was through, I thought it best to have another shower and pull myself together for the big event.

Cleaned, freshened and feeling all the better for it, I decided that I was going to dress for the occasion. My hand luggage had been dominated by my suit for the funeral and I only included a couple of other shirts, a sleeping t-shirt and clean socks and pants.

However, I had become a master of using what I had to at least fake making a good impression. I tucked my shirt in, rolled down my sleeves and, for the first time in weeks, combed my hair into a respectable shape.

I made my way downstairs and found Mindy and Gerry in the kitchen, fussing over the veg. They had pulled the ham joint and roast beef from the oven and were letting it settle on the table. The meat smelled great, wafting aromas of the juices filling the kitchen and making the whole place feel like a lived-in family home. That was what it was after all and those of us in it deserved to have that happiness.

'Well, well, well,' said Mindy, peeling potatoes. 'Don't we

193

look smart this evening,' she smiled.

'Bloody hell, is Brad Pitt coming to dinner?' chimed Gerry, battling with the broccoli.

'Oh, you,' I said, batting my eyelids. We all enjoyed the laugh until my sister's obsession with planning snapped back into action.

'Right, Robbie, I need you to help Rob and Abi with setting the dining room table.'

'The dining room table?' I asked.

'Yes,' Mindy confirmed.

'We have a dining room table? We have a dining room for that matter?'

Mindy looked up from her spuds and shook her head. She continued to slice off the skin, dangerously close to her fingers at breakneck speed.

'Honestly, Robert, I think you need a reality check now and then.' How right she was. 'We converted the old sitting room into a dining room. Mum bought a table and we've used it for occasions, Christmas and birthdays, that sort of thing.'

The second sitting room had always been a room I'd avoided. Mother had kept it as a private shrine for her and Dad to spend time away from the kids. Everything in there was neat and tidy and unused. No sticky hand prints, no writing on the walls, no life. Over the years, I had simply forgotten about its existence, no reason whatsoever to venture inside it.

The idea it had been turned into something practical made me smile. I wondered just how long after Dad's death it had taken for it to be converted. I wasn't in the mood to ask, but I supposed almost instantly.

'Shall I take anything in?'

'Yes, the condiments, the kids are setting the cutlery and

things. Let's get a move on, it's gone six, the rest are due in half an hour.'

I collected the sauces and jars and stalked the hallway until I came to the old sitting room door. Even now, twenty years after I had last been in it, I still had that little trepidation. I had always seen it as a place that children weren't allowed to go, a notion that, unsurprisingly, had stuck through the years. Not through any fear or immature phobia, just a healthy respect for my parents' private lives.

Just how private I didn't quite understand at the time. And even now, after they had gone, I doubted I would ever know the extent of how much they had kept from us.

Breaking down those barriers, though, was important to me and I was glad to know that this room had been changed. For the better, of course, opening it up to the rest of the family as a place of congregation. That was a positive step in my view; give the assets back to the people and all of that Marxist nonsense.

As the little battle finished in my head, I motioned to open the door. While I juggled the pickles and beetroot around between my hands, I reached for the handle but the door opened before I could grab a hold. Almost spilling forward, only the sturdy grip of my nephew stopped me from complete disaster.

'You alright there, Uncle Rob?' he said with a smile. I steadied myself and cleared my throat.

'Yes, thanks, Rob, thank you.' He stood awkwardly close to me, hands fumbling for a place to go. 'You couldn't grab a hold of these could you, buddy?'

'Oh yeah, sorry,' the apologies started again. Rob was a nice kid, just a little mollycoddled.

He was still in that mentality of thinking everything was his fault, a product of growing up with Mindy as a mother. Strict

195

regiments and schedules could do that to a kid. But at nineteen years old, I expected a little more from him.

I wasn't sure if Abi was the same. Four years younger than Rob, I had never really known her. She was at the funeral of course, I had said my reintroductions, but there was only so much a disgruntled, embittered, thirty-something comic could have in common with a teenage schoolgirl. Jack Johnson, on the other hand, and even Jim Currie, would have no problems at all in finding something to talk about. Dirty buggers.

She was laying out the cutlery when we stepped into the new dining room and I was struck immediately how much she looked like her mother. The resemblance was almost uncanny, the same long hair and rail thin body that Mindy had when she was that age. Even her face was ladened with Argyll traits. The dark eyes, the high cheek bones, she had inherited nothing from Gerry.

'Hi, Uncle Rob,' she said, looking up briefly from her duty.

'How you doing, Abi, do you need a hand?'

'No, no I'm just about done, need to get cracking on the plates and the napkins, but I'll race through that no problem and give Mum a hand with the veg.' She was definitely her mother's daughter. Planned, pre-empted and proficient, Abi was already on her way to success.

Resting the jars and tubs of sauce and butter on the table, I milled around a little until I could make myself useful. I knew already I was surplus to requirement; Abi was in complete, competent control.

Rob bumped into me from behind, hauling a chair in from the kitchen. I stepped out of his way and offered to help.

'No, no, I'm alright. Sorry,' he kept on apologising. I tried to remember what I was like as a nineteen year old. I couldn't really remember, the boozing and late night parties, every night parties, had obliterated most of it. Only hazy stories and moments remained. Although, judging by my behaviour the other night I wasn't surprised my brain had gone into remission over the whole thing.

It was an odd age by all accounts, not quite adult and certainly not child. The final year of teenage life, an already difficult period anyway, was usually spent in a strange limbo between the worlds of reality. Maybe that was why he was so feckless. I felt bad for judging him and decided to reach out with my newfound olive branch of connection.

'So, how's uni treating you, Rob?' I asked as he shuffled around the long, mahogany table that dominated the new dining room.

'Oh, not bad,' he said quietly. He reminded me of the toffs that featured so heavily in the P.G Wodehouse novels. Delightfully muddled with nothing much between the ears.

'Rob's band is doing really well, they're playing a gig tomorrow night,' Abi chirped, again just like her mother.

'Really?' I said. 'So what do you guys play? I thought your song at the funeral was really good,' I wasn't going to critique him there and then, nor admit I hadn't bothered to listen.

I leaned on the back of the chair at the head of the table and tried to look relaxed. Not that I was relaxed, I had always been self conscious around young people, youths and the like. My arm had made it safely down to the wooden top without slipping off the edge, but I immediately thought how rubbish it looked.

My only other option was one leg on the seat as I leaned on my knee. Very bargain basement music lesson instructional video. All I needed was a bowl cut haircut and a seventies moustache to complete the look. I decided to stay where I was.

'We mostly play indie stuff, Mumford covers and stuff like that.'

'Ah,' I groaned, suddenly aware of how old I was.

A good rule of thumb I had adopted, when speaking to youngsters, was to go on the offensive. Guiding the conversation back into my comfort zone was usually a winner. They very rarely had a clue what I was talking about and I felt better about myself.

'You ever do any old stuff?' hardly a great start.

'Old stuff?' Rob asked. My namesake nephew seemed genuinely interested, a rare treat.

'Yeah, like The Eagles, AC/DC, a bit of Kiss?' I strummed an air guitar and poked my tongue out, just like Gene Simmons.

Abi laughed and Rob smiled, looking a little embarrassed. Why wouldn't he, his uncle was behaving like an arse, talking about dinosaur bands that nobody under the age of twenty-one had even heard of, let alone enjoyed. So what, I still loved 'Detroit Rock City'.

'No, we don't do any of that,' he said humbly.

'Pity,' I said, stopping my strumming. 'Might kick things up a notch with the audience. You need to give them something, a bit of a jolt, you know.'

Rob nodded. He was listening, I could tell that, but only out of politeness. Whether through some vision of his band unique only to him or sheer cringe worthy shame that he was named after me, his manners were impeccable.

'You guys excited about tonight then?' I cut my losses and moved onto something else.

'Yeah, sure,' said Rob.

'Definitely,' answered Abi. 'Mum says it's the first proper big dinner we've had together in years.'

'You know, I think it is,' I said. I liked Abi, she was the type of girl, young woman, you could have a conversation with. None of this flash-in-the-pan boy band, reality TV show nonsense. A good girl with her head screwed on. Oh, where had the likes of you been when I was growing up?

'Mum says you've got a lot of apologising to do, though, Uncle Rob.'

I cocked my eyebrow at her. 'Does she indeed?'

Abi nodded silently, adjusting the cutlery so they lined up perfectly. 'She says you've been away for so long and come clattering in with your big boots on and disrupted everything.'

When she spoke like that I was reminded just how young she was. And she was right, of course.

'Well,' I laughed. 'I can't really argue with that.' I tucked my hands in my pockets and felt a moment coming on.

'You know, guys, this is probably the longest amount of time I've spent talking to you since you were little babies.'

Both of Mindy's kids stopped what they were doing and stood to obedient attention. I wasn't there to lecture them; I knew what that felt like all too well. I just wanted to tell them I was sorry. This had been a trip of apologies, of regrets, of crushing realisations. I wanted my new start to encompass every reach of the family.

These kids weren't just Mindy's children; they were my flesh and blood, too. Looking at them across the room, in a place I had been forbidden from entering, I realised that they were the next generation of my family. Sure they didn't carry my name, but there was enough DNA shared between us to still make it worthwhile.

The Argyll genes were strong in them, one look at them and I could see the resemblance of myself and Mindy in them both. Even a dash of Wendy's cherub cheeks from her early teens was there. They were my family too, the pioneers who would take the name forward into a future I was already struggling with.

'I guess all I'm saying is, I'm sorry,' I said. 'I'm sorry I

199

haven't been much of an uncle, sorry I've been utterly useless as a person to you guys and above all else,' I had to lighten the mood, they were kids after all. 'I'm sorry I never sent you birthday cards with big fat cheques in.'

Rob and Abi laughed and nodded, sensing the change in the atmosphere. They were good kids, I could see that in them and I knew they would grow up to be great adults. Better than me certainly, but that wouldn't be hard. I wanted to help them in any way I could. Fresh minds, keen to be moulded.

I rounded the table and took them both in my arms for what was probably the most awkward, unexpected group hug in the history of human kind. After a tense second or two of not knowing where to put their arms, they settled and hugged me back.

When I released them they were still smiling. I choked back a little tear and clapped my hands, rubbing them together.

'Right,' I said, 'Are we ready to rock and roll? You know what I'm talking about,' I pointed at Rob who looked a little surprised. 'What do you think, Abs, does he know how to rock and roll, get jiggy with it?' I nudged her in the shoulder as Rob's face flushed with blood.

'Oh, definitely,' she played along.

'Shut up, you two,' he said, fixing the chairs. I let out a loud whoop and thumped my foot on the carpet.

We were all laughing and enjoying ourselves and for that I was grateful. When the hilarity died down I wiped away the sly tear I had choked back earlier, sure that nobody saw me.

'Kids, your Aunt Wendy is here!' came Mindy's voice from the hallway.

Rob and Abi looked at me, their smiles still broad across their faces. I pulled a gurn like an old man and stuck out my tongue. It was a natural reaction, a projection I had no control over. Inside I was shitting myself.

'Well, if that's settled then,' I said. 'I better put my best brown-nosing act on then, hadn't I?' I looked at the kids and they both smiled knowingly.

Two down, two more to go. Not bad for an evening's work.

Chapter 21

Making peace with two teenagers was all well and good, but it stood for very little if I couldn't replicate the success with Wendy. Frankly, she wasn't much different from a teenager, only that the date on her birth certificate showed she wasn't still in that age bracket. Everything else was almost exactly the same.

Granted, she wasn't exactly like Rob and Abi, they were well behaved. Wendy still possessed that rebellious streak that only came about from a lack of growing up in people her age. As I stepped out into the corridor to greet her, I expected the full backlash of that built up rage.

'Hello, Robert,' she said calmly. To my surprise she didn't slap me across the face or kick me between the legs. In fact, her whole appearance was mildly alarming.

Her hair was straightened and neat, styled even into something remotely passable. Even the shorn bits of stubble were covered by her dirty blonde locks looking glossy for a change. She wore a neat dress and cardigan and a pair of short heels. I think it was the first time I had ever seen her feet in anything other than pumps or sandals.

She gave me a hug and held me close. I leaned in closer to her and whispered gently in her ear.

'I'm sorry, Wendy,' plain and simple.

'I know, Robert. And I forgive you,' she said. Any tension or apprehension I had was released in a single, wonderful moment. I stepped back and she smiled warmly at me, something I was glad to reciprocate.

Dave stepped forward and shook my hand, breaking the quiet little moment we shared. I tried my best to keep my animosity at a minimum, but it was incredibly difficult. Just as hard as anything I had battled over the past few days.

I looked at him and then back to Wendy. There was a suppressed yearning in her eyes, a silent plea for me to at least accept his role within our family. His growing role at any rate.

'Good to see you, Dave,' I forced through gritted teeth.

'You too, Bob,' he shook my hand and almost pulled my arm out of its socket. Nobody ever called me Bob, something I was whole-heartedly glad of. I wasn't a nicotine stained snooker commentator after all. Not yet, at least.

Mindy and Gerry were behind us and exchanged their greetings, the kids standing quietly at the back of the group. The soft murmur of conversation hovered in the air and for just a moment, I thought that things might just be alright.

I quickly pushed any notions out of my head. Jinxing things was a terrible habit of mine, the fates having never played with anybody as much since Ulysses.

'I hope you're all hungry,' Mindy announced.

'Starving,' said Wendy.

'You're in for a treat, then. Tonight's dinner comes courtesy of our brother, the soon to be world famous, Rob Argyll.'

'I thank you,' and took a jester's bow. 'And it's Rab Argyll onstage,' I corrected.

'Yes, sorry, Rab Argyll,' said Mindy, shaking her head. 'Why don't you take the guests into the dining room then, *Rab,* and I'll start serving up the entrée.'

I gladly obliged and stood to one side with my arm out, gesturing towards the open door. Dave pushed in first, followed by Gerry and then the kids. Wendy slid her arm into mine and walked with me down the hall.

'Why do you call yourself Rab anyway?' she asked quietly.

'It sounds more Scottish, the punters love all that,' I answered, plainly.

Wendy nodded in agreement and kept her smile firmly intact. We glided into the dining room where everybody had taken their seats.

Mindy came in shortly behind carrying a tray, seven prawn cocktails served in tall glasses balanced delicately on top. I moved out of her way and hovered around, unsure exactly where I was to sit.

When everyone had helped themselves, Mindy pulled the chair out next to Gerry at the opposite end from me and looked up.

'What's the matter?' she asked.

The only seat remaining was the one at the head of the table. Somehow it didn't feel right that I should be sitting there. I wasn't quite sure why, but it felt like I was stealing the limelight.

Maybe it was a guilt thing, the last remorse of not being there for the rest of them for so very long. This was to be the first full family dinner in decades, why should I get the place of honour? Staring out at the rest of them, though, made me feel whole, complete, and safe to know that they were there, in this house, the place that had stayed constant throughout all of our problems.

My glance fell back to Mindy who was still staring at me. She must have been able to tell from my body language that I wasn't comfortable. But she carried on as she always did, the would-be matriarch of the family now thrust onto the throne. Her entire life had been spent in preparation for the passing of the torch and when it came to keeping us calm and collected, there was nobody better.

She nodded and blinked slowly and I knew then that she approved of me. Not just sitting at the head table but in my life and how that factored into the rest of the family. That one gesture wiped clean the slate and I instantly felt renewed, purified, ready to start again.

Second chances were rare, usually rarer than first ones. I had been very lucky to get such an opportunity; I certainly wasn't going to balls it up.

Slowly, I pulled the seat out from beneath the table and sat myself down. Like a newly crowned king, I oversaw my loyal subjects as they tucked into their starters. They were blissfully unaware of the turmoil I had just wrestled with. All of them except Mindy, she always knew and always would.

I quite liked sitting here, it was the first time I had ever been placed at the head of a table in my life. Dad had always taken up the prime real estate when we had gone for dinner at plush restaurants, all on the bill of the firm of course. He didn't even pay for a nice meal for us, the cheapskate. What a real piece of shit.

We all demolished the prawns and gorged on the succulent meats and juices of the ham, roast beef and veg. Maybe I was just being sentimental, but it was probably the best meal I had ever eaten in my life. If I ever ended up on death row and, knowing my luck, that was never impossible, I wanted that to be my last dinner in this mortal realm.

When dessert rolled around, a delicious cheesecake with fresh cream, I was fit for bursting. I reclined in my chair like a zealous Henry VIII, ready for the night's entertainment.

Mindy had excelled herself as host and I was hugely appreciative of the effort. As much as this was meant to be my making up dinner, I had invested very little into the whole process. Maybe I could have lent a hand here and there, making the gravy, peeling the potatoes, that type of thing. But I knew she would only have batted me away, insisting I was doing more harm than good.

'I must say, Robbie,' Wendy started. 'You make a damn good dinner.'

'He wishes,' Mindy snorted, sipping on the last of her wine. We all laughed, the type of tittering reserved only for adult dinner parties. No guffawing or chortling allowed, a neat and polite laugh that kept the ambience light.

'It's true,' I said humbly. 'I can't take all of the credit. Gerry washes a mean dish.'

Gerry tipped his glass and nodded with a tired acknowledgement. Still one of the good guys, the best.

'So, how's your act coming along?' asked Dave, much to my surprise. In the few short days I had known the guy, he had shown zero interest in anything I did.

'Not too bad actually, thanks, Dave,' I said, the surprise evident in my voice.

'Wendy says you've got a show coming up next month.' What was this? He sounded almost interested.

'Yeah, yeah, man. My agent got me on the bill at a small gig in Hammersmith.'

'Ah, right. When is it?'

'First week in December, I forget the exact date.' I kept it close to my chest.

'Great. Well, Wendy and I are going to be down round about then, maybe we could come along,' he had mentioned the trip.

I shot a quick glance at Wendy but she didn't react. No flinch, no wink, not even a twitch in her cheeks.

'Of course, I'll get you on the guest list. No probs, would be good to see you.'

'Tell us about this trip, then,' Gerry jumped in with both feet. I wasn't sure if he knew what we did, but he had opened the can of beans now. He was slurring a little, hence the out of character blurt. No doubt he was overcome with the familial bliss, the rare familial bliss. I buckled myself in and prepared to hold on.

'Wendy and I are going on a 'round the world trip for six months,' said Dave. His shark-like grin had returned, clean-shaven face shining in the lamplight, making him look like he had a sheen of slime over his skin.

'Oh wow, bloody hell!' said Gerry. He hadn't drank a great deal, but it was evident from his enthusiasm it was more than enough. 'That sounds fantastic! Where abouts are you going?'

'Around the world, Gerry,' Mindy said. There was venom there and I knew that things were about to get rough. Call it a sixth sense or just plain paranoia, I sensed that things were all about to kick off.

'Yeah, I know but whereabouts, what countries, I mean?' He stood up for himself.

'We get the Eurostar from London to Paris, spend a few days there before heading east towards the UAE. Then from there we get a railroad across India, heading towards Hong Kong, down to Perth, Sydney, then to Los Angeles, across to New York and then back home about twenty-four weeks later.' Dave had his plan set out and I had to concede that it sounded like a great trip. I wasn't sure the others at the table were going to be so interested.

'That's a big undertaking,' said Mindy, swirling the last of her wine. 'How are you getting the time off?'

Dave shrugged his shoulders and smiled. He took Wendy's hand in the first sign of genuine affection I had seen between the two.

'Some things are more important than work.' I was a little surprised by his answer. Maybe he did care for Wendy. Either that, or he was the best actor I had ever known.

'I was thinking more about your course, Wendy,' said Mindy. Ruthless and straight for the jugular.

'The Uni is deferring my studies for another year,' she said plainly.

'Another year?' Mindy asked, her face contorted into a sneer. 'That'll be yet more time spent at that place. Do you think you'll ever leave?' The question was half jocular, but I could tell Wendy was in no mood for laughs.

'It'll take as long as it takes, Mindy,' she said defiantly. 'I want to go on this trip with Dave, it's important to us both and we might not get the chance to do it in the future. Or ever again, for that matter.'

Standing up for yourself, giving as good as you got, never being told, they were all traits of the Argylls. Sometimes it got us into trouble, me more than most, but they weren't bad attributes to have in life. Watching two well matched foes like Wendy and Mindy go at it would have been a great spectator sport. If I wasn't directly involved.

I was going to calm things down, but they were beyond my control. My sisters continued their barrage; the first stages of full-blown argument were complete.

'All I'm saying is, you've been at university for almost double the time you were planning to be.' Mindy was protesting. 'Maybe it's about time you grew up a bit.'

'So what if I've been there? Surely it doesn't matter if it's what I wanted to do,' Wendy volleyed back.

'But it means nothing if when you get out of there you're a middle aged woman.'

'That's not for you to decide. It's my life, I'll spend it how I want,' Wendy snapped.

'Maybe we should all just calm down a bit,' Gerry tried to simmer things down.

'Good idea,' Dave confirmed. I rubbed my forehead, knowing all too well their efforts would be lost amongst the shouting.

'And this trip is just making things worse,' Mindy pressed

onwards, relentless, I envied her energy.

'How will it be worse, we want to enjoy ourselves before we're too old, got too much responsibility.'

'Responsibility?' Mindy laughed. 'What would you know about responsibility? You've never been in charge or been held accountable for anything in your life.'

'How dare you!' Wendy raised her voice to a shout.

'It's true, Wendy, don't pretend it's anything other than that. You've been spoiled rotten, by Mum, by Dad, you never had to work for anything.'

'And you did, I suppose?'

'I'm a lawyer, darling.' There was finality in her voice.

'Big deal,' Wendy snorted.

'All I'm saying is that you shouldn't be postponing things any longer for trips you can't afford.'

'But I'll be able to afford it no problem when we sell the house.'

Not even Mindy saw that one coming. In truth neither had I.

Wendy's statement cut the conversation's throat from ear to ear. Her words lingered in the room like a bad smell and created an elephant so big, it may as well have climbed on the table and started doing the Charleston.

I had overheard them in the living room the other night, but I was starting to think my imagination was running away with me. There had been no outward signs of them pushing through with their plans and my own paranoia was running rife. To hear her finally say it, I wasn't sure exactly how to feel.

Life had been centred on this whole place for as long as I could remember. Growing up in it, my parents living and dying in it, even my own rebellion was in some small way

209

running away from the place. To imagine that it wasn't ours or that I couldn't walk up that path, lie in my room, throw lighters into the back garden, was alien to me.

Would I be able to handle things if it went? How would I cope, knowing that it wasn't always going to be here? I hadn't really given its absence any thought.

Mother's will had been confusing enough and I was still to clarify the details. But I had come to realise over the past few days that controlling everybody wasn't the way to go. Not for me, certainly, but even for everybody else. If Wendy and Dave wanted to sell their share, I suppose there was little anyone could do to stop them.

Mindy, on the other hand, looked devastated at the news. I had told her earlier, but I suspected she hadn't been listening. My pressing feud and the as yet to be announced engagement must have taken her mind off of it. Either that or she had chosen to point blank ignore what I had told her. Certainly, it wouldn't be the first time.

Hearing it from the horse's mouth evidently had a very different effect on her. She sat with her mouth hanging open a little before remembering where and who she was. She snapped her jaw shut and I could see her tense, shoulders high enough that her pearl necklace stuck out a little on top of the tendons in her neck. This wasn't good.

'There you have it,' said Wendy, draining her glass and pouring another from the bottle of claret. 'That's what we plan on doing.'

Dave kept his eyes firmly on the tablecloth, his hands clasped together, lips rolling over each other. Gerry on the other side of the table had turned white, all colour now gone from his cheeks. Rob and Abi looked thoroughly uncomfortable down the far end of the room. Two innocents of war, dragged onto the battlefield for stakes they had no say in, win or lose.

'Kids, would you go and prepare the coffee please,' Mindy

said. 'Slice up some cheese and bring it all in with crackers and things.'

My niece and nephew shot up from the table and hurried out of the room as quickly as they could. I wanted to go with them.

Their brief exit lifted the atmosphere for the quickest of moments. When they closed the door behind them, the tension returned. Mindy stared at the remnants of her wine, her teeth grinding with either anger or upset, I wasn't sure which. Wendy was the first to crack under the pressure.

'Well?' she asked. 'Aren't you going to say something?'

'I'm surprised,' said Mindy, nodding. 'Surprised that you've got your plans all laid out without even asking the rest of us if it made sense.'

'It's my money, Mindy,' Wendy replied and for the first time in the evening she showed her age, or lack of it.

Up until then she had been holding her own in the big bad argument for adults. Simply put, she was still a child. Mindy's accusations earlier had been spot on, right on the money, when she described our baby sister as having no responsibility. Maybe it was just the rules of the game, what happened with the youngest child of the family. Regardless, Wendy Argyll was a twenty-seven-year-old woman who was still at university and didn't have to worry about a thing.

'Some of us had plans for that inheritance, Wendy,' Mindy started.

'Some of us?' Wendy repeated. 'You mean you.'

'I can only speak for myself. Whatever Robert wants to do with his share is completely up to him.'

'The same as me,' she was adamant.

'Of course. But you've made a pretty big decision in what you want to do with yours and haven't even bothered asking the others if they would be okay with it.' Once again Mindy's logic was sound.

'You don't even know what you want to do with it!' Wendy said, looking at us both. 'Do you?' she reached out for me.

I was about to answer, but Mindy got in before me. I was relieved.

'As it happens, I do.' I looked at her, as confused as I probably looked. She hadn't said anything to me about it, but I suppose I wasn't surprised. Good old Rob, always last to know. Just like Del Amitri. This was getting interesting.

'What?' Wendy dismissed the whole notion in an instant. Mindy hesitated for a moment and looked at Gerry. Could this have something to do with his failing business? I had thought a nice pot of cash from this old place would have been useful for them. At least, that's what I had believed they would have gone for.

And how could I ever stand in their way of that decision. My mind had raced through ways of helping them ever since Mindy had opened up to me about their troubles. If selling the family house would in some small way alleviate their strife, then I would leap at the opportunity. Not for my own conscience but for the overall well-being of the family. Of my family.

But it wasn't going to be the case. At least, that was what Mindy was saying now.

'So, what do you want to do with it?' I asked, speaking for the first time since the whole shooting match had kicked off. Almost fifteen minutes, it had to be a new record.

The two of them looked at each other and Gerry took his wife's hand in his. He nodded at Mindy and she smiled.

'We want to open a bed and breakfast.'

'Where?' I asked, before I realised I had asked it.

'Here, Robert,' Mindy said, keeping her frustration to a minimum. 'We want to sell up our place, move in here and convert some more of the rooms, open up the attic, our old rooms, Mum and Dad's room. We've been thinking about it for years and we have just enough to push it through. But it'll take your support. Both of your supports.'

The Mindy I knew had disappeared and in her place was a woman more fragile and tender than I had ever seen. High flying, tough talking, legal eagle Mindy Dawkins had been swallowed up and spat out by this new woman sitting at the dining room table. Meek, humble, and on her last throw of the dice, my sister looked like a woman who had come to the end of her options.

Gerry sat beside her and looked exactly the same. They were a pair of proud people, hard working people, a couple who deserved every break they got. I wasn't sure if Wendy knew their financial plight, I hoped that Dave didn't. It hardly mattered, I knew.

I also knew that this went deeper that just some hopeful dream, a secret ambition they had shared for a long time. This was a chance for them to save their lives and that of their children. To finally plug the gap and make amends for the mistakes that had cost, and were still costing, them their livelihoods.

Pride had always been something I had seen as little more than a way of getting you into unnecessary trouble. When you could have backed down but didn't and the consequences were destructive. Mindy and Gerry sat as a testimony to that attitude, their pride and arrogance almost bringing about an end to the life they had built up around them. Worse still, tainting the futures of their children, the ones who would be punished without having any involvement.

I didn't know the business behind this B&B scheme, but I knew that it was a do or die effort for both of them. They had gambled before and lost and I could only hope, and indeed pray, that they would get it right this time around.

Wendy and Dave were as quiet as I was. I was no mind reader; my people reading skills had never come across a situation like this before. I doubt many had.

They sat across from the others and remained perfectly silent. Everybody around the table was scared to make the first sound, fearing what the consequences might be. And with good reason, there was an awful lot at stake. I had been nervous before about the dinner. Now I was bloody devastated.

Chapter 22

While it may not have been the way I was expecting things to go, the great, big family reunion dinner was worth its weight in entertainment value. Perhaps not for the players involved but certainly from the outside looking in.

As I lay on my bed, trying to will myself to sleep, the strangest notion that the whole thing would have made great reality TV got me thinking.

One of those silly, spiralling out of control thoughts that never seems to end. I had the whole thing planned out in my head, even going as far as mapping out how it would look. Shiny, glossy, cameras everywhere, the world would marvel at the quirky, quarrelsome, sometimes questionable antics of the Argyll family.

We would all move into a big mansion in LA and Mindy, being head of the household, would get loaded up with more Botox than Gordon Ramsay's chin. It would make her look like a permanently enlarged puffer fish, but twice as ugly. Gerry would let his hair grow down his back but keep his bald crown, a handle bar moustache bleached blonde to match Hulk Hogan.

Wendy and Dave were perfect candidates for the trouble making youngsters. She would have to be constantly pregnant and he would need to be on his phone all the time, dropping celebrity names here and there. Rob and Abi would be the hell-raising youngest of the brood, drugs, drink, DUIs, the works.

That only left me, the outsider. Tall, gangly and with high cheekbones, maybe I could be the only sane one amongst them. This was television baby, anything was possible.

Lying in the darkness I could even see the opening credits. Lampooning all of the old fifties and sixties shows from the States, *I Love Lucy* and all that nonsense. The theme tune would be an old classic, rehashed by a new, hipper artist that would cost the network a fortune. But money was no object, we would take MTV by storm.

The only trouble I could foresee was keeping up the intensity of the dinner party's action. As messed up and inharmonious as we were, I doubted even *we* could keep that type of behaviour up for a twenty-two episode season. The drugs and copious amounts of booze would help, though. That's how The Osbournes did it. For the Kardashians, I'm sure the oil tankers full of money helped too.

My wild-eyed dreams of conquering American TV were, of course, keeping me from sleeping. I could feel the fatigue hanging off of me, making me feel limp and weak. I hadn't slept the night before and, save for a few moments while watching *Countdown*, I was running on fumes.

I was too tired to sleep and much too tired to stay awake. I occupied that strange netherworld known as insomnia. I had pitched battles in this land before and always, eventually, overcome it. But the interim periods were always the worst. Sweaty, greasy nights spent tossing and turning, aching limbs, a lethargic weakness all over. It was like being hungover without the joy of getting rat-arsed before.

The house was too warm, which didn't help, and I was baking beneath my duvet. I pushed it down to the foot of the bed and tried to let some air pass over my sweaty body. I could see little beads of sweat on my arms and thighs, reflecting in the light from the street outside, my t-shirt pasted onto my chest and stuck beneath my arms. I hated the heat, almost as much as I hated not being able to sleep.

I rolled over, then back again, only to roll over a third time. I flipped the pillow, basking in the coolness at first then making that side just as warm as the first. I tried counting sheep, counting to infinity; counting how many counting techniques I could think of. Still nothing.

Someone had once told me the best way to get to sleep

was to try and stay awake. The information had felt like sound advice at the time. Now it made me furious. What a bloody stupid thing to say.

After my fourth botched attempt at trying to find a comfortable position, I conceded that the night was wasted. I didn't want to look at the time because I knew it would hurt my head to realise how long I had wasted with these futile efforts.

In the end, I sat up, threw my legs over the side of the bed and sat, staring into the dark, swirling abyss of my carpet. The problem wasn't insomnia, I knew it was just a symptom of something much bigger and more terrible.

The events of the dinner party had spiralled way out of control. For what had initially been designed as an opportunity to patch things up, to make a positive step towards the future, had descended into chaos.

By the time Mindy and Gerry had said their tight-lipped goodbyes, I felt even further adrift from the rest of the family than I did before we kicked off. That thought made my stomach lurch. Robert Burns had once written that the best laid plans of mice and men often go awry. John Steinbeck ripped it off for his own work a few hundred years later. Now, sitting in the darkness, staring at my feet, I knew exactly what they had both meant.

Extrapolating the evidence, Mindy wasn't the only one who could do it, I came to the conclusion that my interference had probably caused this whole debacle. Shoving my nose into everybody else's business wasn't my usual attitude, but this trip had been unlike any other I had ever put myself through.

Granted, the death of one's mother is hardly an everyday occurrence, but I still felt wholly responsible for the way things had played out. If I had come back home and stayed for a day before scurrying off again, chances were that none of this debate would have even taken place. Mindy and Wendy would have both been in opposing camps, I would have had my cheque forwarded on to whatever rock I was hiding underneath and the world would have carried on as normal.

As things had turned out, I had been responsible for the conflict. Perhaps not solely responsible, but more than a driving factor behind the week's circus. By choosing this moment to become more involved in my family's affairs, I could very well have destroyed the already delicate balance.

Was it bad that I wasn't ashamed of that fact? I was hardly proud of it, but I didn't hold much regret for at least trying. And that was the key difference in this whole sordid affair.

My own effort to be a part of things, to become more involved. As selfish as it was, for the good of my own conscience and sanity, I had to do what I had so unhelpfully did. Otherwise I was sure that I wouldn't just be dealing with insomnia, things would be much worse, perhaps even deadly.

Thinking on it, a sudden realisation popped into my head. I was standing at a crossroads, and not for the first time on this trip. Honestly, if I were a road map, I probably would have been a giant bloody junction. Easy to draw for the boffins at Ordnance Survey, I suppose.

All of my meddling and interference had put me slap, bang in the middle of the chaos with a simple, but very important, choice to make. And I understood the maths of the situation for what was perhaps the first time ever.

There were three children and two of them had very different ideas for what they wanted to do with their inheritance. As the third party in a cake sliced three ways, whoever I decided to back would ultimately get the majority ruling. That made me the dragon, the boss, and the one with the most pressure.

Both arguments were sound when I thought about them. Typical, really. For a man who always looked for the quick fix, I was devastated as much as I was angry that there was no easy way around this.

For some strange reason, I was attacking the problem logically. I remembered an old school report, the scourge of my childhood, that had once claimed I didn't know how to apply logic to problem solving situations. At the time I had dismissed the idea as nonsense, what did they know after all? Those who couldn't do, taught, I knew that much.

Yet bizarrely, the comment had stayed with me all the way through school and into later life. Like some ravenous monkey on my back, whenever anything remotely close to solving a problem had to be done, I was reminded of the spiteful comment from whatever little person had had the bollocks to tell my parents they were effectively not doing their job.

I'm sure they would defend their decision by claiming it was reverse psychology, but I knew that was way beyond their imagination. While the end result might have been the one intended, the application of more logic at the time had hindered me more than helped.

I guess I should have been more grateful now, when it really mattered. I was being as logical as I could. Chemical equations and mathematical algorithms were all fine and good for putting a man on the Moon, or in a film studio in the Nevada desert. When it came to the people I loved and called my own, that was something altogether more important. I had to get it right.

For some reason, completely unknown to me, I pictured a boxing ring. Not the type seen in modern fights, laced with advertising and a titty model parading about with the round board. Something more traditional, like in *Rocky* or *Rocky II*.

In the red corner was Mindy, heavyweight champion of the family, a real hard slugger and one of the best to ever don the gloves and trunks. She pulled no punches, held no remorse and was capable of a knockout at any given moment. She didn't get the nickname 'Dropper' Dawkins for nothing.

Facing her was the young pretender for the championship crown. 'Whistling' Wendy Argyll, the baby-faced assassin.

With no knockouts, no victories and no losses to her name she was the great unknown. Would she float like a butterfly or sink like a dead weight?

And in the middle of it all was the referee for tonight's bout. Mr Robert Argyll: washed up cynic, sometimes comic and a whole lot of dead weight to be throwing around the ring. The announcers would be running out of superlatives to describe the action. And worst of all, I couldn't enjoy any of it. I would ultimately decide the winner.

They both made convincing cases and each had their own reasons behind their motives. Would it really fall on my shoulders to decide the fate of my family? Was this the reality we were living in, where a man who had shunned all responsibility and sense of familial harmony for a selfish existence ultimately called the shots on its future? It was a pretty sad state of affairs really, that being the case.

My road to redemption was barely a week old; I had only just set foot out of the door. Yet, here I was, facing a decision that would shape the course of not just my own life, but six other human beings and perhaps countless more.

My problem was simple: decide who to give my share of the will too. Nothing difficult about that.

For Wendy it was a route of escape, or so I figured. She had always been a prisoner in this place. Stuck under the ever-watchful eyes of my parents when she was younger, her jail sentence lasting all of her life. The rooms of the house would always hold a different light for her than they did for Mindy and myself.

Hardly her fault and I certainly couldn't blame her for trying to be rid of such torrid memories. If I had spent my youth and the better part of my twenties shackled away, hidden from the world because of my ailing mother, I wouldn't want much to do with it either. Hell, that was why I had stayed away for so long.

Wendy could have done the same, but she didn't. For that she would always be braver than I could ever hope to be. Sure, she had it cushy here, Mother would run after her every whim and had done during her turbulent teens and beyond. Lifted and placed back down wherever, however and whenever she wanted.

The cost had been her unquestionable obedience and I knew she was beginning to think it hadn't been worth it. Selling up and moving on would give her an independence that went beyond a few quid in her back pocket. She would finally be freed from a life that had kept her back for so long and maybe, just maybe, let her become the woman she had always wanted to be.

Wendy's case had to be that. Dave wasn't short of cash, or at least he acted as if he wasn't. Flash suits, big car and a job at some firm he had yet to disclose in the city. Or at least, that was how he was showing himself off, projecting to the world. I didn't trust him, I never would trust him. My sister's sudden urge to be gone and into the wide blue yonder was about so much more than money.

It had to be, didn't it? If she was in any way being moulded and shaped by Dave, or anybody else for that matter, then my mind would be made up. But I had to trust her; I had to give her the benefit of the doubt. She had never danced to anybody else's tune, apart from Mother's, and I was sure she wasn't now.

Or was I? How sure could I be? How sure could I ever be?

I could spend an eternity mulling over her case, but I didn't have that long. There was already too much in my To-Do pile, I couldn't keep adding to the blasted thing.

My mind shifted to Mindy's plight and my head began to throb. Hers was completely different, a motive that went beyond anything I could have ever imagined. The once proud woman who had always been independent was now reduced to little more than a begging pauper. Well, maybe not quite as bad as that, but it was getting a little ropey in the Dawkins household.

I felt for the kids, Rob and Abi. They were lovely children, young adults now, of course, and they didn't deserve to be punished for their parents' shortcomings. No child ever deserved that and I could say with a little pride, but mostly relief, that I had never been restrained by my own Mum and Dad.

Gerry's business was broke and they needed cash quickly. This bed and breakfast idea of theirs sounded good on the surface, but then again, what did I know about any sort of business venture. To me, business was what people talked about when they were unemployed and looking for anything to keep them off the streets. An unfair branding, no doubt, but there were too many so-called entrepreneurs out there with absolutely nothing to show for their populist job title.

The problem facing my decision was Gerry and Mindy's track record. Again, I wasn't privy to the workings of his failed electrician's venture, I had always thought they were making a killing in a world that had turned its nose up at manual and physical labour. It was a new golden age for the bricky, the chippy and the sparky.

Somehow, he hadn't been able to make a go of it and that was a pretty big factor in my view. Of course I was surprised, Mindy had one of those brilliant minds that should have seen disaster coming. Maybe she had been blinded by love, masked to the potential downfall through her devotion to her husband.

I could understand that. What wife wouldn't want to see her partner succeed beyond their wildest dreams? But success had been hard to come by for them, regardless of the motive or their best intentions.

Could I really trust them to make a go of this new scheme? Desperation was a strange fuel, some thrived on it, others cracked under the pressure. Sitting at the dinner table, they looked like a couple that was out of ideas. Was I really prepared to hammer in the final nail in their coffin by giving them free reign to follow another harebrained idea?

I would help them in every way I could, that had, after all, been the big reason behind my sudden change in attitude. What I wouldn't be responsible for would be their ultimate demise. As clichéd as it was, sometimes you had to be cruel to be kind. To save both my sister and her own family, I was prepared to make any sacrifice, even if that meant dashing their hopes.

What a terrible situation I was in. Emotionally, I had no doubt that it was the worst I had ever experienced.

During my affair I hadn't wrestled with my conscience nearly as much. Reflecting on it now, that made me feel terrible, of course. Jack had so adequately pointed out a whole other level of selfishness in that small footnote of my life, the great friend he was.

I would never forgive myself, of course, but that was aside. I couldn't help but feel now that this might offer me some sort of salvation from my previous failures.

I was in no way spiritual, I had always been critical of that way of thinking. But even I could see the poetic justice, the pseudo Greek-tragedy circumstances of my plight. Surely this type of thing never happened in real life? A week ago I would have laughed the thought out of the room, more than any of my audience members certainly.

Yet, here I was. Faced with a decision that was emotionally tearing me apart. I had to break somebody's heart, and in the process, I knew that mine would break too.

There was, of course, a third option. I could keep my own share and run to the hills, let the others battle it out. But that wasn't really ever going to happen. Even in my darkest moments, I doubted I would have been so callous and self absorbed. Perhaps not one hundred per cent sure, but close

223

enough that it didn't figure. A close call for my conscience, though.

I felt like the whole room had gotten a little bit darker, the shadows gathering around me like I was a half arsed black hole. I didn't feel any better for listing the good points and bad, if anything, I felt worse. The sheer scale and size of the task ahead was enough to make my head burst. Or implode. I wasn't even sure which would be more painful.

Minor technicalities, there were more pressing problems. The thought made me hungry, although dinner had clogged my intestines up so nicely that would take at least two days to clear. I resolved to have some scraps and clear my mind, maybe even getting some shuteye in the process.

Chapter 23

Best behaviour always came easy when you weren't the one under the spotlight. Like a dog that is finally freed from his leash and let loose in the park, or a field or anywhere he can shit without barriers. This whole strange ordeal had left me feeling liberated.

Sure, the thought of having to make The Decision, as I was calling it, hung over me like a dark cloud, one that wouldn't blow away. But having the advantage of being the hammer, not the nail, was enough to keep my pecker up. So the old phrase so colourfully went.

Sleeping had helped. The past few nights had been a hellish torment whenever I closed my eyes. After a big night out you don't really sleep, not in the restful sense anyway. More like a mild coma, you can wake up the next day feeling like the past six hours never happened.

Usually that feeling extended to the next night, too, although much better by comparison. Normality wouldn't return until the night after that. As it happened I would have gladly enjoyed the rest when it came, but things had spiralled a little. Whenever I put my head down on the pillow, I was haunted by whatever latest disaster had befallen the family.

Much to my surprise then, when I actually enjoyed a solid night's sleep. I woke at around 10 am and felt thoroughly refreshed. Even the impending thought of The Decision wasn't enough to discourage me.

I found the house empty when I eventually made it down stairs. There were no notes, no messages and the phone hadn't gone as far as I was aware. The post had been gathered and neatly stacked beside the door. Wendy, who had taken to staying in the house since Mother had died, must have left early.

There were no cars outside, the old driveway sitting empty.

The house was silent and warm and comfortable. Had I not been suffering from cabin fever quite so badly, I probably would have enjoyed a relaxing day. That was boring, though, and I hated boring. While I may moan and whinge about needing time to myself, the truth was I quite liked having people around.

Even in the current throes of The Decision, having somebody to talk to would have been nice. But their lives went on and I seemed to be left behind.

I stood at the front door and peered out through the window. I didn't look at anything in particular, just the space between the spaces. My thoughts wandered to the others and what their opinions were on the whole scenario.

Were they as bothered about it as I was? Of course they were, it was their future. I wondered if they were at all angry with me in the whole thing.

If they were, I couldn't and didn't blame them. I tried to imagine what it would have been like from my perspective if I wanted something bad enough and had to rely on their decision. It would drive me bloody mad.

A strange buzzing filled the room and I looked around, searching for what it could be. When my brain decided to start behaving normally again, I realised it was my phone, lost somewhere amongst the clutter of the sitting room.

Throwing cushions about and checking beneath the couches, I eventually found it, wedged down the arm of the big chair near the fire. Wasn't that always where these things ended up? There was a joke in there somewhere.

'Hello,' I said, not looking at the number.

'Oi oi polloi, if it isn't Robbie the jobbie,' came a booming voice from the other end.

'Ah, good morning, Mr Johnson, very nice to hear from you,' I settled into the chair.

226

'Good morning to you too, sir. And how are we this morning?' he was in a chirpy mood. Something was wrong.

'Been better, Jack mate, things aren't good here, doing my head in.'

'Nothing to do with the other night, I take it?'

'What about it?'

'That little red head I saw you chatting up in the club.'

'We were in a club?' I asked, trying to avoid the memories of Angela, second time around at least.

'Oh dear, you really were plastered. Well, I won't spoil any surprises for you then.'

'Trust me man, you won't.' I laughed a little.

'Anyway, I've got something I need to tell you.'

'Jack, can I stop you there, mate. If this is to do with the other night, I don't want to know. Can we just scratch it up to experience and move on please ... ' I tried to sound sincere without being a prick.

'No, no, jeez, get off your high horse, Argyll. It's about your Wendy's man, Dave.'

I sat up in the chair. Something rippled through me, like I had put my finger in a socket. What was going on?

'Go on,' I said with a little trepidation.

'Remember we were talking about him at your old lady's wake?' said Jack, his voice steady and, for the first time in our relationship, serious.

'Yeah,' I breathed.

'Turns out I knew his face, I just couldn't remember where from that night. So when I sobered up, eventually, I realised how I knew the bastard ... he's a shyster, a con man.'

'What?' I blurted.

'Yup, came into one of my gaffs in Govan about six months ago, trying to sell us some carpets or rugs or whatever, some upholstery. Wasn't something I would have entertained, but he gave it large with a lot of rubbish, saying he could get bespoke handmade products from the Middle East at a fraction of the price and we could sell them online. Of course I snapped it up, you know what I'm like with a bargain … '

'Anyway, we agreed a sum, a hearty sum, for his services and contacts, paid half up front and never saw the bastard again. Vanished by all accounts, no phone number, nothing. Our finance department tried to track his whereabouts, trace where cheques were cashed, but the money had been dispersed and put through more phoney accounts than a Nazi war criminal hiding out in Brazil. The money we'd paid him was nothing compared to the legal fees we would have forked out to try and get the blighter and, not to toot my own horn, I'm not short of a hundred grand or two. Buttons to me, really, so I very promptly forgot the maggot!'

'A hundred thousand pounds!' I gushed, 'You handed over a hundred thousand pounds?'

'It's business, Robbie. Anyway, I thought I recognised his face, name didn't ring a bell, though, but that makes sense. I'd had previously met him as David *Armstrong*. He wouldn't go about using his real name anyway. I'd like to get my hands on the bugger now, though.' My head was thumping. This was too much to take in.

I had always held suspicions over him but never to this degree. Who was to say that he'd stopped, or even started, with Jack. And ripping off a hundred grand wasn't small change. He was a bloody criminal. I began to panic.

'Jack,' I tried to steady myself. 'Jack, I need you to think very carefully about your next answer.'

'Uh huh,' he said.

'Are you sure, are you a hundred per cent sure, that this

guy, Dave Thatcher, is the same man that stole all that money from you?'

'Robbie, I might be stinking rich and it means nothing to me, but I thought I vaguely recognised him that night, he's buffed up a lot since then though. But, yeah, I'm sure that's him. Sorry I would have phoned sooner, but I've had a rough couple of days, met two Miss Scotland contenders … well, I think that's what they said they were … '

'Thanks, Jack.' I cut him off, before he got into too much detail. 'I'll call you in a while.'

I hung up and stood numbly in the middle of the sitting room. Taking all things into consideration, the whole messed up affair was a giant cluster of disasters that had happened, were happening and waiting to happen. A quantum bomb of endless nightmares.

A small robin floated down from the hedge and began to walk across the damp chipping on the driveway. It pecked at the weeds that were sprouting out of the ground in great chunks. Waddling along, it seemed endlessly happy in its own little world.

I could do that, I could be a robin. Or any kind of animal, really. Things were so much simpler for the rest of nature. When you were hungry, you ate. When you were in danger, you fled. When you were randy, you had sex. Sometimes I thought the human race worked better as animals. The day we became self-aware was arguably the worst moment in our long and storied history.

The little robin hopped up and down the driveway. It ruffled its feathers and came to a stop not far from the door. I had half a mind to let it in, we could have some tea and a scone and talk about a swap of professions. Sure, the money wasn't great but the hours were fantastic. His job sounded good, too.

I tapped on the glass and the little bird's head twitched towards me. I tapped it again and it came trundling towards the door.

Quicker than I could see, a ginger mass of fuzz leapt on the little robin and it was gone in an instant. I jumped backwards, startled, gasping for breath. When my heart retreated back down my throat and I started to breathe again, I stared, wide-eyed, looking at a fat, old ginger tom-cat pawing at the porch step.

Like some Warner Bros. *Loony Toon*, the cat chewed down on something before swallowing. It stretched its mouth and flashed its fangs, satisfied with its meal.

I was shocked and a little frightened. Nature was all well and good when it was on the Discovery Channel. You hardly expected, or needed to see it at your front door.

I opened the door and shooed the cat away. It walked away at its own, casual, cocky pace. With a belly full of robin and a swagger to match even the most confident of nightclub sharks, I was a little jealous. Not of the cat, of the bird making its way through his digestive system.

The ginger Tom disappeared around the edge of the front gate and I was left, alone, in the cold, again. I turned to go back into the house but thought against it as soon as I saw how gloomy and dark the hallway was. I could be doing with a smoke, or at least a breath of fresh air. A quick inventory check and I was reminded of the cigarette box shaped hole in my pocket.

The urge was tempting, but I thought better of it. Maybe it was my conscience again, that annoying little voice who had found a megaphone from somewhere in the depths of my mind. Regardless, she was telling me to be more proactive, do something better and healthier for me. Gemima Cricket, the bitch.

I grabbed the keys from inside the door and threw on my boots. The garage was around the side of the house, just beyond the back door of the kitchen. I had always hated the place; it stank of varnish and old paint.

After trying the fifty different keys on the ring, I found the right one and opened up the door with a screech. That familiar gust of stagnant, chemically putrid air hit me and I choked down a swallow of bile. Much to my surprise, and a little disappointment, I found what I was looking for.

The tyres were flat, the chain had come off and the saddle looked like a real nutcracker, but my old bike was still there. I wheeled it out and rubbed the spokes and frame with my hand, pulling away a layer of dust as thick as birthday cake icing.

The pump was attached to the frame and, again to my surprise, still worked. Working up a sweat, I breathed life back into the tyres, checked they were secure and replaced the chain. My mind was made up. I was going for a cycle.

Keys, wallet, phone, and trainers, I was ready in five minutes. No crash helmet, I would run the risk, and a pair of old shorts and t-shirt from one of the drawers in my room. Pretty I wasn't but willing, you bet.

Setting out on the road, I gave a quick glance over to the Campbells', hoping to get a glance of Philippa doing her morning exercises, by the window, in the nude, everything on show. No such luck, so I set my wheels in motion.

The useful part of Glasgow's South Side had always been its relative friendliness to cyclists. In London, there was a daily battle between those who took to two wheels and the others on four. North of the border, or indeed anywhere outside the capital, that war had come to an end long ago. I suppose that was partly behind my rash decision in the first place, sheer availability to do it.

Usual traffic, usual faces, the normal humdrum activity of the suburbs was unfolding as usual, regular as clockwork. When I rolled up to the traffic lights, I had to force my mind to remember what day it was. Friday, end of the working week. I smiled a little.

There was a slight tingle of anticipation in the air. For a city like Glasgow, Fridays and Saturdays were the wildest nights in a town where there was always a party in full flow. Since the days of the hard working industrial mills and shipyards had dominated the economy, there had always been room for heavy drinking and fighting. Once those whistles went at five o'clock at the end of the week, it was a feeding frenzy.

The weekend lunatics and their selfish, violent antics had ravaged whole families down the decades. Alcoholics, gamblers, football hooligans, they all came out to play under the bright lights of Scotland's city of sin. Shipyard grafters and skivvies had given way to new forms of unhinged young men. Call centre workers, tellers, or just the plain unemployed on jobseeker's allowance, they still had a place to go at the weekend.

Bars would be packed out, clubs thumping to a collective beat. Money earned with blood and guts, sweat and toil over the five working days before would be frittered away in a matter of hours. Then, when the greedy owners had had their fill, the punters were thrown out onto the street; a takeaway and a fight before home to bed and a chance to sleep it all off.

I could feel the change in the air even out as far as the suburban outskirts. Drivers moved that little bit quicker, the pedestrians had that bit more of a spring in their step.

While their work was just coming to an end, mine would usually be starting. Fridays, Saturdays, even Sundays I would usually have a gig. On occasion I would perform in a big club, but mostly it was in local bars and venues who looked a little kinder on my current state of affairs. Being on TV once had its merits: it gave you an almost guaranteed soapbox to shout from, no matter how small the venue.

As I cycled onwards towards the countryside, I wondered how different things were up here. When I first started out, there had only ever been two very different places to perform comedy: student unions, where the uni types were more open to fringe material, and working man's clubs, who liked their humour blue and saucy. While the audiences were night and day, my job had always been the same. Make them laugh or learn to duck.

I was sure it was different; brave new world and all of that. Glasgow's cultural revolution had been in full swing since the early nineties and people were learning to mellow out a bit more to the arts. The city had a famous reputation for being notoriously difficult for performers.

Stephen K. Amos once said that if the Scots like you, they like you. And he was right. If it went the other way, then you were usually in a lot of trouble. There was no prejudice, either.

I had never considered myself particularly patriotic. I wasn't hugely anti-patriotic either, I had once begged Mother for a Scotland football shirt, only to wear it once then resign it to the cupboard. Both my parents were Tory voters; I had never been registered, so there was a strong British identity in the house.

But Scottish crowds, Glasgow ones in particular, held no special reserve for you if you were 'one of their own.' If your material stank, they were going to tear you limb from limb, regardless of your accent. It made for a fearsome reputation and a lot of my colleagues were usually nervous about coming north of the border.

The challenge was still there, though, and like in most professions, you got gluttons for punishment. To conquer the Dear Green Place, or 'Glesga' as locals knew it, was to get a badge of honour. True, it might be carved into your chest with a broken beer bottle, but the scars would heal and leave you with something you could be proud of.

I had mine, albeit small and insignificant. More like a faint scratch that didn't rival my measles jab. I still had one though, my little battle won when I was barely out of my teens. As small as it had been, it had still been enough of a launch pad for me to make a career out of comedy.

Running on automatic, I hadn't been paying attention to where I was going. All around me the houses had gotten bigger, more luxurious and, of course, more expensive. I had almost reached Mindy's, but I wasn't stopping, I wanted some country air.

For a city so built up, you never had to travel very far to get into the wilderness. Through in Edinburgh it was even less time, something I missed living in London. The freedom of the rolling hills and outstretched farmlands had always been a favourite of mine. Not an outdoors person by nature, I still liked the solitude and sheer peace and bloody quiet that it afforded.

The further I pushed on, the more I was convinced this had been a good idea. The Decision was eating away at me, but the exercise was keeping it at bay, at least until I stopped. By that time I would be in the middle of nowhere with only my thoughts for company.

Slowly the houses began to dissipate, the space between them getting bigger, wider and filled with fields. The roads got straighter and newer, cycle lanes dotted along the inside track to keep me out of trouble and motorists out of court.

I could smell the difference in the air. I wasn't sure how long I had been going for, but it couldn't have been an hour. Yet already there was a change in the freshness, the scent of everything around me. At home things were better than the City Centre, and positively perfect compared to London. Yet out here, amongst the bucolic kingdom of fields, trees, bushes and shrubs, it felt good, cleansing even.

My thighs burned and my back hurt, but I didn't care. The old t-shirt was sticking to my back, beads of sweat trickling down through my hair as I pushed on through the agony, the ecstasy. My lungs were wheezing and I could barely breathe, but I kept on going, knowing the pain, the agony, the sheer exhaustion was good for me.

Veins bulged in my arms, my knuckles white around the handlebars, temples throbbing from my gritted teeth. I began to roar as the road climbed upwards into a single lane country track. I looked up at the crest of the hill and knew that was where I wanted to go. I needed to go.

I hunkered down, dropped gears and hammered the pedals with legs like pistons. The world raced past me, I could feel the machine between my legs straining, its old joints and workings getting more activity now than they had in the past decade. But it held on, as I held on, smashing through the barriers that gravity, time and all of existence put in front of us both. We were bigger than all of them put together, better, and we wanted our reward.

When I reached the top of the hill I started breathing again. The road levelled out for a short way and I let the bike gently coast to a stop, the wheels clicking in that imitable way all bicycles do. The chorus of the Tour de France.

I came to a stop at the side of the little lane and dismounted. The bike collapsed on the frosty grass and I fought the urge to do the same. I sucked in air through my nose and out through my mouth. I paced around a little, feeling the adrenaline and blood course around my body. It was good, it was refreshing, I could almost feel the saggy, lack of fitness leaving through my pores.

A thin layer of steam was coming off my bare arms and legs, making the air around me foggy. I heaved in a big gulp of air and immediately started a coughing fit. Doubled over, I coughed up a glob of greeny, brown phlegm and deposited it on the grass.

The brief lapse into bad health passed and I regained myself. Only then, was I able to take in the sheer beauty and tranquillity of the place.

And oh, how beautiful it was.

From the top of the hill I could see out across the city and all of the surrounding countryside. Away in the far distance, through the murky, cold air of the winter morning, were the towering glass and steel buildings of Glasgow City Centre. The cathedral and university spires acted like bookends to much newer structures, chimneys spouting great plumes of thick, white smoke into the morning sky.

From there things flattened out, everything I had come to expect from the world during my adolescence and youth. The suburbs were neatly laid out in rows and packed tightly into their own designated areas, boxed between the inner city curmudgeon and the rural bliss of the country. The home of the middle classes, stuck where it should be, right in the middle.

Then there was the splendour all around me. Rolling hills, ploughed fields, the odd herd of cows grazing on the morning grass. Mist rolled along the tops of the higher rises, spilling down their gentle slopes and disappearing into the ether at the base.

The pale morning light seemed to add a strange glow to the whole world, like it had just been born into existence. Everything seemed brand new, virginal almost. I had never seen anything quite like it and it took what little breath I had left away from me.

There was something else there, too. Standing in the middle of nowhere, gazing out across the landscape so drastically different, I realised that I had made my choice. An epiphany, a completely random slotting together of ideas had formed and, being too distracted, I hadn't been able to fight them.

I pulled my old bike up from the grassy verge and clambered on for another testicle crushing journey. It hardly mattered, though. I was fuelled by a new sense of purpose and drive.

The Decision had been made. I had to let somebody know before it blew up inside my head. Or worse still, disappeared altogether.

I started down the road, peddling as fast as I could. Like Charlie with the golden ticket, I was going to tell my family the good news.

Chapter 24

Chocolate factories and magical trips around them were one thing. Breaking the news to my family, as they were, was something altogether more daunting. And a lot less sweet to swallow.

The cycle home proved easier than before if not a bit more problematic. Half way down the road I got into a scuffle with a ten tonne bus, its driver voicing off as I peddled away as fast as I could before I could be squashed beneath the wheels.

I had never understood why some of the sturdiest, heaviest, damn near indestructible vehicles on the road were allowed to drive in the same lane as bicycles. Not since *David V Goliath: The Showdown* had there been a more mismatched pair.

The near death experience aside, I had always enjoyed a flare for the dramatic, I returned home and hobbled into the house. Going from no physical exercise, at all, to cycling close to twenty miles, in one day, on the hop, without a warm-up had left me a quivering wreck.

For the purposes of anybody who asked, I was fine, could take it all in my stride, didn't know what all the fuss was about. By the time I reached the door to my room, I was weaker than a baby kitten, and not anywhere near as cute.

I might have enjoyed a quick nap, or just a little rest, but it wasn't to be. The front door swung open and I heard voices, angry voices, coming from the hallway. I sat bolt upright up on my bed, I knew there was trouble.

I dashed to the door and headed for the stairs. I could have stopped and listened, peering through the gaps in the banister like I had done so many times before. Only then it was my parents arguing; this, I feared, involved me much more directly.

I reached the bottom floor and caught a glance of Gerry scuttling into the kitchen. I raced after him and found that the whole family had congregated there. This was wholly inconvenient, I thought. My plan was to tell them all individually, but it seemed that fate had, once again, conspired against me.

'You never understood me!' Wendy was screaming, although pouting would have been more accurate. 'You were always trying to hold me back.'

'How dare you. How *dare* you!' Mindy matched her anger but it was much more controlled, levelled even. 'You've been given nothing but opportunities and chances by us and this is how you repay it? With this holier than thou attitude that makes you think the world owes you a living? Grow up, Wendy.'

'Fuck you!' Wendy volleyed back. I was a little shocked with the malice and I was more than annoyed.

I was aware of how difficult Mindy could make life for each of us, but she didn't deserve to be spoken to like that. I motioned to intervene, but the slug out was still in full swing.

'And who are you to tell me what to do anyway?' Wendy pressed. 'You were always the one who cried independence. Now when I get a chance to be like that, you're all for clipping my wings. It's blitzkrieg man, you're a total fascist.'

'And if I wasn't like that you'd still be in India, or Timbuktu or wherever the bloody hell you're wanting to go. You're almost thirty for God's sake, don't you think it's time to give up on the whole living like a grotty student act?'

'But I like the way I live.'

'Nobody likes the way you live. Not even tramps in the street live in the same squalor as you.'

And so it went on, round and round and round until everybody was dizzy. Since my decision to become a better, more productive member of the family, I had fought plenty of urges. Some to lesser degrees than others, but I'd always had the will power.

239

Standing in amongst the chaos of the kitchen, my sisters going at it like two drunken hen party women, was almost enough to push me back. I had never been more tempted just to turn around, walk out of the front door and never come back. I could take the bike.

I didn't, much to my surprise, instead choosing to stay put and get The Decision off of my chest. I was king of the castle after all; I deserved the audience at least once.

'Enough!' I shouted. Gerry flinched in his seat, snapping out of whatever daydream fantasy he had slumped into to escape this drama. Mindy and Wendy both stopped shouting and turned to me. Dave looked nonchalant.

'That's more than enough, from all of you,' I said. 'I want you to shut your traps and listen to what I've got to say. Capisce?' I shouldn't have added in the slang at the end, it weakened my authority.

'In case you had both forgotten, that will wasn't divided up between the two of you, I was included in it, too.'

If my sisters were ashamed of their selfishness, they certainly weren't showing it.

'Robert, we know that, it's just … '

'Enough!' I held up my finger and stopped Mindy before she could launch into another tirade. This was my moment, I wanted to enjoy it.

'I know you two know this, I'm not accusing you of anything,' I lied. 'But I also think you should know that I've been taking this whole thing very seriously. To the point where I even went cycling this morning, as you can probably tell,' I passed my hands over the dishevelled, sweat soaked outfit that was stinking up the air as I spoke.

'But I've come to a decision. Now I'm not wholly sure what the legality of these things are, I know you'll be able to take care of that,' I nodded to Mindy. 'But I think that what

I've got planned is the best for the whole family. I know you both want your share for very different reasons, and I also know how important those reasons are to you both.

'Wendy, I know that you and Dave are wanting to go away, escape it all and I'm aware that this place, or at least your share, will be more than enough to set you up nicely.' Wendy nodded, Dave remained stoic. 'I'm not wholly sure it's the right idea, but I do know it's what you want. And, as such, I respect that and will do all that I can to give it to you. You're my baby sister and I want to look after you as much as possible. I love you.' Wendy beamed back at me, her mouth pulled into a smug grin.

'And, Mindy, I also know what the share means to you, and to Gerry.' I looked at the two of them in turn, tears welling up in Mindy's eyes. 'And it's not just you two, it's your kids, too. I know I don't really know them, but I want that to change. You've both done a great job of raising them and I know they'll do you proud. Rob's a lovely guy and Abi is sharper than the point of a needle, they're both going on to greater things. And this house, this place, I know you've both got big plans for it and you need the majority in your favour. But you'll both agree that your track record for businesses and things like that isn't fantastic and that's what worries me.'

'But, Robert, we … ' Mindy tried to get in, but I wouldn't allow it.

'Let me finish. You're my big sister and I've always looked up to you, and I'm so proud of what you do for this family. But I have to go with my gut instinct on this one and that's why I've made my decision.'

I was sweating, nervous tension. My stomach was churning, flipping over and over on itself. Maybe it was all the exercise, my body finally rejecting itself for the sheer bloody hell I'd put it through this morning. Maybe I was having a heart attack, or a stroke, or a combination of the two. My lifestyle certainly ticked enough boxes for that to be more than a possibility. It would just be my luck, delivering the keynote speech of my life only to keel over and die before I finished.

I looked out at my family and reaffirmed in my own mind what I had decided. Every last possibility, eventuality, projected outcome, they all raced through my mind in that still, silent moment. I knew then that it was the right thing to do.

'Well?' said Wendy, 'What's it to be?'

'Oh,' I stuttered, woken from my living coma. 'I've decided to … ' One last check before it went live. God knows how newspapers did this.

'I've decided to let you two decide.'

A long, drawn out silence descended on the room. I was no stranger to audiences not getting the joke, but this was just taking the piss. I stood still, sweat running down the back of my neck and suddenly feeling very stupid. Had this been the right decision after all? Was it even a decision in the first place? I was altogether very self-aware.

'That's it?' said Wendy, the first to speak up. 'That's your big decision?' she sneered.

There had been plenty of times where I could have punched my little sister in the face. None of them compared to right then. The urge was so great, my knuckles cracked under the strain of my clenched fist.

'That's what you've been thinking about all of this time?' she was mocking me, making me look like an idiot. I was getting angrier.

'No offense, Robert, but that doesn't sound like too taxing an effort on your part. I mean, what do you think *we've* been doing all of this time?' she snorted and looked at Mindy for support.

The blood coursing through my veins felt like boiling hot

242

lava. Every pump of my heart forced more and more of this fiery venom around my limbs, stretching to my fingers and toes. I didn't consider myself a particularly angry person, but I could have ripped her head clean from her shoulders at that moment.

How dare she make a mockery of this? How could she be so immature with this whole thing? Didn't she know how much this had strained me, how much of a soul searching, harrowing, over dramatic mess I had made of The Decision?

I was about to respond, not quite sure what I was going to say, when Mindy intervened. She always knew just when to put her nose in.

'I think what Robert is trying to say, Wendy, is that this decision is one for the whole family.' Wendy fired her a look of discontented petulance.

She wasn't getting this, she really *was* that immature. I could only imagine what Dave was thinking of the whole thing, watching on silently but seeing, hearing, knowing everything. Maybe he knew it all already, maybe that was the big attraction? I knew his dirty little secret.

'But we've been doing that for days now. He's just being over dramatic,' she waved me away, dismissing me from the whole conversation.

'Maybe it's what we've needed, a fresh approach, somebody to tell us exactly what we need to do.' Mindy was trying her best, but I was still mad as hell.

'So, what do we do then?' asked Wendy.

'We make a decision, right here. We all know what we want to do with the place, it's up to us to figure it out.'

'I know what I want,' Wendy snapped. 'I want to sell up and leave this dump behind, forever.'

The words stung my chest. I knew they were the truth, I

243

think that was what was so hurtful about them. I also knew the reasons behind them, but that didn't make it any easier to swallow. The Argylls were certainly no chocolate factory.

I looked at Mindy and hoped that she would make the right decision. Whatever she chose would determine the future of her family, of our family. Wendy wasn't budging; I knew that something had to give.

'Okay,' she said softly.

'Okay?' Wendy and I said together, both a little in disbelief.

'Okay,' Mindy said, moving over to her husband and resting her hands on his shoulders. He took a hold of her and they both looked at us, united in their decision. 'You get what you want, Wendy. If Robert is happy with it, then we sell the place up. We'll cut you a cheque and you can do what you want with your share.'

She had started to cry but was battling through the tears. I saw her grip on Gerry's shoulder tighten, her husband looking sadder than I had ever seen him. For a man who had always been so strong, so jolly, so happy-go-lucky, the pain and disappointment had suddenly come to the fore. In those last few moments he had aged a hundred times over, ravaged by the unfolding events.

'But I want you to know something, Wendy,' Mindy sniffed. 'I'm doing this for us. I'm doing it for all of us. If handing over the rights to the house, to Mum's inheritance is enough to keep you happy and a part of this family, then I'd sign it over to the Devil himself.'

Her words were ladened with emotion, every syllable pushed past her lips with the feelings she had been bottling up for God knows how long. I had no idea how it must have felt to do something as brave as that. I doubted I ever would.

We were her family, but we were also stretching her to her very limit. To give up everything she had was one thing, to mortgage her future for the sake of keeping us all together was nothing short of staggering. In her one simple gesture she had given me everything I had wanted, yet still surprised me by actually doing it.

I took a long, deep, broken breath and hoped I still had the strength to keep from crying. Any sadness I had for ever doubting Mindy was replaced in an instant by disgust when I looked across at Wendy.

My sister, the youngest of the three Argyll children, was sitting on the lap of her partner, and soon to be fiancée by the looks of things. She wore a look of quiet, unashamed smugness that made her eyes look like little more than slits. I was half expecting her to start clapping, loud, mocking slaps with her hands. But she didn't, she spared us all that indignity at least.

Mindy sniffed and moved away from her husband towards the sink. She ran the cold water and filled a glass, draining it instantly. When she was finished, she turned back to us all, her eyes bright red, mascara in long streaks down her cheeks.

'Robert, I want you to get dressed and we'll head down to the lawyers'. Let's get this whole thing cleared up as soon as possible.'

'Good,' said Wendy, jumping up to her feet and clapping her sides.

Dave moved with her, always lurking, always leering, ready to make a killer bite with those fangs he called teeth. They gathered up their coats quicker than I had ever seen two people move. My heart thumped hard and loud, filling my head and making me angrier than I ever thought possible.

Then I remembered why this was happening. I had the power, I was in control. Nothing could go ahead without my say. Maybe my body was telling me this all along, but I had been too blind, or stupid, to notice it.

My heart wasn't thundering around behind my rib cage

because I was angry. It was doing an improvised conga line on its own because I had the trump card. Like some fat cat poker player who has lured in the rest of the table with his bluffing, I was about to show my hand. And what a devastating hand it was going to be. All aces, all high.

Not that it mattered anymore, we had gone beyond the looking glass, the point of no return was a dot in the distance.

I tried to compose myself and make my thumping heart behave itself. Big breaths, in through my nose, out through my mouth, anything to calm me down. My limbs were shaking with the anticipation, the adrenaline, the sheer exhaustion they had been put through. I could feel my chest quivering, my stomach roaring as it cannibalised itself.

I was ready. Now or never, the chance to be the hero I had always wanted to be. Cometh the man, cometh the hour.

'I don't think so, somehow,' I said, Wendy and Dave now itching to leave by the door. They looked at each other and then towards me.

'I'm sorry, what?' my sister asked.

'I said, I don't think we'll be going down to the solicitors' right away.' I was aware I sounded like a bad Bond villain. More Mouldfinger than Goldfinger.

'Come on, Robbie, stop your messing around,' Wendy laughed a little.

'I'm not going, not with you two, anyway.'

That got their attention. Their faces dropped a few pegs, the arrogant self-belief slipping away like a wax mask held too close to a candle flame. They shared another glance at each other and then over to Mindy in the corner.

'This isn't a joke, Robbie,' said Wendy, stepping forward towards me.

'Do you know something, Wendy,' I said. 'That's the first

intelligent thing you've said all day.' Now *that* was a killer line.

I walked around the table to enjoy the moment, never taking my eyes off the pair of them by the door. Dave's face was turning a shade of scarlet, much like it had done a few days before. I couldn't imagine what this was doing to him, but I was going to find out.

'You see, I've been doing a lot of thinking, like I said. Big picture stuff, fate and all of that jazz,' I tapped Gerry on the shoulder, his face still two-hundred years old. 'And I figure I have a pretty big decision here on how things are going to work out. But, I'm no power mad dictator and when the shit hits the fan, I do actually care about how my family takes care of itself. I know that you've all got big plans for your inheritance, but I've got to think of everybody's well being, too. Now, I know I've been a terrible brother in the past, but if this trip has taught me anything, it's that I have been given a second chance. And that's why I'm signing over my share to Mindy, so she can open up our house, *our* family home into something that will stay in the family and mean something.'

'What!' Wendy shouted, her voice startlingly loud.

'You heard me, Wendy,' I levelled at her. 'And it's okay, I forgive you.'

'You can't *do* this to me.' Flecks of spit flew from her mouth. She stamped her foot and fumed across the table, a fully-grown woman having a hissy fit like a five-year-old.

I would have pitied her if I knew there was any use in it. As it was, I knew things would get worse before they got better.

'I forgive you for being selfish, Wendy, and I forgive you for acting like this. But most of all, I forgive you for being led by this worming snake, slime bag piece of mucus you call a boyfriend.' I looked across at Dave, his face now a colour of purple so deep, he looked like a giant penis.

Wendy stopped her stamping and looked at him. She turned back to me, her face slack, veins still bulging in her temples.

'What did you say?' she asked.

'I said I forgive you for being taken in by this bastard. He's a top catch, I'll give you that but he's also a two-faced liar who I'm sure has got some serious plans for your share of Mum's money.'

'Robert,' Mindy touched my arm. 'I don't think this … '

'Robert,' said Wendy. 'How dare you say that about him, how *dare* you,' she seethed. 'You haven't even bothered to get to know him. How could you say that? Do you know something, Robert, you're so full of shit, I've had enough of all of your bollocks. How fucking *dare* you say that about Dave. You're a right prick, do you know that?'

She turned her attention from me to the others.

'I've had enough of this fucking family and do you know something better? I'll be looking about getting myself a new lawyer and we'll see how this ends. That money is mine and Dave's.' Wendy moved to usher her boyfriend out of the back door.

'Wendy!' I shouted. 'Will you please just sit down? Do you really think Mum would have wanted us to end up like this?'

The room fell silent. Wendy stood near the door, her hand resting on the handle. She turned slowly to face me, eyes watery and beginning to go bloodshot.

'And how would you have known what Mum wanted? You were never here.'

Her words hit me hard, but I had to remain strong. She was right of course, they always were. But this wasn't about me, this was about the family.

'I know that, Wendy, really I do,' I said. 'But I'm damned if I'm going to let you walk out of here and for me to lose you

248

too. Because you see, it's not about him, it's not about this bloody house. None of that matters, Wendy, none of it. It's about us. We're all that's left.'

As much as I would have liked to, I couldn't hold back the tears. Once the first few fell, it opened the floodgates and I tried desperately to cram them back into my eyes with the backs of my hands.

'Alright, Rob,' said Wendy, cutting through the silence. You've got my attention. But don't bullshit me now. Don't even fucking dare.'

I cleared away the snot and spit on my sleeve and blinked.

'Do you see him,' I said, clearing my throat and pointing at Dave. 'He's been at it, Wendy. He's trying to get our money. He doesn't love you, not like you love him. You're just a gig, the latest in a long line. I'm sorry, Wendy. He's a gold digger, a con man.'

She stood like a statue and blinked. Her mouth hung open and she blinked again, vacant.

'What?' she asked.

'It's true, every word of it,' I said. 'He's a con man, he's playing you.'

'You can't be serious,' she fired back, her face still flush with anger. 'What do you think this is? *Eastenders*? Just because you're in show business ... '

'Give over, Wendy,' I spat. 'Ask him yourself.'

'What?'

'When did you meet him? I'm guessing it was after Mother got sick, no?'

She stood silently and didn't answer.

'And I assume you had spoken about what would happen if things turned for the worst?'

'Do you know what you're saying, Robert?' Wendy asked, curtly.

'I do,' I nodded solemnly.

'After all that I've told you, everything you know about me and him, this is what you're saying?'

I stepped around the table and took her hands. They were cold, trembling. She had never grown up, not really. Everything had always been done for her, laid at her feet. She was still an innocent to the ways of the world and it was up to me, in the most basic of big brother roles, to look out for her.

'Please, Wendy, please,' I said quietly. 'Just ask him for me. Just ask him for yourself.'

'What if you're wrong?' she whispered, staring up at me with glassy eyes.

'Then I'm wrong,' I shrugged my shoulders. 'But you have to know, we have to know.'

She turned from me, a single tear dripping from her eyelid and dotting her woollen jumper. She gasped for breath, her shoulders bobbing up and down in little fits.

'Is this true?' she asked. Dave stood still in the doorway, his shoulders squared and jaw now set. He flexed his hands, open and closed, open and closed and looked pretty intimidating.

'Of course not, Wendy, don't be stupid,' he said with a smarmy smile half laughing, his face still beaming.

'I got a phone call this morning from my old friend Jack Johnson,' I said with pride. At the sound of his name, Dave's colour began to drain. 'He said you were in one of his outlets a few months ago, trying to flog some dodgy carpets. Only you took a hundred grand of his and were never seen again.'

The atmosphere in the kitchen was thick and dense and taut enough that it felt like stretched muscle. Every atom in the room was watching on and I was sure I could see the air

250

shimmer.

'Is this true?' Wendy screamed.

Dave bowed his head and shook it, light dancing across his slicked back hair. When he looked back up, his face had returned to a normal colour.

'Wendy, come on … ' he pleaded. She continued to stare at him.

'Yeah, it's true,' he said coolly after a long pause.

Wendy's mouth opened and closed repeatedly, like a fish stranded on dry land. She remained silent, unable to form any words or even any sound. She swayed slightly and fell into my arms and began to cry uncontrollably. Her body shook and shivered and looked like a balloon that had been sucked of all air in an instant.

I helped her into a chair as Gerry and Mindy raced to be by my side. Mindy grabbed our sister and held her close to her, Wendy sobbing into her shoulder, arms draped around Mindy like a rag doll. I stood back up and had to force myself to be strong, for a little moment longer at least.

I turned to Dave and raised my chin. He met my gaze, dark eyes filled with a malice I hadn't ever experienced before in another human being. This wasn't the first time he had seen something like this happen, I could tell. Watching another person break down in front of you wasn't the type of scenario you casually brushed off. Dave was a veteran, a serial heartbreaker and a cheat.

'How did you know?' he breathed. Every word of his was like poison, polluting the air of my family home.

'I didn't,' I said casually.

'What do you mean?' he asked, looking confused.

'I didn't know you were a gold digger. I didn't even know you were only in it for the money. I had a hunch, a gut instinct, up here,' I tapped my temple, cocky and brazen. 'You see, I might not have the fancy degrees or higher education that some folk talk about. But when you spend your life watching others, you tend to be a good judge of character.' I had my Poirot hat on now, all I needed was the curly moustache.

'I know my sister, she's never been street savvy. But I wasn't going to see her bury her future by lining your pockets. So I think it's probably best you leave, and we'll say no more about it. That call from my mate Jack. Bit of serendipity, of course.'

Dave snorted in disgust. He straightened his tie and moved to leave the kitchen.

I didn't see him coming, his turn had been too quick. My instincts were still rubbish even though I was fresh from a fight. Where was Bonnie Tyler when I was finally ready for her?

What was more important was, I didn't see Gerry take flight from behind me.

Dave was stopped dead in his tracks with a finely placed crack on the jaw. Gerry had swooped up from the table and taken out the man twice his size, three times his weight and almost half his age. Like a Pringle jumper clad Batman, his well-aimed strike felled the giant with one blow.

Dave reeled backwards and clattered into the bin by the door. He tripped and fell over, pulling the trash with him. Onion skins, carrot peelings and old teabags fell on top of him as he tried to haul himself up. His expensive shoes slipping on rotten potatoes.

He turned and looked at us, wiping away a trickle of blood from his lip with the back of his hand. He levelled a finger at us all and sneered.

'I'll get you back for this, just you wait. You fucking weirdos!'

And with that, he was gone. Like a pantomime villain, cast into the darkness, he vanished down the hallway and slammed the front door behind him.

We all remained silent for a moment before Wendy started crying again. Mindy held her tightly and hushed her, the pair rocking back and forth gently, the way mother used to do when we had nightmares. I let out a long breath of choked up air and blinked for the first time in what felt like three days.

Gerry turned around, his fighting stance relieved. He shook out his hand, a nasty red lump of swollen flesh forming around his knuckles.

'Is everybody okay?' he asked.

I leapt forward and hugged him. Gerry was one of the good guys. He was also a great fighter.

Chapter 25

A broken heart wasn't something I ever wished on anyone. I had been lucky, my heart was still in one piece. My self-obsession and preservation had meant that stone had replaced natural tissue. Watching the aftermath of Wendy's breakdown was enough to make it bleed for the first time.

In all of my grand splendour as master of the ceremonies, I hadn't factored in the pain and distress that would come in the aftermath. Very stupid of me, I know, it seemed too easy to spot now. Especially when my sister hadn't left the house in three days.

Keeping people at a safe distance was fine, but I had learned that those types of attitudes also bred a vicious scepticism. To spend one's life going through the motions, never feeling that connection was a tragic waste of time. Love hurt, sure it did, but the pain would ease and in the end a person would emerge stronger and less naive.

When Wendy finally came downstairs on the morning of the fourth day, she didn't look any stronger. I would have said she looked weaker, more fragile, like a woman who had just had her heart ripped from her chest and splattered across the room. Colourful, as ever.

'Good morning,' she croaked, large bags under her eyes where the skin had been saturated.

'Morning, Wendy,' I said solemnly.

Mindy had taken up residence in the old house, too. Her transformation into our mother was all but complete, only the age and embittered wisdom were missing. I was resigned to knowing that those would come in time.

'Would you like some breakfast?' she asked, Wendy slipping into a chair beside me.

'No, no, thank you,' the same answer had come every

morning. 'Actually,' Wendy added, just as I was taking a gulp of tea. 'Do you know something, I'd love a fry up. Bacon, eggs, sausages, beans.'

Mindy looked around from the sink and smiled a little in disbelief. I almost choked on my tea, gurgling it back into the mug and wiping my mouth.

'You sure?' I said.

'Black pudding and potato scones, too?' Mindy was beaming.

'Yeah, why the hell not. Lump it all on there,' Wendy had a determined glint in her eye, one that was trying its hardest to break through the defeated visage that had consumed her completely over the past few days.

'I'm bloody starving,' she added, sinking back into her chair, dressing gown and pyjamas bunched about her shoulders and chest like a bag of old washing.

'I'll get right on it then,' said Mindy, making a direct line for the cupboard that stored the old pots and pans. 'Are you wanting any, Robbie?'

'Damn straight!' I laughed. I shook Wendy's shoulder and tried to raise another smile from her. It came at last, when I kept on pushing and pulling, her head lolling like an orange on a toothpick.

'Get off,' she laughed eventually, batting me away with a tired paw.

'Are you alright, kiddo?' I said, when the hilarity died down.

'Yeah,' she replied with a sad smile. 'Yeah, I am. Or I will be at any rate. It was just a surprise, that's all. I never ... I never thought he was like that, you know?' Another river of tears began to dam in her eyes before she let them go.

'I'm fine, I'm fine, honest,' she sobbed, sniffing big, wet

255

snorts. 'I just, I just feel like such a bloody idiot, that's all.'

'Hey,' I said, shaking her arm. 'You weren't to know. It wasn't your fault, Wendy.'

'Of course it wasn't,' chimed Mindy, wrestling with a packet of bacon near the hob. 'The guy was a creep, a total shark. We should have all spotted it earlier; we should have known he was up to no good. I think we should all be grateful that your big brother had the foresight to call him on it when he did.'

I was no fisher of praise and I hadn't gone about this whole escapade for gratitude. I wasn't a huge believer in altruism, and certainly these past few days had little altruistic motive behind them, certainly not for me. But I did feel good about myself, there and then. To hear Mindy vindicate my gamble, my ad lib crusade against my young sister and her money grabbing fiancé/boyfriend was very amicable and sat well with my conscience.

In fact, it probably breathed life into the little lady, she had been suffocated long ago. Pillow to the face in the dead of night, all cloak and dagger stuff. Nasty business.

'Thank you, Robert, thank you both so much,' she leaned across the table and hugged me. She felt weak, empty, like there were no muscles beneath her skin, only a skeleton.

I couldn't help but think that there might be a fad diet in there somewhere. The Argyll Diet, get your heart broken, lose two stone in four days.

'Don't thank me, sis,' I said into her ear. 'I've been a terrible brother to you and Mindy but I'm changing all that now. From here on in I'm going to be here for you both, do you understand?'

She pulled back from me and nodded. Her tears began to dry up and she wiped her eyes and cheeks on the cuff of her fuzzy, pink dressing gown.

'That goes for you too, Mindy,' I said. My older sister looked around from the sizzling sausages and smiled warmly.

'I'm here for both of you and I always will be. Whenever you need me, I'll be a phone call away and never much further than that. You two are all that I've got left and I can't afford to lose that. I'm sorry for everything that's happened and if I could change it then I would, in an instant.' I snapped my fingers. 'But I can't and what's done has been done and can't be changed. But that doesn't mean I can't make the future a bit better for us three, for all of us, Gerry and the kids included. I'm going to be here for you all, day and night and I want to be a part of your lives more than I ever have been. So, if you'll have me ... '

I stood up and stretched out my arms. Yes it was corny, yes it was worse than on TV, but I needed to do it. Mindy and Wendy, my two lovely, beautiful, pain-in-the-arse sisters looked at each other and then back to me. They came around the table and joined me, there, in our old kitchen, in the house we had all grown up in.

I pulled them both close to me and kept my grip around their shoulders as tight as I possibly could. I began to cry and I think the others did, too. It didn't matter; nothing else mattered, only that my family was around me, together and happy. There was still a lot of work to do. I was investing myself into them and I knew they were doing the same for me. In fact, they had never stopped; only I had forgotten that they had always been there.

I wished that the moment would last forever. In those few seconds, a minute tops, I was happier and more full of joy than I had ever felt in my entire life. To have that sense of place, of purpose, of knowing that there were other human beings out there who gave a damn. That had been what I was searching for all of these years.

The comedy, the failure, the misspent youth, it all added up to the same conclusion. I had been scared, terrified, of what I would become. Whenever anybody reached out to me I had spurned them, fearing they would end up disappointed in me.

Only now, when there was nothing left to prove to these people, did I realise that it had been the complete opposite. My sisters, my family, they didn't care about failures and successes. All they wanted was to have me be part of them. Good or bad, they had always been there and now I was going to be just as faithful and dedicated to them as they were to me.

My sisters stepped away and wiped their own faces of tears. This whole crying thing was getting out of hand, we just couldn't stop ourselves. So much for the 'tough guy' reputation of the Argyll kids. Even the bruise on my cheek had started to fade, I no longer looked like a thug.

'I love you, both,' I said softly.

'We love you too, Robert,' said Mindy.

'Of course we do,' added Wendy.

'Talk about an emotional rollercoaster,' I said, shivering.

'I know,' replied Mindy.

'We wouldn't be the same without it,' Wendy laughed a little.

'I'd love to see us try,' I said.

'Tell me about it.'

We all stood silently for a moment, basking in our family love like some sixties hippy commune. I could only imagine what our parents would think if they could see us. I didn't want to know and that was okay. They were gone now and we had mourned them, now it was time to get on with our lives, however we wanted to play them out. I took a great deal of solace in that thought.

'Mindy, Wendy,' I said, my sisters looking at me.

'Yes?' they said in unison.

'I hope you won't mind me saying this,' I started, acting coy and bashful. 'It's a bit embarrassing.'

'Go on, Robbie.'

'You can tell us anything.' They both looked concerned, Mindy reached out to take my hand.

'It's just a bit sensitive is all,' I said.

'You can tell us, come on. We're a family, remember?' said Wendy, taking my other hand.

'Okay,' I said, raising my head to meet their looks of concern. 'I really hope you guys like your sausages and bacon burnt to a crisp.' I couldn't hold it in any longer as I burst out laughing. Maybe it was nerves or just a sheer relief to be rid of all the pent up remorse and unhappiness, but I couldn't stop myself.

'Oh shit!' Mindy shouted, racing over to the pan and running it under the tap, a scream of hisses erupting from the burning breakfast.

'Robbie!' Wendy said with a smirk. She punched my arm and I recoiled, rubbing it.

'Ow,' I said. 'You swing better than Dave!'

'I hit harder than that twat, too,' she said and I knew then, with that simple little gesture, that things might just turn out to be okay after all. I could always live in hope.

She reached over and hugged me again and kissed my cheek. I could get used to all of this affection, thirty years spent avoiding it had been a bad decision for so many reasons.

'You're a good big brother, Robert Argyll,' she said. 'And an even better man.'

'I will be, sis, I will be,' I said humbly.

'Right,' said Mindy, serving up the remnants of the chargrilled fry. 'Tuck in, you two, we've got business to take care of.'

'Mindy,' Wendy started.

'Yes?'

'Maybe you'll let me do the cooking in the B&B, you couldn't serve this to the guests,' she motioned to the plate.

Mindy's face lit up as she smiled.

'Sounds like a great plan to me.'

Chapter 26

I remembered reading a novel when I was younger called *Kingdom By the Sea*. In it, a young boy thinks his family has been blown up by a German bomb during the Second World War. Surviving with his dog, the young protagonist embarks on a journey to secure some sort of refuge with the only family he has left.

The main character, Harry, has to come to the dreadful realisation that he is all alone in the world, with nobody left to take care of him. The book deals brilliantly with his isolation and I remember reading it in complete horror.

Back when I was a child, barely in double-digits, the thought of never having a family was truly dreadful. I admitted that I didn't get on greatly with those who shared my blood. But being without them was something that I couldn't even comprehend.

Home Alone had a similar moment. When Macaulay Culkin creeps down the stairs from his attic, he searches the house for the rest of his family. When he realises that they've gone and left him behind, he embarks on every child's dream of running the house on their own.

Every child but me. That elation soon turns to sadness when he comes to terms with his affection for the others. It's classic Hollywood hogwash, the happy ending that very rarely comes true. Yet, sitting in Fraser's office, ready to sign the appropriate documents, I couldn't help but feel just a little bit proud of myself.

It didn't help I was wearing a plaid shirt that looked almost exactly the same as Culkin's pyjamas in that scene. Talk about an overactive ego.

'Now, I'm required by law to make sure you all understand this, so bear with me,' droned the old solicitor, looking over his spectacles.

He licked his dry thumb with what looked like an even dryer tongue and began to paw through the mounds of paperwork stacked on his desk. After a moment of quiet contemplation, more like fifteen moments, he finally spoke again in his long, drawn out tone.

'You, Robert Gladstone Argyll, do hereby sign over your inheritance left by your legal guardian to one Amanda Wellington Dawkins, nee Argyll.'

'I do,' I said, feeling like the world's weirdest groom in the world's most diabolical marriage. Where were the TV cameras when you needed them?

'And!' Fraser raised his hand to signal the important bit. 'Are of sound mind to be committing these acts of legality?'

I hesitated, unsure what the right answer should be. Surely somebody who was mad would never freely admit it, in a solicitor's office, during the middle of the day. It was like being drunk. No boozer who had had too much to drink, anywhere, at anytime has ever thought they weren't completely sober.

'It's just a formality,' Mindy whispered beside me.

I gawped at her, but she ignored me. Wendy tittered behind somewhere, lost amongst the filing cabinets.

'Again, yes, I do … I mean, I am. Is that right?' I asked the room. Nobody answered.

'If you would sign on the dotted lines, then that should take care of things nicely and Amanda here will be in sole possession of your share of your mother's inheritance.'

I took the pen, a fountain number with green turtle shell design along the shaft, and stared down at where my signature was about to go. I paused for a moment, considering all that had happened.

Somehow, I had imagined this would have been more difficult than it was proving. Not that I would feel any differently or be reluctant to hand over my share. I figured that when it finally came to the act I would be more concerned about my own well-being. This was, after all, a financial opportunity that could potentially lend me a little breathing space for a few years.

The money generated from the sale of the house could take care of my lifestyle for almost a decade, give or take a few years either side. It was more than enough time to try and crack the big time, finally make that big push that I'd been waiting for.

Yet here I was, on the verge of signing the whole lot away on a whim and a prayer, a half-baked dream that could see the whole lot flushed straight down the toilet. I didn't care.

This venture, turning the old house into a bed & breakfast, was merely the tip of the iceberg. It had kept my family together and gave me the gift of a second chance. How could I not take that with both hands?

I signed my name and looked at the writing beneath me. When I handed the pen back to Fraser, Mindy took my hand. She was smiling again and, for the first time since I had arrived, she had a look of relaxed confidence about her.

That same guile had been missing, probably for a lot longer than the past few days. Now it was back and I was sure that she was going to be okay. This was a small gift I could afford to give. I only wished there was more, but that would come, with time and with trust.

Wendy was read her rites in the bizarre wedding ceremony and signed on the dotted line, too. She sat back in an old squeaky chair and made a sigh of relief that almost blew the papers off of Fraser's desk. The old lawyer checked our signatures and stacked the pile with a satisfied clap.

'That's all for now, ladies and gentleman,' he said.

'Is there nothing else you need from us?' Mindy asked.

'No, no, not today. There will be some processing time and the appropriate documentation will be posted out to you in due course, but that's all I need from you all for the moment.'

He straightened his shoulders and clasped his hands over the papers in front of him. Fraser was a man of few pleasantries and I could tell he was ready for us to leave his sanctum. I took the hint and stood up, heading for the door as the others joined me.

We passed through the teabag brown office, the two drones still ploughing away mindlessly at their computers, and out into the breezy street. My sisters joined me and we all looked at each other.

A long, still moment passed before Mindy began to sob. Wendy and I reached out and held her tightly.

'I'm fine, I'm fine, it's okay,' she said, digging out a handkerchief from her handbag and dabbing at her eyes. 'I'm okay, honestly, I'm just so relieved.'

The three of us were united at last, standing in the middle of the street. This had been a long journey, for us all.

When her tears finally stopped, she kissed me on the cheek and gave Wendy one to match.

'Thank you, both,' she said.

'Anytime, sis,' said Wendy.

'Anytime,' I smiled.

She sniffed a little then composed herself, straightening her coat and readjusting her perfect hair. Satisfied her composure was back, she took a hold of Wendy's shoulders and stared intensely into her eyes. I stood back a little and watched my sisters.

'I want to thank you, Wendy,' Mindy started. 'I know that you had your own plans for the money and I also know you wanted to fly the coop and you will my darling, you will. But this is very important to us all and I am so very grateful of what you've done for me today. I can never thank you enough.'

I smiled and felt that familiar sting behind my face. My sisters embraced each other, hands clinging on tightly to each other before turning back to me. I nodded to them both, so very, very happy to be with them.

When they were ready, we started down the street, heading towards the car. I walked in the middle, Wendy on one arm, Mindy on the other, flanked by the two most important people in my life. Not even Satan himself could have wiped the smile from my face, I was in my element.

Everything had slotted right into place. Maybe not in a conventional way, or indeed the way I had planned, but they were there and that was all that mattered. I had a right to feel smug; I was where I wanted to be. And for the billions on the planet who spent their lives searching, I felt nothing but compassion. Not because I was rubbing it in, but because I knew how lucky I had been.

We walked down the pavement, three grown adults skipping like Dorothy and the others on the Yellow Brick Road. We drew looks from the other pedestrians, but I didn't care and neither did my sisters. We were about to start the rest of our lives and I, for one, couldn't wait.

'So,' I said. 'What do we do now?'

Chapter 27

Central Station hadn't changed since I had arrived. In fairness to construction workers and Network Rail, there was very little they could do in just over a fortnight.

December had arrived and with it was the dreadful weather that, in any other month, would have seemed like a punishment. But Christmas was just a matter of weeks away and everybody in the city seemed adamant that it was a good thing. I blamed the copious amounts of festive spirit hanging in the air. Vlad Vodka and Glenmorangie mostly.

The whole family had made the treacherous journey into the City Centre to see me off. By the time we had all clambered out of the car, skied our way up Union Street and reached the safety of the station, I was just about ready for the rest of a lengthy train journey.

The train to Euston was on time and I prepared to say my goodbyes. No matter how hard I tried to remember that I was coming back up in less than ten days, I was still finding the whole thing dreadfully difficult.

Rob and Abi bid farewell to their uncle with a sturdy handshake and hug respectively, gestures I appreciated. Christmas was no time to be spent in the doldrums with your soppy relatives, they should have been out getting pissed, like I used to. I told them as much and they agreed politely.

Gerry patted me goodbye and insisted on taking my bag to the train. I tried to protest, hoping for a quiet moment before I boarded to choke down any tears, but he was adamant he would help me. I didn't have the heart to tell him 'no'.

Wendy was the first to say her goodbyes. She had started to eat again and was getting over the whole debacle with Dave at a good rate. I was happy to see her in a better place although I knew there was still plenty left to do.

The rat hadn't been in contact, much to my surprise, but that wasn't a bad thing. She had taken to not answering her phone anyway, returning to her books in preparation for completing her course, on time and within schedule.

'You have a safe journey, okay?' she said, adjusting the lapels of my new coat. 'Give me a call when you arrive to let me know that you're safe.'

'I will,' I replied.

'I never truly thanked you, Robert, for all that you did.'

'I didn't do anything, Wendy,' I said. 'You would have found out sooner or later. But I'll always look out for you kiddo. Always.'

'I know. I'm missing you already, can't wait to see you in a couple of weeks, I know how soppy that is. We'll have some wallpaper samples for the B&B for you to look at when you come back.'

'Oh great,' I rolled my eyes with a wry smile. 'You know how I love wallpaper samples.' We both laughed and she looked at me sincerely.

'But thank you. Thank you for everything … just … thank you.'

She gave me a kiss and stepped back to be with Gerry and the kids. I gave her a little bow and kept my bottom lip from trembling. That was until Mindy stepped forward and draped herself around me.

'I'm going to miss you, Robert,' she whispered.

'I'll hardly be gone before I'm back again,' I said through short breaths. 'Then you'll have to put up with me all over Christmas.'

'Always,' she said tearily. 'You give me a call as soon as you get in, not a moment later,' she added, trying to be stern.

'Honestly, this family,' I said, wiping my nose. 'You'll have me bringing down BT at this rate.'

She laughed and I did, too. My sister held my hand for a long moment and then let it go, blowing me a kiss as she went to be with her own children.

'I love you all,' I said, straining hard to speak at all with the tennis ball caught in my throat. They all waved me off as I turned towards the platforms, the train steaming and ready to take me away from them.

Gerry and I trudged up the length of the gangway until we reached the open door to my carriage. He stepped onboard with my bag and returned as I gasped for air.

'That's you all sorted,' he said. 'Bag's above your seat. Have you got your ticket, pal?'

'Yeah,' I just about managed.

'Right, well, you take care of yourself, alright.' He said, his eyes glistening in the hard electric light of the station. 'And give your sisters a ring when you get in. They'd appreciate that.' He took a deep breath and I could see he was struggling, too.

Gerry and I hadn't ever been very close, but I felt that we had built up a strong rapport in the past week. Not the best circumstances to be under, but that hardly mattered. I hadn't ever appreciated just how much Gerry did for my sister, or for the whole family. I was going to miss him, I would miss them all.

'Right then,' I said trying to smile. 'Thanks, Gerry, for everything,' I offered him my hand, but he refused it, instead stepping forward and giving me a big, tight bear hug.

'Don't do anything daft now, Robert,' he said, voice muffled by my coat. 'You come back. You come back to us.'

'I will, Gerry, I will. I promise, man.' He released his grip and my feet returned to the platform. 'And look after them, will you? You know what they're like, couldn't run a piss-up in a brewery that lot,' I thumbed back down the gangway at the rest of the family. He nodded.

'I'm off, then,' I clapped my sides and stepped onto the train, giving Gerry a wave as I did so.

The electric door hissed closed behind me and I found my seat. My bag was above me in the overhead rack, just as Gerry said, and I settled in beneath it. I stared for a long moment out of the window, glad that it looked out onto the other side of the platform. My heart was aching enough, I couldn't bear to sit and watch the train pull away from the rest of them.

My head hurt and my stomach churned, business as usual then. Being on the train, heading back down to a gig I wasn't even sure I wanted to do anymore, something kept ticking over in my mind. Questions after questions, always gnawing away. Was I doing the right thing? Had I already done the right thing? What was the future going to hold for us all? Completely endless.

I pulled my coat off and stuffed it down the side of the seat. A complimentary magazine sat in the cargo net in front of me, I foolishly picked it up. On the front cover was a picture of an atomic explosion, all light and cloud and ominous premonition. The headline was simple: 'When will it end?'

I let out a small chuckle and shoved the magazine back into its pocket. The chuckle kept going, ascending in volume and effort until it was a full-blown laugh. A tired, weary, how did it come to this kind of hoot that drew the stares from some of the other passengers.

'Don't worry,' I said to quietly to myself, 'I'm a comedian.'

Chapter 28

'Nice to see you all out tonight. I guess we can tell who the real alcoholics are. Drinking on the third of January, you people need help,' I took a sip of the bottle of imported beer that sat on the stool beside me. A comfortable flutter of laughs went around the room and settled my nerves a little.

'So it's a brand new year, again, anybody made any resolutions?' a few yeses from the crowd. 'Well, good luck with that one. Kept to them, have you?' A little less of a response but still mostly positive. 'You're dirty, rotten liars.' That brought in the applause. I was such a tart for applause.

'Yeah, I don't get it with resolutions, every year we're encouraged to make a resolution, but it's like a red rag to a bull. I reckon making a resolution makes you more likely to break it. So I say, make daily resolutions, that way you'll be an overweight, alcoholic, chain-smoking heart attack waiting to happen. Otherwise known as a Glaswegian.' Now they were really getting into things.

'As you can probably tell, I'm from that neck of the woods, yes, thank you. I was up there at Christmas, great town, great city. The kind of place that makes you glad you can speak English, you know. Because it usually means none of the natives will understand a word you're saying.

'But on a more serious note, I've just gotten back together with my family after a long break-up shall we call it,' a round of applause that I really wasn't expecting. 'Thank you, thank you. And I can honestly say, now that Christmas and the New Year is over, I can't wait … to never see those moaning bastards ever again,' the hilarity was genuine, even if I wasn't, but that was all part of the game.

A great writer once wrote that perhaps we're all a little mad, we who don the cap and bells and tread beneath the proscenium arch. And it was true. You gave it your all and presented yourself in a way that would draw the best results. I was keeping my personal life to one side, I was only glad I had a personal life to keep there.

I wrapped things up, took my bow and made my way off of the stage. The whole area beyond the lights was quiet, only the nervous rookies daring to go out in this weather. I did it because I wanted to, because I had better plans.

'Good set, man,' said one of them, all spots and grease.

'Cheers, buddy, enjoy.' I clapped him on the shoulder and headed for the fire escape.

The usual gust of icy cold air slapped me in the face as I shut the door behind me. I walked a little down the back alley and dug around for my cigarettes, my own resolution broken at half past midnight on January first.

I found them and pulled them out of my pocket along with a fountain of change. Suddenly my phone began to vibrate, much to my surprise. Nobody called me during a show. This seemed awfully familiar.

Pulling it out, I didn't recognise the number and with a little trepidation, hit answer.

'Hello?' I said, not sure what to expect.

'Robert?' came a voice I didn't recognise.

'Yes,' I answered.

'Robert, it's Angela.'

'Angela?' I asked. 'Angela who?'

'Angela Crosby,' came the voice, irritated. 'Wendy's friend, you know, your sister.'

'Oh, Angela,' I was surprised. It seemed she hadn't quite had enough of this particular shithead after all. 'How are you, Angela, good to hear from you.'

'Yeah, whatever,' she sounded angry. 'Listen, I've got

something to tell you and I don't think you're going to be happy.'

'Sure, go ahead,' I wasn't paying attention, instead fumbling with a cigarette from the mashed up packet.

'You're going to be a Dad ... '

You know that way where life just seems to stop in an instant? Everything completely freezes and the whole mechanics of existence come to a grinding halt. That was just about how I felt when she delivered the news.

And worst of all, I was lost for something clever, creative or even remotely funny to say.

'Shit.'

END

Some other books from Ringwood Publishing

All titles are available from the Ringwood website (including first edition signed copies) and from usual outlets.
Also available in Kindle, Kobo and Nook.
www.ringwoodpublishing.com

Ringwood Publishing, 7 Kirklee Quadrant, Glasgow, G12 0TS
mail@ringwoodpublishing.com
0141 357-6872

Memoirs of a Feminist Mother

Carol Fox

As a committed feminist, Carol Fox has achieved success for very many women, but her greatest battle described in this book was very personal. Following serious fertility problems, Carol made the positive decision to become a single parent by choice, to have a child while she still could. Refused access to fertility treatment in Scotland she had no choice but to move to London.

Through sheer determination and tenacity, Carol obtained treatment in England in the early 1990s and her daughter was born in 1992, following extensive fertility treatment and battles against judgemental attitudes which appear almost vindictive to us 25 years later.

Her story has attracted media coverage, sparking debates on motherhood and the right to be a single parent in the UK.

Written as a memoir addressed to her only daughter, the story has been, and continues to be, of interest to a wider audience of women, young and old, mothers and non-mothers, as the chapters record the changing social attitudes towards single parents during the past 25 years.

ISBN: 978-1-901514-21-6   £9.99

Torn Edges

Brian McHugh

Torn Edges is a mystery story linking modern day Glasgow with 1920's Ireland and takes a family back to the tumultuous days of the Irish Civil War.

They soon learn that many more Irishman were killed, murdered or assassinated during the very short Civil War than in the War of Independence and that gruesome atrocities were committed by both sides.

The evidence begins to suggest that their own relatives might have been involved.

ISBN: 978-1-901514-05-6 £9.99

Silent Thunder

Archie MacPherson

Silent Thunder is set in Glasgow and Fife and follows the progress of two young Glaswegians as they stand up for what they believe in.

They find themselves thrust headlong into a fast moving and highly dangerous adventure involving a Scots radio broadcaster, Latvian gangsters, a computer genius and secret service agencies.

Archie MacPherson is well known and loved throughout Scotland as a premier sports commentator.

"An excellent tale told with pace and wit"

Hugh Macdonald -The Herald

ISBN: 978-1-901514-11-7 £9.99

Calling Cards

Gordon Johnston

Calling Cards is a psychological crime thriller set in Glasgow about stress, trauma, addiction, recovery, denial and corruption.

Following an anonymous email Journalist Frank Gallen and DI Adam Ralston unravel a web of corruption within the City Council with links to campaign against a new housing development in Kelvingrove Park and the frenzied attacks of a serial killer. They then engage in a desperate chase to identify a serial killer from the clues he is sending them.

ISBN: 978-1-901514-09-4   £9.99

A Subtle Sadness

Sandy Jamieson

A Subtle Sadness follows the life of Frank Hunter and is an exploration of Scottish Identity and the impact on it of politics, football, religion, sex and alcohol.

It covers a century of Scottish social, cultural and political highlights culminating in Glasgow's emergence in 1990 as European City of Culture.

It is not a political polemic but it puts the current social, cultural and political debates in a recent historical context.

ISBN: 978-1-901514-04-9   £9.99

Good Deed

Steve Christie

Good Deed introduces a new Scottish detective hero, DI Ronnie Buchanan.

It was described by one reviewer as *"Christopher Brookmyre on speed, with more thrills and less farce".*

The events take Buchanan on a frantic journey around Scotland as his increasingly deadly pursuit of a mysterious criminal master mind known only as Vince comes to a climax back in Aberdeen.

ISBN: 978-1-901514-06-3   £9.99

Dark Loch

Charles P. Sharkey

Dark Loch is an epic tale of the effects of the First World War on the lives of the residents of a small Scottish rural community. The main characters are the tenant crofters who work the land leased to them by the Laird. The crofters live a harsh existence in harmony with the land and the changing seasons, unaware of the devastating war that is soon to engulf the continent of Europe.

The book vividly and dramatically explores the impact of that war on all the main characters and how their lives are drastically altered forever.

ISBN: 978-1-901514-14-8   £9.99

Black Rigg

Mary Easson

Black Rigg is set in a Scottish mining village in the year 1910 in a period of social and economic change. Working men and women began to challenge the status quo but landowners, the church and the justice system resisted. Issues such as class, power, injustice, poverty and community are raised by the narrative in powerful and dramatic style.

ISBN: 978-1-901514-15-5   £9.99

The Malta Job

Alywn James

The Malta Job follows the story of John Smith, a young Scottish journalist with literary aspirations, who is sent to Malta to complete a sequel to the very successful MacMurder, a round-up of Scotland's more infamous homicides. Once on Malta, with the dead author's notes, he gets involved in a gripping set of circumstances involving high romance, exciting adventure and a bank heist crime.

"The Malta Job is a highly literate, greatly accomplished fictional debut by an author well known for high quality non-fiction works like Scottish Roots and Other Men's Heroes".

ISBN: 978-1-901514-17-9   £9.99

The Gori's Daughter
Shazia Hobbs

The Gori's Daughter is the story of Aisha, a young mixed race woman, daughter of a Kashmiri father and a Glasgow mother. Her life is a struggle against rejection and hostility in Glasgow's white and Asian communities.

The book documents her fight to give her own daughter a culture and tradition that she can accept with pride. The tale is often harrowing but is ultimately a victory for decency over bigotry and discrimination.

ISBN: 978-1-901514-12-4   £9.99

Scotball
Stephen O'Donnell

Scotball is a searing examination of the current state of Scottish football and the various social, political and economic forces that combine to strangle its integrity and potential.

ISBN: 978-1-901514-13-1   £9.99

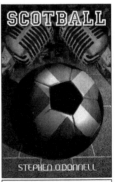

Paradise Road
Stephen O'Donnell

Paradise Road is the story of Kevin McGarry, who through a combination of injury and disillusionment is forced to abandon any thoughts of playing football professionally. Instead he settles for following his favourite team, Glasgow Celtic, whilst trying to eke out a living as a joiner. It considers the role of young working-class men in our post-industrial society.

ISBN: 978-1-901514-07-0   £9.99